SPIRIT MARKED

AURAS & EMBERS BOOK 2

GWEN DEMARCO

CHAPTER 1

Gideon hovered his palm over the corpse's chest and closed his eyes. The crematorium faded away – the ash, the lingering scent of industrial cleaners, the mechanical hum of the furnace – as he concentrated on what lay beneath his fingertips.

He focused – not with his eyes, but with that other sense he'd been developing.

A prickling sensation spread up his arm like static, raising goosebumps despite the room's warmth. The dead man's magic buzzed against his skin – hot and dry like desert sand on sunburned skin and rough as a cat's tongue, with an undercurrent of viscous black tar.

First, he detected feathers, but a leonine aspect dominated his senses – a rolling, muscular warmth that pushed against his palm with the phantom sensation of coarse fur, triggering some primitive part of his brain that recognized the presence of an apex predator.

Beneath that sensation flowed something different – a scorpion element, bitter and metallic. It stung his senses – the toxic magic designed to paralyze and destroy.

These signatures fused perfectly with the man's essence – predatory strength interlaced with piercing venom – creating something that was neither entirely bird, feline, or scorpion but entirely unique.

"Feels like some sort of animal. Pretty strong magic. I'm getting feathers, I think. So, some type of bird." Gideon tilted his head and pushed on his magic. "Wait, not just feathers. I'd swear I'm also sensing fur. And – something like that basilisk we got last week? But it's not snake-like, if that makes sense – I'm not picking up any scales. The venom, maybe."

Gideon opened his eyes and stared down at the mummified-looking corpse. "A hippogriff? I think I was reading about them the other day."

Silas gave him a good-natured nudge, and the satyr's magic brushed against Gideon's senses. "You're close, but no cigar. This guy was a manticore."

Gideon gave Silas a blank look, having never heard of that type of Mythical. Silas gave him another grin, his eyes bright and pleased at having stumped Gideon. "A manticore has a human head with the body of a lion. It has wings and a tail with venomous spikes."

"Huh," was all Gideon could think to say. He put the lid back on the box and helped Silas slide the manticore into the retort.

"Man, you're getting good at this," Silas said, looking over Gideon's shoulder as he documented the manticore's magical signature in his notebook. The pale light of dawn was beginning to creep through the windows, signaling the end of another quiet night shift. "I've never actually met an auramancer before, but from what I hear, you're picking up magic reading crazy fast."

Gideon shrugged, trying to hide how pleased he was by the compliment. Working at Tranquil Haven, the Conclave-owned funeral home had been a revelation. For the first time, he felt like he belonged somewhere. The work fascinated him, his coworkers were genuinely kind, and the pay exceeded anything he'd previously imagined possible. Even all the paperwork couldn't dampen his enthusiasm. Best of all, the steady stream of Mythical creatures passing through their doors allowed him to track and catalog a diverse array of magical signatures.

A familiar fiery sensation suddenly washed over his senses,

making the hair on his neck stand up. His head snapped toward the door a moment before it swung open, revealing a petite figure.

"I had the guy totally cornered with his pants down. *Literally*. Found him in a bathroom stall at a rest stop right off I-75," Dacey was saying into her phone as she strode in, somehow managing to look dangerous despite the pink cardigan and sensible shoes. Her eyes lit up when she spotted Gideon, and a grin spread across her face. "I've got to go. I'll send in my report later."

She ended the call and bounded over to him, throwing her arms around him in an enthusiastic hug that made his heart skip a beat. "Giddy! I've missed you! Talking to you on the phone just isn't cutting it."

"I've missed you too," he said, awkwardly patting her back with one hand. He was acutely aware of Silas watching them with poorly concealed interest. "It's been, what – a month? Why are you dressed like an elementary school librarian?"

Dacey stepped back and grimaced, plucking at her flowery blouse. "Very funny. I needed to blend in for my last assignment. Don't ask – it involved too much time in a Sunday school room." She glanced around the quiet morgue. "Still burning the midnight oil, huh? Why haven't you switched to days yet?"

"I'm used to the hours," Gideon said, stuffing his hands in his pockets to keep them occupied. "Plus, it'll work better with my schedule when I return to college in the fall."

Gideon suddenly remembered his manners. "Uh, Silas, this is Dacey Menet. She works for the Savannah Conclave. Dacey, this is Silas, my coworker and friend."

"Nice to meet you," Dacey said, extending her hand. "Gideon's told me a lot about you."

"Likewise," Silas replied with a knowing grin that made Gideon wish the floor would swallow him whole. They shook hands, and Silas's grin widened. "Well, I should get back to work. These death certificates won't file themselves."

As Silas headed for the door, he caught Gideon's eye, pointed at

Dacey's back, and gave an enthusiastic thumbs up. Gideon kept his face carefully neutral, though he could feel heat creeping up his neck.

"What are you doing here?" Gideon asked, turning from Silas to grin at Dacey, delighted by her unexpected visit.

She gave him a bright, mischievous smile that he'd missed so much it made his lungs ache. "I've got a case, and I could use your help... It's gonna be fun."

"Fun, huh? I've heard that one before," Gideon teased, trying to ignore how his pulse quickened at the prospect of working with the bennu shifter again.

"We've got a situation in central Florida," she explained. "Five deaths in the past month. No obvious cause of death – no signs of trauma, magic, or poison. The victims just... stopped living. Most of them fell unconscious first and just never woke up. Actually, I should correct that – one victim had been in some kind of fight, but the medical examiner was adamant it hadn't been the cause of death. They were all perfectly healthy one minute, then a corpse the next."

Gideon frowned. "Any connection between the victims?"

"Not as far as we can tell. Different ages, different backgrounds, different parts of town. Some human and some Mythical. The latest victim was the mayor of Millhaven's sister – that's what finally got the Conclave involved. Local law enforcement is stumped, and the medical examiner is about ready to tear her hair out trying to figure out what killed these people."

"You think it's something magical?"

Dacey nodded. "That's our working theory. But we need to know for sure before we justify dedicating resources to a full investigation. That's where you come in." She fixed him with an intent look that made his stomach do a slow flip. "The Conclave wants you to examine the bodies and see if you can detect any magical residue that might tell us what we're dealing with."

Gideon ran a hand through his hair, thinking it through. His heart leaped at the chance to work with Dacey again, but responsibility won out over desire. "I'm still in training, Dacey. Maybe Vena would be better for this?" It pained him to suggest his auramancer mentor instead of himself, but he knew Vena was endlessly more qualified. "She's got years of experience that I don't. I'm not sure how much I'd be able to pick up."

"Vena is out on an assignment already. I think you're ready for fieldwork, and my bosses agree. Come on, Gideon – no more excuses! Let's do this! I'm so excited to work with you again. We make an awesome team!"

Gideon refrained from pointing out that he'd been set on fire the last time they worked together. Instead, he asked, "Do you think this will take more than a day? If so, I'll need to request time off."

"Already cleared it with your supervisor," Dacey said with a slight smirk. "And you're the best shot we've got at figuring out what's going on. Five people are dead, Giddy. If we don't figure out what's causing this, there will probably be more deaths."

"Don't call me Giddy," he said automatically, putting up a token resistance, knowing it was futile to get Dacey to stop.

Despite his protestations, they both knew he was going to say yes. Ever since that day in the woods with the demons, he'd stopped fighting what he was and started embracing his power. He saw more Mythicals walking among the mundane world each day – their magical signatures blazing like bonfires in the dark. His abilities were growing, whether he was ready for it or not.

"When do we leave?" he asked.

Dacey's face lit up with that fierce grin he remembered so well. "How fast can you pack?"

"I need to finish up some paperwork here first. Give me a couple of hours?"

"Perfect. I can pick you up at your place around eight. We can grab breakfast on the road."

"Sounds good." He stifled a yawn. "And maybe I can catch a few hours of sleep on the drive."

Dacey's phone chimed, and she glanced at the screen. "Oh, the mayor's office messaged back. They can see us at five. That gives us plenty of time to get to Millhaven." She slipped her phone back in her pocket. "Pack something nice – we'll need to look professional."

"By 'nice,' do you mean 'looks like I shop at Librarians R Us'?" Gideon couldn't resist asking, giving Dacey's outfit a raised eyebrow.

She gave him an arch look, tugging her cardigan with a flourish. "I'll have you know that I rock the schoolmarm look, *thank you very much*."

Gideon snorted, giving her a teasing eye-roll.

"Hey, by the way... I haven't heard from you in a while. Everything okay?" Gideon said, trying to keep his tone casual despite the knot in his stomach. Two weeks of near silence had him second-guessing everything. He'd sent a few casual texts, not wanting to seem clingy, but her sparse replies were a sharp contrast to their usual back-and-forth. Maybe he'd been fooling himself that their friendship meant as much to her as it did to him.

Dacey's expression turned sheepish. "Yeah, sorry about that. My safe house burned down."

"Your what? Wait – what happened? Did you...." Gideon lowered his voice, thinking of Dacey's fiery bennu shifter nature. "Did you set it on fire?"

"No, nothing like that," Dacey said with a light laugh. "I wasn't even there when it happened. Fire department's still investigating, but it looks like an electrical problem or something equally mundane."

She shrugged, tugging on the sleeves of her cardigan. "It's mostly just paperwork and hassle at this point. The place was insured, and I didn't keep most of my important things there anyway. That's the whole point of a safe house – it's disposable."

"Right," Gideon said, unsure how he felt about that information but deciding to move on. "Hey, what should I tell my mom about where I'm going?"

Dacey paused, hand on the doorknob. "How about we tell her you're helping me with another consulting job? It's technically true."

Yeah, she'll be thrilled *to hear that after what happened last time.* However, Gideon kept that thought to himself.

"Be ready by eight," Dacey said, tapping her watch. "Pack light – I'm hoping we won't be gone more than a day or two." She pulled open the door, already stepping through it.

"See you soon," Gideon called after her retreating form. The door clicked shut, leaving only the faint scent of her shampoo and the lingering warmth of her magic signature in the air.

Gideon winced, remembering his mother's thinly veiled hostility toward Dacey after their last investigation had landed him in the hospital covered in burns. His mom's opinion of Dacey went well beyond mere dislike, but he didn't have the heart to tell her. He'd have to come up with a different story to tell his mother about his trip to Millhaven – mentioning Dacey would only trigger endless lectures and worry.

Sooner or later, he'd have to have an uncomfortable conversation with his mom about Dacey being a permanent fixture in his life. But not today.

Silas poked his head back in almost immediately. "So… that's the famous Dacey, huh?"

"Don't start," Gideon warned, but he could feel himself blushing again.

"Hey, I'm just saying – a girl who can kick ass and looks that good in a cardigan? Don't let that one get away." Silas waggled his eyebrows suggestively.

"There's nothing… It isn't like…" Gideon growled and shook his head at himself. "Don't you have paperwork to file?"

"Fine, fine, I'm going." Silas started to turn away when he paused and glanced back at Gideon. "Hey, do you think you'll still be able to make training the weekend after next?"

Gideon shrugged. "I don't think it'll be a problem. Dacey thinks this investigation will be wrapped up in a few days, but we'll see."

Gideon had been spending a few weekends each month with Silas at a Conclave training facility in Tallahassee, working to become a full-fledged agent. The program was intense – weapons training, physical conditioning, hand-to-hand combat skills, and more. He'd even gotten to work face-to-face with Vena twice now. He felt lucky because she had to fly from South Carolina for the training sessions. He'd told his mom he'd joined a hiking and camping enthusiasts club, knowing her dislike of camping would prevent her from ever wanting to tag along or ask too many questions.

"Ah, well," Silas grinned. "At least you get to work the case together. Make the most of it. Seriously, man, you should—"

"Goodbye, Silas."

Once he was alone, Gideon pulled out his phone and typed out a quick message to Vena: *Going on my first official investigation for the Conclave. Might need to call/text if I run into unfamiliar magic. Just wanted to give you a heads up.*

His phone rang almost immediately, Vena's name lighting up the screen.

"Congratulations!" Vena's warm voice came through, though there was an undertone of concern that made Gideon picture her worried face, brow furrowed beneath her wispy silver hair. Sometimes, he felt like Vena was the grandmother he'd never had. "But I wanted to warn you to be careful out there."

"I will be," Gideon assured her.

"I mean it," Vena's voice turned serious. "Don't tell anyone outside the Conclave what you are. In my younger years, I had two younger cousins whose parents were attacked, and their children were stolen."

Gideon's breath caught. "Because they were auramancers?"

"Probably. We never were able to find the culprits or any sign of my cousins. It was decades ago, but the danger is still real." Vena sighed heavily. "The why and how don't truly matter – it could have been someone wanting them for their abilities, to steal their power, or even for a blood sacrifice. Who knows? Just be careful. Auramancers are rare, and our magic is powerful and coveted. People will want to use you, and not everyone who does has good intentions. Being able to sense and identify even hidden magic is a powerful tool – it makes you incredibly valuable to both allies and enemies. That kind of power always comes with risk."

"I'll be careful, I promise," Gideon said softly. "I won't tell anyone about my ability."

After ending the call, Gideon bit his lip, his mind racing with possibilities about what they might be walking into. His last "consulting job" with Dacey had ended with him rolling into a bonfire and facing down incorporeal demons. He wondered what awaited him this time.

Gideon pulled his notebook out of his pocket and thumbed through the pages filled with careful observations about magical signatures. In the last few months, he'd documented over thirty types of Mythical beings that had passed through the crematorium, in addition to all the strange magical artifacts Vena kept mailing him to study. He'd learned more about magic in the past two months than he'd known existed his entire life before. But book learning and carefully controlled observations were one thing – going out into the field and putting that knowledge to use was something else entirely.

At least this time, he was going in with his eyes open. He knew what he was getting into – mostly. And he had actual training now, plus a much better understanding of his abilities.

Still, as he started gathering his paperwork, he couldn't shake the feeling that they were about to step into something big. Five mysterious fatalities with no apparent cause of death? That wasn't just unusual – it was deeply unsettling. Even in the weird world of Mythicals, people didn't just drop dead for no reason.

His phone buzzed with a text from Dacey: *Pack running shoes. And maybe something fireproof. lol.*

Gideon texted back: *Haha very funny*

Sorry, Giddy. Too soon???

Gideon stared at the message for a long moment, then shook his head and smiled. Whatever they were walking into, at least it wouldn't be boring.

CHAPTER 2

Gulf Breeze Hardware stood as a testament to old Florida, from when the state was still more swamp than useable land and before Disney's arrival. The squat cinder block building had weathered countless hurricanes, its windows protected by metal shutters battle-tested through decades of storms. The parking lot was cracked but clean, with faded yellow lines and patches of stubborn weeds pushing through the asphalt.

A bell chimed overhead as Gideon pushed open the door, breathing in the familiar mix of paint, potting soil, and WD-40. The store was a maze of tall metal shelves packed with everything from power tools to flower seeds, each aisle meticulously organized despite the constant stream of contractors and weekend warriors who filtered through each day.

Stella Bean stood behind the counter, her light brown hair – the same shade as Gideon's own – pulled back in a practical ponytail. Even in the store's navy polo shirt, her tall, thin frame carried the kind of wiry strength that came from years of hauling buckets of paint and heavy bags of mulch. The gold cross pendant she never took off caught the fluorescent light as she leaned forward, explaining something to a customer with the patience of someone who'd spent over a decade helping people figure out exactly which nail or bolt they needed.

The "Manager" designation on her name tag was new, and Gideon felt a familiar surge of pride. His mom had earned every letter of that title, working her way up from part-time cashier through sheer determination and grit.

She caught sight of him over the customer's shoulder, and her face lit up with a smile that held just a hint of ever-present maternal worry. Ever since he was little, Gideon had never quite fit in with his peers, and his mother's concern had only grown when he'd suddenly dropped out of college a few years ago. After the demon attack, when Gideon had set himself on fire to save them, it was as if all his mother's worst fears had materialized at once. The burn unit stay had amplified her anxiety to unbearable levels, and only now, months later, was she beginning to find some semblance of calm. He couldn't bear to tell her he was taking another case with Dacey – the very thought of reigniting her panic made his stomach twist. Eventually, he needed to have a real conversation about his plan to become an agent, but watching her now, he wasn't ready to tackle that difficult conversation yet.

Gideon gave her a reassuring smile and waited by a display of work gloves while she finished ringing up the customer's purchase, trying to ignore the guilty twist in his stomach.

"Honey, what are you doing here? Is everything alright?" she asked once the customer had left.

"Everything's fine, Ma," Gideon said, leaning against the counter. "I'm just stopping by because I need to leave town for a few days. The company I work for needs some help in Millhaven, near Orlando."

"Oh, is their crematorium short-staffed too?" His mother asked. "I bet it's that flu that's going around. Half my staff has been out this week with it."

Gideon felt a twinge of discomfort. He hated even this small deception, but he couldn't bring himself to correct her. Better than worrying her unnecessarily.

"I should only be gone for a few days," he said instead. "It's a good opportunity to show them my worth. Plus, they're offering a pretty good bonus."

"That's wonderful!" His mother beamed. "I'm so proud of how seriously you take your job. Do you think you'll be back before Saturday? I'd hate for you to miss the party. I'm so excited to throw our first Fourth of July barbecue. It's a good excuse to get to know the neighbors better." She adjusted her cross absently. "We finally have a proper backyard to host a party. Plus, Pastor Simon was especially looking forward to seeing you."

Gideon kept his expression neutral, though inside, he wouldn't mind having an easy excuse to miss another well-meaning lecture about his declining church attendance. "I'm not sure if I'll make it back in time. I'll try, though. But if I don't, tell Pastor Simon I said hello. I'd hate to miss the barbecue – knowing Mrs. Henderson, she'll probably bring enough fried chicken to feed us for a week."

His mother laughed. "You know she will. That woman thinks everyone in the neighborhood is too skinny." Her expression softened. "I'm just glad we're finally in a real house. Even if it is just a rental, it's so much better than that awful apartment."

A customer appeared at the end of the counter, clutching a handful of PVC pipes with a confused expression. "Excuse me, but do you know where I can find—"

"I should let you get back to work," Gideon said. "I need to go pack anyway – they're pretty backed up and could use the help as soon as possible. I'll call you when I get settled, okay?"

He circled the counter to give her a quick hug, breathing in the familiar scent of her shampoo mixed with sawdust. "Love you, Mom. I'll see you in a few days."

"Love you too, honey. Be safe." She squeezed him tight for a moment, then turned to help the customer with their plumbing question.

As Gideon returned to his car, the lie he'd told his mom sat heavy in his chest. But it was better than the alternative –telling her he was headed into another potentially dangerous situation with Dacey. At least this time, he was more prepared. Probably.

He hoped.

CHAPTER 3

A car horn and muffled cursing jolted Gideon awake. He blinked, disoriented, as his mind struggled to make sense of his surroundings. The late morning sun beat down on Dacey's car, which was currently trapped in a sea of crawling traffic.

"How long was I out?" he asked, working out a crick in his neck from sleeping awkwardly against the window.

"A few hours." Dacey drummed her fingers against the steering wheel, her long black hair falling in a curtain over one shoulder as she craned her neck to see around a semi-truck. "We're not far from Millhaven now, but I swear to god, I-4 traffic makes me want to murder everyone." Gideon could see ghostly flames rising from her arms, visible only to his magical sight – a manifestation of her growing annoyance. She glared at the endless line of cars stretching ahead of them. "Especially that guy," she added as an SUV cut across three lanes without signaling.

Gideon couldn't help but grin as he watched her, struck by how someone so pretty could look so murderous. The ethereal flames dancing around her only enhanced the effect. "I can literally see how annoyed you are – there are actual flames in your pupils right now."

Dacey's head snapped toward him, her expression startled. "Wait, what? You can see my flames?"

"Yeah." Gideon tilted his head, focusing his magical sight more intently on her. "There's even fire rising from your arms right now. And if I concentrate, I can make out the ghostly shape of your flame wings."

"That... that should be impossible. With my sigil tattoo, no one should be able to detect my bennu shifter heritage."

"Sigil tattoo?"

Before Dacey could answer, the car in front of them slammed on their brakes for no apparent reason. Dacey hit the horn, the flames on her arms flaring for a brief moment. "Learn to drive, asshole!"

Once they were moving again – if you could call inching forward at a snail's pace "moving" – she explained, "A sigil tattoo is magical inkwork. Most Mythicals get them to hide their true nature from humans." She glanced around at the surrounding cars, then shoved up her sleeve with one hand, revealing an intricate tattoo of flame wings that spread across her upper arm. "This tattoo contains and conceals my fire until I consciously release it."

Gideon had noticed Dacey's tattoos before – how could he not? The intricate designs had caught his eye more than once. But he'd always assumed they were just artistic expression, never considering they might serve a magical purpose.

Gideon leaned closer, fascinated. When he focused his auramancer senses on the image, the tattoo had an otherworldly shimmer, like heat waves rising from hot pavement. Without thinking, he reached out and touched the inked skin. A spark of sensation danced across his fingertips, reminiscent of Fae magic – bright, wild, and ancient – melded with the heat of Dacey's magic.

"That makes sense," he said, trying very hard to focus on the magical signature and not how soft her skin felt under his fingertips. "It feels like Fae magic."

"Good catch," Dacey replied with an impressed look. "The artist who tattooed this on me was Fae."

Gideon reluctantly withdrew his hand and pulled out his notebook, determined to document the unique magical signature while it was still fresh in his mind. The familiar act of taking notes helped ground him, pushing away the lingering sensation of Dacey's warm skin beneath his fingers.

The Fae magic in Dacey's tattoo reminded him of the case dossier he'd been reading before he dozed off: five deaths in total. The first victim was Marcus Chauvin, a well-known Fae tattoo artist. Only now did Gideon realize that Chauvin had likely created tattoos infused with Fae magic, just like the ink on Dacey's skin. The next victim was Brandon Cho, a sun bear shifter from the neighboring town of Lake Mary. The third was Eleanor Preston, a wealthy human socialite known for charitable work. Fourth was a homeless man identified only as "Joe." The final victim was the mayor's sister, Willa Wagner, a witch who was a professor at a local university.

After reading the victims' backgrounds, Gideon agreed with Dacey's earlier observation that these people shared no apparent connection.

"Oh, thank god," Dacey breathed suddenly. "There's our exit. I'm starving, and we've got about an hour before we need to meet the mayor. Enough time to eat if we grab something quick."

They turned off I-4, and the tension in Dacey's shoulders visibly eased as the traffic thinned out. Gideon stared out the window as they drove into Millhaven proper, taking in the historic downtown that looked like it had been frozen in time around 1950.

The town's main street ran parallel to a large lake, its old brick buildings housing an eclectic mix of antique shops, cafes, and bars. Red, white, and blue bunting draped the storefronts, and American flags fluttered from every lamppost in preparation for the upcoming Fourth of July celebrations. The afternoon sun cast long shadows between lamp posts, where unlit strings of lights crisscrossed overhead, waiting for evening to transform the street into something out of a postcard. The lake peeked between buildings, and Gideon caught glimpses of a riverwalk that meandered along the waterfront.

They turned onto Palmetto Avenue, passing more brick buildings with wrought iron balconies and colorful awnings. Through the gaps between structures, Gideon could see a marina where everything from small fishing boats to yachts bobbed gently in their slips. A few people were dotted along the riverwalk, either out for a stroll or fishing off the seawall.

"It's like stepping back in time," Gideon murmured, watching a family of tourists taking pictures in front of an ornate courthouse that looked like it belonged in the previous century.

"Millhaven's proud of its history," Dacey said, navigating around a horse-drawn carriage filled with camera-wielding tourists. "The downtown area had fallen on hard times for many years, but in the last decade, there's been this huge revitalization push. Now, all these old buildings have new life. Empty storefronts are now restaurants, boutiques, art galleries, and so on. It's also a pretty Mythical-friendly town; even the mayor is a Mythical."

"Really?" Gideon instinctively reached out with his magical senses, scanning the pedestrians they passed. Most registered as purely mundane, but here and there, he caught flickering signatures that marked someone as not quite human.

They pulled into a parking spot in front of a cornflower blue clapboard building with the sign Millhaven Food Depot out front. As they headed for the entrance, Gideon paused to read a placard: "Built in 1887, the Millhaven Train Depot served as the town's primary railway station until 1965. This historic landmark has been lovingly restored to house our community's finest eateries."

Inside the building, a spacious hall was lined with food vendors along both sides. Strings of Edison bulbs crisscrossed the open central corridor between vendor stalls, and high windows let in natural light. The different vendor stalls offered everything from ramen to pizza to tacos and craft beer.

"I'm going to grab a sandwich," Dacey announced, checking her phone. "We have just enough time to grab something to eat so we don't show up hungry."

They split up to grab food, meeting back at a long communal table near the center of the food hall. Gideon returned with a pizza loaded with pepperoni and mushrooms. Dacey's plate held two plump, steaming bao buns and a strange-looking corndog, its crispy coating crisscrossed with drizzles of red and white sauces.

Dacey bit into the corndog, revealing stretchy, melted cheese instead of the expected hot dog. She caught Gideon staring and offered it to him with a smile.

"You gotta try this. Have you ever had a Korean corndog?" she asked. "The cheese inside is incredible."

Gideon hesitated for a moment, his heart skipping as Dacey held the food out to him. He felt a sudden, wild impulse to bypass the corn dog entirely and press his lips to her fingers, the thought sending an unexpected jolt through him. He leaned forward and took a bite instead, hyper-aware of her fingers inches from his lips.

The crispy exterior gave way to molten mozzarella, and he made an appreciative sound. Their eyes locked, and the noisy market seemed to fade into silence. The warmth in her gaze held him there, suspended in an unexpectedly intimate moment that quickened his pulse.

Stop it, he chided himself. *She's just being friendly. We're here to solve murders, not... whatever you want this to be.*

"So... what's our game plan now that we're here?" he asked, deliberately turning his focus back to his pizza.

Dacey popped a piece of bao in her mouth, chewing thoughtfully. "Mayor first, then the coroner's office. I'll handle all the questioning while you scan for unusual magical signatures. I hope the bodies will still have residual traces we can work with."

"What do you know about the mayor?"

"Mayor Winnifred Thorne's been impressive here in Millhaven. She's behind all this revival – turning the town into a tourist spot while preserving its historic charm. Rumor is she's planning a run for the governor's office next year." She took another bite before continuing. "The Conclave is invested in getting this solved quickly. They want more Mythicals in positions of power, and having one of our own as Florida's governor would be huge for the community. She's a witch like her sister Willa was." Dacey's expression sobered at the mention of the murdered woman. "Their family came from the

Appalachian backwoods. They're direct descendants of a Granny Woman."

Gideon frowned. "A what?"

"Mountain witch," Dacey explained, gesturing with her remaining corndog. "They're powerful witches who lived deep in the Appalachians. Draw their magic straight from the mountains themselves. Old, powerful magic. Wild magic."

Gideon's eyes lit up. "I wonder if her magical signature will differ from other witches I've encountered. Last week at the crematorium, we had a hedge witch come through. Her magic felt like a garden and new green growth."

"Well, you'll find out soon enough." Dacey glanced at her phone and quickly gathered their trash. "We should head out if we want to make our appointment."

Dacey lowered her voice, leaning closer across the table. "One more thing – don't tell anyone you're an auramancer. The second people know they'll try to mask their magic."

"What should I say if someone asks what I am?"

A mischievous smile played at the corners of her mouth. "Nothing. Just act mysterious."

Gideon snorted into his final bite of pizza. "Right. Because I'm so good at being mysterious."

"You'll figure it out." Dacey grabbed his now empty plate, still grinning. "Come on, Mr. Mysterious. We've got a mayor to interview."

They walked back into the afternoon heat, leaving behind the food hall's air-conditioned comfort. Before they reached the car, Dacey pulled two items from her purse and handed them to Gideon.

"I almost forgot. Your ID for this mission and your badge."

Gideon examined the driver's license first. The photo was his, but the name read 'Gideon Nash' with an address in Jacksonville he'd never seen before. The badge was sleek, silver, and professional-looking, identifying him as an investigator for the Savannah Special Investigations Unit.

"What, no gun?" Gideon asked with a playful grin.

Dacey chuckled. "Not until you're a full agent. For now, you're just considered a 'consultant'. It's protocol," she continued, holding up her own badge. "I'm Candace Santiago for this one, but you'd better still call me Dacey."

"Sure thing, Candy," Gideon said with a smirk.

Dacey rolled her eyes, but he caught the hint of a smile as she turned away.

CHAPTER 4

The city hall building matched the historic charm of downtown Millhaven, its red brick facade adorned with white trim and tall windows that reflected the late afternoon sun. Inside, the walls held framed black-and-white photographs chronicling the town's history: paddlewheel steamboats on the lake, the old railway station in its heyday, and proud townspeople in period dress standing before newly constructed buildings.

A security guard directed them up a curved staircase to the second floor, where polished hardwood floors gleamed beneath their feet. When they reached the landing, Gideon was hit with a wave of raw magic that nearly made him stumble. It felt ancient and primal, like moss-covered stones and mist-shrouded hollows – the kind of magic that sang with thunderstorms and grew in dark, misty places. The magic's aura had soaked into every corner of the floor, leaving a residue of wild energy that made his skin tingle.

Gideon followed a sign down the corridor toward the mayor's office. He arrived at a corner suite, where elegant gold lettering on frosted glass spelled "Mayor Winnifred Thorne."

A middle-aged man in a navy blazer greeted them at the reception desk, his nameplate identifying him as Michael Torres, Executive

Assistant. A stark streak of white cut through his otherwise black hair, rising from his left temple. As Torres rose from his chair in greeting, Gideon detected the distinctive shimmer of magic. He extended his senses toward the man, trying to identify the signature – not quite warlock, but similar, perhaps sorcerer. Wild magic also clung to Torres like morning dew, its presence so potent that Gideon suspected he would leave this meeting with traces of it attached to him.

Gideon made a mental note to ask Vena about the difference between the various types of human magic users. He'd been meaning to learn more about the different magical practitioners but hadn't found the time yet. He'd mainly been focusing on types of shifters since the majority of Mythicals were shifters of one kind or another.

"Agent Santiago and Agent Nash," Dacey announced. "We're here to see the mayor."

"Please, have a seat," Torres gestured to a pair of antique chairs outside the mayor's office. "I'll let Mayor Thorne know you're here."

The chairs were more comfortable than their Victorian appearance suggested. While Torres knocked on the mayor's door, Gideon pulled out his small notebook and jotted down: "Torres – warlock/sorcerer? Ask V difference between types."

He tucked the notebook away as Torres opened the door.

"Your five o'clock appointment is here, Mayor."

"Thank you, Michael." The mayor's voice carried clearly – precise and professional but warmed by a hint of Southern twang. "Would you let them know I'll be just a minute?"

Torres emerged and relayed the message, but in his haste to return to his desk, he didn't quite close the door. Through the gap, Gideon could hear muffled voices. A man spoke in low tones, his words indistinct, but the mayor's response came through clearly, thick with emotion.

"I don't know if I can do this without Willa. It doesn't feel real. I just want to wake up from this nightmare." Her voice cracked slightly. "I just… what am I going to do without her? This was *our* dream – to do it together. I don't want to do it without her. It all feels pointless."

Gideon glanced at Dacey, whose expression had softened with sympathy. The man's voice grew louder, more distinct.

"Willa would want you to finish your mission, Winnie. People need you. You can help them." There was a pause. "I want to see you in that governor's office, and I know Willa would feel the same way. She'll be there with you, even if not physically. I love you, and I'm so proud of you."

Gideon and Dacey exchanged small, sad smiles at the tender moment. They heard the mayor blow her nose, followed by the man's voice again. "I'll get your guests."

They quickly straightened in their chairs, carefully arranging their expressions into polite neutrality. The door opened fully, revealing a handsome man with salt-and-pepper hair, dressed in a crisp button-up shirt and gray slacks. Smile lines creased the corners of his eyes as he greeted them.

"Winnie will see you now."

"Thank you," Dacey said, rising smoothly to her feet. Gideon followed her into the office, where late afternoon sunlight streamed through tall windows overlooking the lake. Mayor Winnifred Thorne stood behind an impressive mahogany desk, her brown bob framing a face that appeared calm and placid, though her red-rimmed eyes betrayed recent tears. Her charcoal suit was impeccably tailored, a small silver locket at her throat catching the light.

"Agents." She stepped forward to shake their hands. "Welcome to Millhaven."

"Thank you for meeting with us, Mayor Thorne," Dacey replied. "I'm Agent Santiago, and this is Agent Nash from the Savannah Conclave. First, I want to express our deepest condolences for your loss."

Gideon had to suppress a tremor as he shook the mayor's hand. He was nearly overwhelmed by the power radiating from the woman. Her aura pulsed with raw magic, as untamed as a storm rolling down from mountain peaks. It felt ancient and primal, like gnarled pine roots gripping weathered granite, the kind of magic that crackled with autumn frost and flourished in shadowy ravines. Despite its wild nature – or perhaps because of it – her magic had an almost magnetic pull, drawing him in even as his instincts warned of its dangerous potential. The sheer strength of it had seeped into every corner of the office over her years of occupancy, turning the space into a kind of magical sponge that fairly hummed with stored power. The dichotomy struck him – this wild, free energy contained within such a polished, professional exterior, like lightning bottled in a crystal decanter.

"Thank you. Please call me Winnie," Mayor Thorne said, gesturing for them to take seats across from her desk. "And this is my husband, Gregory Thorne. He's an engineering professor at the University of Central Florida."

The man who'd let them in stepped forward with a warm smile, extending his hand first to Dacey, then to Gideon. "Greg, please," he insisted as he shook their hands. His grip was firm but not overpowering, and his gold wedding band matched the one on the mayor's left hand. He then stood behind his wife's chair, his hand resting supportively on her shoulder.

Gregory radiated a faint echo of his wife's wild mountain magic to Gideon's magical senses, absorbed over years of marriage the same way the office walls had soaked up her power. Though fully human, living so long with such potent magic had left its mark on him. Gideon wondered if the professor knew his wife was a witch. He likely did – their introduction as Conclave agents suggested as much since the Conclave's existence was only revealed to humans already aware of the magical world.

The mayor settled back into her plush office chair. "I appreciate the Conclave sending their agents to help." She took a deep breath as if in preparation for an ordeal. "Please let me know what I can do to assist your investigation. Do you think there's... foul play involved?"

"That's exactly what we're here to determine," Dacey said, her voice gentle but professional. "We're going to look into every angle, and if foul play was involved, we won't stop until we've uncovered the truth. I know this isn't easy, but I have some questions that might help us piece things together. Would that be alright?"

"Of course. I'll help however I can." Mayor Thorne's fingers went to the silver locket at her throat, twisting it slightly.

"When was the last time you saw your sister?"

"We were at the Edelweiss Hall restaurant, having a dinner meeting to finalize some details for the Fourth of July celebration." The mayor's gaze drifted to the window. "As we were wrapping up, Willa mentioned feeling exhausted." Her voice caught slightly. "I… I teased her about it. Said she was just a professor and should try being mayor – that I was tired forever. I should've paid attention and taken her complaint seriously. I should've realized… Instead, I made a joke."

Dacey leaned forward, her expression compassionate. "That's a normal interaction between sisters."

"We always teased each other like that." Tears welled in the mayor's eyes. "But I should have taken it more seriously. Willa never complained – she had an amazing work ethic. I should have realized something was wrong."

"What happened next?" Dacey asked softly.

"She went home right after. I texted her goodnight, just to check on her." Mayor Thorne drew a shaky breath. "When she didn't text back, I thought nothing of it. I figured she was sleeping. It wasn't until the next day when one of her fellow professors called me, worried because Willa hadn't shown up for her class…."

"Your sister was a professor…" Gideon prompted when it looked like the mayor wasn't going to continue.

"Yes, she was in the mathematics department at UCF." The mayor's voice filled with pride despite her grief. "She is – *was* – a brilliant mathematician."

Gregory squeezed his wife's shoulder. "That's actually how I met Winnie. Willa and I met at UCF, where we both worked and became friends. Willa introduced us thirteen years ago."

"What did you do when you found out Willa hadn't shown up for class?" Dacey continued.

"I called her, but it went straight to voicemail." The mayor's fingers tightened around her locket. "I pushed back my meetings and went to check on her. Her car was in the driveway. We have keys to each other's places, so I let myself in when she didn't answer the doorbell." Her voice grew thick. "I called out, but there was no answer."

As she described going to her sister's bedroom, Mayor Thorne's composure began to crack. Her words came haltingly. "At first... I thought she was just sleeping. She looked so peaceful...."

"I'm so sorry for your loss," Gideon said quietly. "If you need a minute to gather yourself, please let us know."

The mayor shook her head, though tears slipped down her cheeks. "She was cold. Long gone. I called the police, and that was that. I only found out last night from the coroner that her death...." She swallowed hard. "That it doesn't seem natural."

"Did you notice anything strange at your sister's house?" Dacey asked. "Was there anything else unusual about her behavior that night or in the days leading up to it? Anyone new in her life? Was she dating anyone?"

"No, nothing like that. Willa was single." Mayor Thorne wiped her eyes with a tissue her husband had quietly provided. "The only strange thing was that she hadn't changed into her pajamas – she was still wearing the same clothes from dinner the night before."

"Did your sister have any enemies?" Dacey asked. "Anyone who might have wished her harm? Anyone at work that she didn't get along with?"

Mayor Thorne shook her head emphatically. "No, absolutely not. Everyone adored Willa."

A soft knock interrupted them. The assistant opened the door partway. "I'm sorry to interrupt, Mayor, but Detective Voss has arrived as requested."

"Ah yes, thank you, Michael. Please send him in." The mayor straightened in her chair. "I asked Detective Voss to join us. He'll be your liaison with the police department during your investigation."

A tall man in a navy suit entered the room, his blonde hair neatly combed back from his forehead. His movements were precise and deliberate as he approached the desk. At first glance, he appeared completely human. However, when Gideon focused his auramancer abilities on him, he could see past the man's glamour, revealing vertical pupils like a viper's that examined them with unblinking intensity.

"Detective Victor Voss," he introduced himself, his voice carrying a slight rasp. "A pleasure to meet you both."

When he shook Gideon's hand, magic zapped his palm. Beneath the detective's human exterior, Gideon sensed something reptilian. He was pretty sure the man was some kind of snake shifter – Vena had sent him some lamia relics to memorize earlier in the month.

Gideon struggled to keep his expression neutral, his newfound abilities as an auramancer making the encounter more intense than he'd expected. His skin crawled at the thought of what lay beneath Voss's human glamour. Gideon had never been comfortable around snakes, and not knowing exactly what kind of serpentine Mythical he was shaking hands with didn't help matters.

The detective's grip was firm and cool to the touch.

"Detective Voss will help facilitate anything you need from the department," Mayor Thorne explained. "Just let him know what you require."

Voss took up position near the window, his unblinking gaze moving between the agents as Dacey resumed her questioning.

Dacey reached into her bag, withdrew several photographs, and laid them on the desk. "Do you recognize any of these people? Or know if they had any connection to your sister?"

The mayor leaned forward, studying the photos. Her eyes widened slightly as she recognized one. "Yes – that's… that's Eleanor Preston. Her family has been in Millhaven since the railroad days. She was a prominent philanthropist in town. She died about two weeks ago." She touched the edge of Eleanor's photo. "We served together on the Millhaven Heritage Foundation."

"The Millhaven Heritage Foundation?" Dacey repeated, leaving the question open-ended.

"The Heritage Foundation is one of our most active non-profits," Mayor Thorne explained, visibly brightening as she shifted into what Gideon assumed was her public-speaking mode. "We're focused on preserving Millhaven's historic architecture and character. The Royal

Palmetto project is our most ambitious undertaking yet, but we've already saved several buildings in the historic district – even the lovely blue Victorian on Oak Street where Willa...." Her voice caught slightly before she collected herself. "Where Willa lived. That was one of our first success stories."

"Success stories?" Dacey prompted gently.

"Yes. We buy historically significant properties that are at risk, restore them, and then either maintain them as museums or sell them to vetted buyers with preservation covenants. The Foundation ensures these buildings will be properly maintained for future generations." Pride crept into her voice. "We've helped transform Millhaven from a town of crumbling old buildings into a preservation success story. The Royal Palmetto Hotel is our most prestigious project yet."

"And your sister was involved with this as well?" Gideon asked.

"Oh yes, Willa was our treasurer. She had such a head for numbers...." The mayor's hand went to her locket again. "Eleanor Preston was our president. She'd been with the Foundation since its inception twenty years ago. We were founding members..."

Gregory's hand tightened on his wife's shoulder. "Losing Eleanor will cause all kinds of complications with the hotel restoration."

"Yes," the mayor agreed, patting his hand. "Her loss has been keenly felt throughout Millhaven." She turned her attention back to the photos and pointed to another. "And that's Joe. I didn't know him personally, but he's been a fixture in Millhaven for years." Her expression softened with sympathy. "A deeply troubled man, but ultimately harmless. The town has several programs to assist those experiencing homelessness, but from what I've heard, Joe was never interested in participating. I didn't realize he had died. I hadn't seen him around town lately, but I don't think it was unusual for him to disappear for long stretches of time before reappearing suddenly. Do you... do you think all these people's deaths are somehow related to Willa's?"

"That's what we're here to determine. Can you think of anyone who might have had problems with any of these people?" Dacey asked, gesturing to the photos.

The mayor shrugged. "I'm sorry, but I don't know most of them well enough to even venture a guess."

"What about Eleanor Preston? You said you served on the foundation board with her..."

"We've moved in the same social circles for years, but I wouldn't say we were particularly close – though certainly friendly," Mayor Thorne replied.

"But you worked with her extensively on this hotel restoration project?"

"That's true. Both of us were passionate about the hotel. It's been a passion project of mine for several years now." She brightened slightly, professional pride showing through her grief. "The Royal Palmetto was quite famous in the twenties. All the biggest stars of the silent film era stayed there when they came to Florida. Clara Bow, Rudolph Valentino, and Mary Pickford graced its halls. But like many grand old hotels, it fell into disrepair during the seventies and eighties."

She gestured toward one of the framed photographs on her wall, showing an imposing three-story building with elegant Mediterranean Revival architecture. "We're hoping to restore it to its former glory. It could be such a draw for visitors and put Millhaven back on the map. A few high-end hotel chains have even expressed interest in partnering with us on the restoration." The mayor straightened in her chair. "In fact, many of our Fourth of July celebrations this year are fundraising events for the restoration project."

"Has anyone expressed opposition to the hotel restoration?" Dacey asked.

"No, quite the opposite. The whole town is excited about it," Mayor Thorne replied. "Right now, it's empty and crumbling. Frankly, it's an eyesore. Once it's restored, it will bring jobs and tourists to Millhaven. Once it's completed, we will have it registered as a historic site. It's a win for everyone."

"That sounds very exciting," Gideon said, earning him an approving smile from the politician.

"It really is. Hopefully, Eleanor's loss won't put the project too far behind, but only time will tell."

With a glance at her watch, Dacey began gathering her notes. "This has been extremely helpful, Mayor Thorne. Unfortunately, we have an appointment with the coroner that we can't miss."

"Of course." The mayor opened a drawer and withdrew two business cards. "Please, take my card – it has my personal number. Call anytime if there's any way I can help."

As she handed one each to Dacey and Gideon, Winnie gave them a worried look. "What... what happens next?"

"We'll conduct our investigation and find out what's happening," Dacey assured her. "Could you give me a list of everyone who was at the Edelweiss Hall meeting? We need to interview everyone who last saw your sister." She added in a lower voice, "For now, we're telling the general public that Willa's death was from natural causes."

The mayor nodded in approval and then pressed the intercom button on her desk. "Michael, could you bring me a list of everyone who attended the meeting at Edelweiss Hall?" She released the button and turned back to them. "He keeps meticulous records."

Detective Voss, who had been standing silently by the window, straightened his jacket. "If you'll excuse me, I need to get back to the precinct." He approached Gideon and Dacey, handing them each his business card with a direct number scrawled on the back. "Call me if you need anything at all during your investigation." His vertical pupils briefly caught the light as he added, "Anything."

As Voss moved toward the door, Michael appeared with the printed sheet. They exchanged brief nods as they passed, the detective's movements fluid and purposeful as he exited the room.

The mayor passed the list to Dacey. She scanned it quickly, nodding with satisfaction as her eyes moved down the page.

"This is very helpful. Thank you," Dacey said, tapping the paper appreciatively.

Dacey and Gideon stood, shaking hands with the mayor and her husband before heading for the door.

"Thank you for taking the time to meet with us, Mayor," Dacey said before they exited.

"Please call me Winnie. You're here to help my family during this unbearable loss; there is no need to be formal."

"Thank you, Winnie. We'll be in touch soon."

As they descended the curved staircase, Gideon leaned close to Dacey. "What do you think?"

"I'm not sure yet." Dacey's voice was barely above a whisper. "Did you pick up on any unusual magic?"

"Nothing unusual, but her power is impressive. That mountain magic of hers – it's the strongest witch magic I've encountered – not that I have much experience with it, but still. You could feel it saturating the whole office." Gideon shook his head slightly.

"And what did you think of the mayor?" Dacey asked.

"I liked her. I can't believe I'm saying that about a career politician... but my initial impression is that she actually cares about more than herself and accumulating power. Only time will tell if that remains true."

"I liked her too," Dacey responded, shaking her head at the thought of liking a politician.

Something about Mayor Thorne reminded Gideon of his mother despite the stark contrasts between the women. Where the mayor projected polished elegance and obvious wealth, his mom managed a hardware store in Gulf Breeze and owned one formal dress she wore for both weddings and funerals. She would have been as out of place in that refined office as a hammer on a silk pillow. Yet beneath Mayor Thorne's sophisticated exterior, Gideon sensed a familiar essence – that same combination of maternal caring and iron will. Both women, however different their circumstances, radiated an unshakable strength wrapped in genuine care for others.

CHAPTER 5

Dacey pulled out her phone as they stepped out of City Hall into the punishing heat of a Florida July. She squinted at the map app, then looked up. "The medical examiner's office is just about a mile down the road," she said, slipping the phone back into her pocket. Even at nearly six o'clock, the sun blazed in a cloudless sky, the humidity making the air feel thick enough to swim through. "It's not worth getting the car – if you're up for walking. The ME's office is attached to Lake Monroe Hospital. We can take the riverwalk – maybe catch some breeze off the water."

"Sounds good to me." Gideon welcomed any excuse to stay outside a bit longer. Even in the heat of a Florida summer, a walk sounded better than getting back in the car.

The breeze off Lake Monroe provided welcome relief from the summer heat, carrying the mingled scents of water and sun-warmed wood from the marina's weathered docks.

As they passed the marina, a flash of bright color caught Gideon's eye. A petite woman stood outside a tiny houseboat, reaching up to hang a 'CLOSED' sign beneath a placard that read "Millhaven Sailing School." The late afternoon sun caught her turquoise tank top as she stretched to reach the hook.

"Hey, Captain Sam! How was the sailing today?" A man's voice called from somewhere down the dock.

"It was crap! Not enough breeze. We were just bobbin' and bakin' out on the water," she called back with a laugh.

A loud squawk rang out from behind the woman, and she turned toward a large cage positioned next to the houseboat's front door. "Hush, Athena. Bob wasn't talking to you. Mind your own business." The red macaw ruffled its feathers indignantly.

Gideon couldn't help grinning at the exchange, and when he glanced at Dacey, she was chuckling too. They continued along the riverwalk, where alternating American and state flags snapped in the lake breeze. Palm trees lined the path, their fronds casting shifting shadows on the concrete.

"The lake is bigger and prettier than I expected," Gideon commented, scanning his eyes across the water and back to the marina where sailboats bobbed gently at their moorings.

"Lake Monroe," Dacey gestured across the water, "is pretty much why Millhaven exists. All those steamboats in city hall photos were docked right here. Back in the 1800s, this was prime real estate. Because bigger boats couldn't go further south on the St. Johns River, it gets too shallow, this was their final stop."

"How do you know all that?" Gideon asked, impressed.

"I did some quick research when we got assigned the case," Dacey replied with a slight shrug. "I like knowing the history of a place – sometimes it helps make sense of the case."

Up ahead on their left, across the street from the riverwalk, the hospital's white walls gleamed in the weakening sunlight, its red trim seeming especially vivid against the blue sky. They found the medical examiner's entrance tucked around the side of the building, marked by an unassuming sign.

Inside, the fluorescent lights and institutional flooring felt dim against the sunny afternoon they'd left behind. They approached a window where a man sat working at a computer.

"I'm Agent Santiago," Dacey said. "Doctor Blackwood is expecting us."

"Send them back!" a woman's voice called from somewhere behind the reception area.

The receptionist pointed them toward a door, and they found themselves face to face with a broad-shouldered older woman with silver hair buzzed close to her scalp. "Tabitha Blackwood," she said, extending her hand. Her grip was firm, her hands strong and slightly rough.

Gideon's magical senses tingled as they shook hands. There was something distinctly feline about her energy – some kind of shifter, he guessed, though he couldn't pin down exactly what type.

"The Savannah Conclave sent you?" When they nodded, Dr. Blackwood's shoulders relaxed slightly. "I'm glad they responded so quickly. I was worried they still weren't taking my concerns seriously."

She led them down a corridor, her sensible shoes squeaking against the linoleum. "I first became concerned when Marcus Chauvin was brought in. He'd been in some kind of fight. He'd been found unconscious in a bar's parking lot, from what I understand. His injuries were mostly superficial – nothing that should have been fatal. But he never woke up. I was unable to find a cause of death. At first, since he was Fae, I thought maybe he'd been dabbling in magic he shouldn't have. But now I'm not so sure…."

"Is it unusual to be unable to determine a cause of death?" Gideon asked.

"It's not unheard of, but it doesn't happen often. And I've never had more than two in a month. And now here we are with five…."

"Forgive my ignorance here, but this isn't my area of expertise. Can you explain how there can be situations where the cause of death is hard to determine?" Gideon asked.

"Oh, certainly," Dr. Blackwood replied. "There can be several reasons – advanced decomposition, certain types of magic, toxins that break down quickly in the body. Some cardiac arrhythmias leave no physical traces. Some drownings, electrolyte imbalances, and certain neurological events – they can all be tricky to detect post-mortem. About two to five percent of autopsies end up with an undetermined cause of death."

"What about Brandon Cho, the second victim?" Dacey asked as they reached a set of heavy double doors.

"He was examined in Lake Mary. I only found out about him after Willa Wagner died. I called the other ME offices in Florida, looking for similar cases." Dr. Blackwood pushed through the doors into the morgue. "When Eleanor Preston came in – the next victim I received – I didn't immediately flag it as unusual. She had a history of heart problems. But after Joe...." She shook her head. "I emailed the Conclave detailing my concerns at the time, but apparently, the numbers weren't statistically significant enough to warrant investigation. Not until Willa Wagner."

"Anything else unusual about the victims?" Dacey asked. "Beyond the missing cause of death?"

"Other than Marcus's injuries from the bar fight? No, nothing unusual – no deadly wounds or injuries, nothing out of place. The bruises on his face and jaw were superficial, and the scrapes on his knuckles showed he'd gotten some hits in himself. The rest of the bodies don't have a single mark on them. If they weren't lying here dead, you'd think they just came in for a routine checkup." Dr. Blackwood approached a wall of small steel doors. "Would you like to see them?"

At Dacey's nod, the doctor opened one of the doors and slid out a tray. The man lying there was thin, heavily tattooed, with black hair. Purple bruises mottled his jaw and left cheekbone, and his split lip had been cleaned but was still visible. His knuckles were scraped raw. Dacey glanced at Gideon and raised an eyebrow.

Gideon stepped forward and carefully touched the dead man's shoulder. His eyes widened in surprise. "He's Fae, but...." He trailed off, confused.

"What is it?" Dacey asked.

Gideon slowly waved his hand over the body. "I'm not sure yet. Show me the others?"

One by one, Dr. Blackwood revealed the remaining victims. Eleanor Preston, her white hair slicked back from her face. Joe looked far older than Gideon suspected he was. And finally, Willa Wagner, whose resemblance to the mayor made Gideon's chest tighten uncomfortably.

He passed his hand over each body in turn, his frown deepening. "Doctor," he said finally, "do you have any other Mythical bodies here? Ones not related to this case?"

Dr. Blackwood looked confused but nodded, opening a different door. "This one is—"

"Don't tell me," Gideon interrupted. "I need to test something."

The woman on the tray was severely damaged, clearly from some kind of accident, but Gideon felt her power immediately. "Vampire?"

The doctor nodded. "Even being a vampire won't save you if you won't wear a seatbelt."

Gideon stuffed his hands in his pockets, his expression troubled. "I can barely feel any trace of the victims' magic."

"What about the humans?" Dacey gestured to Joe and Eleanor's bodies.

"Even humans have an aura, though it's usually muted compared to a Mythical. But these bodies...." He shook his head. "Almost all of their magic is gone, both human and Mythicals. I was worried that something was wrong with me or maybe even this room, but I can feel the vampire's magic just fine."

"You're a sensate?" Dr. Blackwood asked, interested. "An auramancer?"

"He is," Dacey confirmed. "But that needs to stay between us. We trust you since you're the one who alerted us to this situation, but we don't want anyone else to know."

Blackwood nodded her head, an understanding look on her face.

"Could it be some kind of spell?" Dacey suggested. "Something that killed them magically?"

"Maybe?" Gideon was already shaking his head. "Although if it was a spell, I should be able to detect traces of that magic. But there's nothing. It's like...." He gestured helplessly at the bodies. "It's like there's just a void where they're lying. I've never seen or felt anything like it."

"Could the bodies be warded?" Dacey asked, brow furrowed. "Some kind of spell to conceal the magic used to kill the victim?"

"I'm still learning to detect wards, but if I know it's there or if I'm looking for it, I can sense that something magical exists there. It's like a wall I'm training myself to push past – to see beyond the concealment. It takes concentration and effort, but I can usually tell when magic is being hidden from me, even if it's too strong for me to break through yet."

Gideon turned back to Chauvin's body on the tray, his hand hovering just inches above the corpse. "But this… this is completely different. There's no wall to break through. It's like a black hole where nothing magical exists." He pulled his hand back, feeling unsettled. "I've never seen or felt anything like it."

Gideon rubbed his eyes, trying to clear the unsettling sensation. Looking at the space where their auras should be felt like staring at the sun. When he looked away, a dark void lingered in his magical vision, and a perfect silhouette of each body burned into his senses like a photograph negative.

"Well, shit. That's not good news," Dacey exclaimed, a frown marring her brow.

"Wait," Gideon said suddenly. "Do you still have any personal effects from the victims? Something they were wearing when they died. I want to send a sample to Vena for analysis."

Blackwood nodded. "Follow me." She led them down a sterile corridor to a secure storage room, pulling out a box labeled 'Chauvin, M.' "Everything's cataloged and preserved."

Gideon rifled through the contents until he found a watch, its face slightly scratched but otherwise intact. "This should work. I'll need an iron-lined box – can't risk the residual energy getting corrupted in transit."

"We keep a few in stock for exactly that purpose," Blackwood replied, reaching for a cabinet behind her. She pulled out what looked like an ordinary cardboard shipping box, unmarked and plain. But when she opened it, Gideon could see the dull gleam of lead lining the entire interior. She grabbed a roll of lead foil tape from a nearby shelf. "Extra precaution for the seams."

Gideon carefully dropped the watch inside and closed the lid with a solid, metallic click. He then took the tape from Blackwood and methodically went around each edge of the box, the metallic tape crackling softly as he pressed it into place. The dull gray strips would ensure nothing got in – or out – during transit.

"If you write down the address, I can send it out today," Blackwood offered.

"That would be great, thanks." Gideon scribbled Vena's details on a shipping form. He turned to Dacey. "In the meantime, we'll have to do this the old-fashioned way."

"Good old detective work," she agreed.

They turned back to Tabitha. "Thank you for your assistance, Dr. Blackwood," Dacey said. "We'll be in touch if we have any more questions."

"Please do," the doctor replied. "And… be careful. Whatever this is, it's not natural."

Outside, the sun had dipped lower, painting the sky in shades of orange and pink. The humidity still hung heavy in the air as they discussed their next move.

"I'd like to check out Willa Wagner's home if you're up for it," Dacey said. "However, if you're too tired, we can get to the hotel and go first thing in the morning."

"Nah, let's get it done," Gideon replied. "The trail's already cold enough."

As they walked back to Dacey's car, she pulled out Detective Voss's card and dialed his number. "Detective? Agent Santiago here. We'd like to take a look at Willa Wagner's house. Any chance you could meet us there to let us in?"

Gideon couldn't hear the detective's response, but Dacey gave him a thumbs up. "Excellent, we'll see you in thirty minutes then."

Once they got into the car, Dacey pulled up Willa's address on the GPS. Instead of pulling out of the parking space, though, she turned to Gideon. "What do you think so far?"

Gideon shrugged, his expression troubled. "I have no idea, but something is definitely not right. I haven't been doing this aura-mancer stuff long, but I've never seen magic just... absent like that. Those bodies had no more magic in them than a piece of rock. Less, actually. It is super weird. And unsettling, to be honest."

Dacey fired up the engine and reached for her phone. Pulling out of the parking lot, she hit "Wiz" on her display and switched to speaker.

"Dacey! Gideon!" A bright, bubbly voice filled the car. "I heard you two are working together again. Dacey's been *so* excited about it."

Gideon glanced at Dacey, trying and failing to hide his hopeful expression. Dacey rolled her eyes dramatically at Wiz's comment, though Gideon noticed she didn't deny it. He tried not to take the eye-roll personally – he knew how Dacey was with any display of affection or emotion.

"Wiz, we've got a situation here," Dacey said, changing the subject. She outlined what they'd discovered so far: the seemingly unrelated victims, the lack of cause of death, and most disturbing, the complete absence of magical energy that Gideon had detected.

"Hmm," Wiz said when Dacey finished. "I think we should loop Leonhard in on this. As a numerai, he might be able to detect a pattern to the victims that we're missing."

There was a brief pause, then a dry, sardonic voice joined the call. "What fresh hell is this?"

Not for the first time, Gideon wondered what the magical numbers man looked like – Leonhard was the only member of Dacey's team at the Conclave that Gideon had never met in person.

They explained the situation again, and Leonhard was quiet for a moment. "I'll analyze the data – deaths, locations, timing, whatever I can find. See if there's a pattern we're not seeing. I'll be in touch." He disconnected without another word.

Wiz giggled. "Lenny really needs to work on his people skills."

"You know he hates it when you call him that," Dacey scolded. "While he works on the victims' connections, can you dig into their backgrounds? We need to know if there are any skeletons in their closets. And see if you can find out who the homeless man 'Joe' really was."

"On it! Good luck, you two. Try not to have too much fun without me!" With that, Wiz hung up, leaving Gideon and Dacey alone in the car once more.

CHAPTER 6

The GPS guided them through Millhaven's historic district, where massive oaks created natural archways over the narrow, cobbled streets. Heavy with Spanish moss, their branches cast long shadows in the deepening twilight.

Less than fifteen minutes from the hospital, Dacey pulled up in front of a blue clapboard house with crisp white trim.

As he stared at Willa's house, Gideon's first thought was of his mother. She'd take one look at this perfectly maintained Victorian with its white picket fence and matching gingerbread trim and launch into her favorite daydream about opening a bed and breakfast. She would adore this house. It even had a wraparound porch complete with rocking chairs and hanging ferns. Ancient oak trees spread their protective canopy over the property, their twisted branches reaching toward the darkening sky.

A gray sedan pulled behind them, and Detective Voss unfolded his tall frame from the driver's seat. Gideon had expected to see police tape across the front entryway, but the house looked perfectly normal – peaceful even. Then he remembered that, officially, Willa Wagner had died of natural causes. Looking at the neat flower beds and carefully trimmed shrubs, he was more certain than ever that there had been nothing natural about her death.

Voss climbed the porch steps ahead of them, keys jingling in his hand.

"Thank you for meeting us, Detective," Dacey said.

"Please, call me Victor." His voice had that same slight rasp, but his tone was warmer than before. Gideon noticed that the invitation didn't seem to extend to him, and he tried not to bristle at the way Voss's gaze lingered on Dacey. He pushed down the flare of annoyance, reminding himself that his unrequited feelings for his partner weren't anyone else's problem. He wouldn't let a slight crush compromise their friendship or his professionalism.

The moment Gideon crossed the threshold, he felt that same wild mountain magic he'd sensed in the mayor's office. It was fainter here, just residual energy that had seeped into the walls during Willa's lifetime, but it was unmistakable.

"I can sense the witch's magic here," he whispered to Dacey. "Even though I couldn't detect it on her body."

Dacey raised an eyebrow. "Interesting."

The interior of the house matched its exterior perfectly – perhaps too perfectly. Every room looked like it belonged in a magazine. The formal parlor featured delicate Victorian furniture arranged just so, with precisely placed throw pillows and carefully chosen artwork. The dining room held a gleaming mahogany table with settings that Gideon had a hunch were never used. Even the kitchen, with its modern appliances, maintained the historical aesthetic with copper pots hanging in perfect alignment and matching canisters lined up on the counter by size.

Stepping into the office, Gideon left the historical theme of the house behind. Against one wall stood a desk featuring a sleek computer station surrounded by multiple monitors. A whiteboard covered in mathematical equations that might as well have been an alien language to Gideon took up another. Floor-to-ceiling bookcases crammed with textbooks and binders lined the remaining walls. The only piece of art in the office was an artistic close-up photo of a fiddlehead fern, the tightly coiled frond a splash of color in the otherwise stark room.

However, even this modern space seemed meticulously controlled – the desk was pristine, the monitors perfectly aligned, and not a single paper appeared out of place. Despite being stuffed full, the bookcases had an organizational system that was evident even to Gideon's untrained eye, with color-coded binders and books arranged by some precise methodology.

To Gideon, it felt more like a museum than a home. He couldn't imagine kicking off his shoes and relaxing here after a long day of work. The whole place felt like a stage, with every item carefully chosen and positioned for maximum effect.

The bedroom, however, told a different story. Here, finally, were signs of real life – and recent death. A pair of heels lay where they'd been kicked off, one upright and one on its side. A designer jacket had been tossed carelessly over a chair, with a leather purse dropped beside it. The bed was rumpled, and the duvet was partially pulled back as if someone had collapsed onto it without fully getting beneath it.

Gideon could picture it clearly: an exhausted woman coming home, shedding her professional armor piece by piece on her way to bed. He moved closer to the mattress, aware of Voss watching his every move. Carefully, trying to look casual, he held his hand over the bed. The difference hit him immediately – this spot was utterly devoid of magic, a dead zone in the otherwise magically saturated house.

"This is where she was found?" he asked Voss, pointing to the side of the bed he was examining.

The detective nodded. "The mayor found her there, still fully dressed from the night before."

Dacey caught Gideon's eye, raising an eyebrow in question. He cut his eyes toward Voss, then back at her. She gave a slight nod, understanding his reluctance to discuss magical findings in front of the detective.

"Did you know Willa Wagner?" Dacey asked, turning to face Voss.

"Somewhat," he replied. "I deal with the mayor quite often, so I inevitably got to know Willa since the two sisters were pretty inseparable."

"What was she like?"

Voss considered for a moment. "Quiet, smart. Somewhat introverted, especially compared to the mayor. She preferred to stay in the background while her sister took center stage."

"Anyone you can think of who might have wanted to hurt her?" Dacey asked. "Any grudges or bad blood?"

"No," Voss shook his head. "Everyone liked Willa. She wasn't the type to make enemies."

"Was she dating anyone?"

"No."

"How can you be so sure?" Gideon interjected. "Maybe she had a secret someone."

Voss scoffed. "Not in this town. Keeping secrets is almost impossible here."

They continued their search through the rest of the house, but nothing else seemed out of place. Dacey opened the refrigerator, examining its sparse contents. "Not much of a cook?"

"She wasn't home much," Voss replied, leaning against the doorframe. "Everyone knew she spent most of her free time either with the mayor, at the university, or at meetings for the Heritage Foundation. The sisters were incredibly close – you rarely saw one without the other at local events."

Gideon, who'd grown up as an only child and had often wished for a sibling, felt a pang of envy at the thought of such a close relationship. Then he remembered the devastation in Mayor Thorne's eyes, and the envy vanished. Having such a deep connection only made its severing that much more painful.

"The mayor mentioned the foundation," Dacey replied, closing the refrigerator.

"The Millhaven Heritage Foundation is *the* social organization in town," Voss explained. "They're leading the restoration of the Royal Palmetto Hotel, along with several other historic buildings. Both the mayor and her sister, along with Eleanor Preston, were active members."

Dacey and Gideon exchanged a look. That was two victims connected through the same organization.

"Would you be able to get us a membership list?" Dacey asked.

"The list from the Edelweiss Hall meeting the mayor gave you will be most of them," Voss said, "but I'll email you the complete membership list first thing in the morning." His reptilian eyes remained fixed on Dacey.

As they prepared to leave, Gideon took one last look around the house. He was disappointed that he hadn't found anything to help their case.

Outside, the streetlights had come on, their warm glow fighting back the gathering darkness. Voss locked up behind them, then turned to Dacey. "If you are looking for a place to stay, I'd try the Lake Monroe Inn. It's just a few miles from here – one of the nicer places in town."

"The Conclave has already booked us there, but I appreciate your thoughtfulness, Victor," Dacey said. "And thanks for your help tonight."

"Any time." He smiled. "Don't hesitate to call if you need anything else."

As they walked back to their car, Gideon could feel Voss watching them – watching Dacey – until they drove away. The weight of the detective's gaze made his skin crawl, though he wasn't sure if that was due to his personal feelings about the man's obvious interest in Dacey or Gideon's instinctive reaction to snakes.

Gideon twisted slightly in his seat, keeping Voss in his peripheral vision until they turned the corner.

Dacey noticed the direction of his focus and asked, "What kind of Mythical is Victor?" Dacey asked, glancing at him. "I thought maybe a shifter, but it's not polite to ask until you get to know someone better."

"Some kind of snake creature," Gideon replied with a barely repressed shudder.

Something in his demeanor must have given him away because Dacey grinned. "Not a fan of snakes, I take it?"

Gideon made a face and shook his head emphatically, which drew a snort from her.

Once they'd put some distance between themselves and Willa's house, Gideon finally spoke about what he'd discovered. "Willa's magic just... stopped at her bed. Where there should have been residual magic, all that was there was a void, just like with the bodies."

"It's got to be related to the cause of death."

"I agree." Gideon agreed, drumming his fingers on his thigh, thinking. "The rest of the house still held traces of her magic, but where she died... it's like that spot is a dead zone. There's just nothing there. I've never encountered anything that could cause that."

"Neither have I."

"I'm going to text Vena and see if she's ever heard of someone's magic disappearing after death."

Dacey's hands tightened on the steering wheel. "Let's hope Leonhard or Wiz can find some connections because we've got more questions than answers right now."

Gideon nodded, staring out the window at the darkening sky. "And not a single decent lead."

Silence settled between them for a moment, broken only by the soft hum of the car's engine and the rhythmic clicking of the turn signal as Dacey changed lanes.

Later that night, Gideon lay sprawled across his hotel bed, staring at the textured ceiling. A ceiling fan spun lazy circles above him, its rhythmic whirring doing nothing to quiet his thoughts. Despite the exhaustion weighing down his limbs, sleep remained elusive.

Every time he closed his eyes, he saw the same images: the pristine Victorian house with its perfect rooms, the void of magic around Willa's bed, the devastation in Mayor Thorne's eyes. And Dacey – always Dacey. The way she'd questioned the mayor, how easily she'd caught Gideon's subtle signals, the grin she'd given him when he'd confessed to hating snakes. He groaned and pressed the heels of his hands against his eyes. This crush was getting ridiculous.

A knock at his door made him start. He sat up, glancing at the clock – 11:47 PM. When he opened the door, Dacey stood in the hallway, case file tucked under one arm and two bottles from the mini fridge dangling from her fingers. She'd changed into yoga pants and an oversized sweatshirt, her dark hair in a messy bun. Even dressed down, she managed to take his breath away.

"Hope I didn't wake you," she said, though her knowing look suggested she'd figured he'd be awake.

"I wasn't asleep," Gideon snorted, stepping back to let her in. "Even though I should be exhausted, my brain won't shut up. This case has me spinning in circles."

Dacey held up the file, her eyes bright with excitement. "Guess what I found?"

"What?"

"After reviewing Brandon Cho's information, I realized he works *in* Millhaven," she said, barely containing her enthusiasm.

Gideon sat up straighter. "Really? So the town connects all the victims?"

"It appears so," Dacey nodded. "He was a nurse at the Serenity Living nursing home on 5th Street."

A grin spread across Dacey's face, her usual mercurial nature settling into something warmer and more intimate. "Want to look it over with me again? Maybe we'll catch something we missed."

"Hell yeah," Gideon said, matching her grin. He gestured to the bottles in her hand. "But first, let's have a drink. We might as well be comfortable while we drive ourselves crazy with theories."

CHAPTER 7

Something tickled Gideon's nose, and he batted at it absently, still mostly asleep. The tickling sensation persisted, and he cracked open his eyes to find his face buried in a mass of dark, silky hair. His heart stopped for a moment as his foggy brain registered that the hair belonged to Dacey.

He froze, afraid to move, trying to piece together how they'd ended up in this position. The case files were scattered across the foot of the bed, and two empty bottles from the mini fridge lay on their sides on the nightstand. They must have fallen asleep while reviewing the evidence.

They were both fully clothed, lying on top of the blanket rather than under it. Gideon realized he should have been cold – the hotel's air conditioning was cranked to arctic levels – but Dacey radiated warmth like a space heater. He'd never met any other bennu shifters besides Dacey, but he wondered if they all ran hotter than an average human.

Dacey made a soft noise in her sleep and rolled over to face him. Gideon quickly shut his eyes, not wanting to be caught staring at her like some creepazoid. His heart hammered in his chest as he waited, barely breathing, but after a moment of silence, he dared to open his eyes again.

Her dark eyebrows formed bold slashes above her closed eyes, and her tanned skin held the warm golden undertones of her Egyptian heritage. A small scatter of freckles dusted the bridge of her nose – something he'd never noticed before. Her full lips were slightly parted as she slept, and a lock of hair had fallen across her cheek.

Glancing past her to the window, Gideon could see the sky lightening, the darkness giving way to the pale gray of early morning. He knew Dacey had wanted to get an early start on the investigation. As much as he wanted to let her sleep – she looked so peaceful, and God knew they both needed the rest – he should probably wake her.

"Dacey," he said softly, reaching out to give her shoulder a gentle shake. "Hey, wake up."

Her eyes fluttered open, confusion clouding them momentarily before recognition dawned. A slow smile spread across her face, and Gideon's heart did that annoying flutter thing it seemed to do more and more around her.

"We must have fallen asleep," she murmured, voice husky with sleep. "What time is it?"

Gideon rolled over to check the clock on the nightstand, trying to ignore how cold the bed felt the moment he moved away from her warmth. "Almost six."

"Good." Dacey sat up, stretching her arms above her head with a jaw-cracking yawn. "I fell asleep before I could set an alarm." Her hair had partially escaped its bun during the night, dark tendrils framing her face. "Let's get showered and cleaned up. Meet you in the lobby in thirty minutes?"

She stood, gathering the scattered case files. Even rumpled from sleep, she moved with that innate grace that made everything she did look purposeful and elegant. She headed for the door, then paused with her hand on the handle, turning back to give him a small smile. "I'm glad you're here to help me work on this case."

Then she was gone, leaving Gideon alone with the lingering warmth in the bed and the faint scent of her shampoo on his pillow.

He flopped back onto the mattress with a groan, pressing the heels of his hands against his eyes. This crush was *definitely* getting worse.

He lay there for another moment, then forced himself to get up. They had mysterious deaths to solve, and he couldn't afford to be distracted by his feelings for his partner. Besides, a cold shower might help clear his head.

Almost thirty minutes later, showered and changed, Gideon stepped out of the elevator into the hotel lobby. The smell of coffee drifted from the breakfast room, pulling him into the space. A few other early risers occupied the scattered tables and armchairs, most clutching coffee cups like lifelines.

Dacey wasn't there yet, so he headed for the coffee station. When she emerged from the elevator, he'd just finished fixing two cups – one black for himself, one with a splash of cream and sugar for Dacey. She'd traded yesterday's suit for dark jeans and a fitted blazer, and her hair was pulled back in a neat braid. She looked fresh and put together as if she hadn't spent the night passed out on top of case files.

"Is one of those for me?" she asked, nodding at the coffee cups in his hands.

"Of course." He handed her the doctored one. "Thought we could use the caffeine after our late-night investigation session."

"Thanks." She took a sip and smiled. "Perfect. You remember how I take it."

"I pay attention," he said with a shrug, trying to sound casual.

"So," Dacey said, pulling out her phone, "I've been thinking about the Heritage Foundation connection. I want to review that membership list Voss promised us as soon as it comes in, cross-reference it against the guest list from the dinner at Edelweiss Hall."

"Good idea. We should also...." Gideon trailed off as his phone buzzed. He pulled it out to find a text from Vena about his magic question from the night before. His expression must have changed as he read it because Dacey stepped closer.

"What is it?"

"Vena says she knows of several kinds of Mythicals that can drain or consume life force, but they all leave magical traces when they attack, plus there would be evidence left behind on the victim's body. She's going to send me a list of all known beings that feed on magic or life force."

"I somehow doubt that we're going to find what's doing this on her list. We would have already solved this case if it was that easy." Dacey's brow furrowed.

"It'll still be good to get the list and rule them out. She will do more research and see what else she can dig up. She said she'll get us a list of all Mythicals that consume life forces before the end of the day."

Dacey took another sip of coffee, then squared her shoulders. "Well, standing here theorizing isn't going to solve anything. Ready to head out?"

"Where to first?"

"I want to visit each location where the victims died, see if we can pick up any trace of magical residue. Plus, we need to talk to all their family members and friends – maybe someone noticed something off in the days before their deaths. Let's start with the first victim."

"The tattoo artist?"

"Yeah, he lived not far from here. I've texted Voss, and he said he'd be happy to tag along with us today and get us access to the victims' homes."

Gideon nodded, schooling his face to hide any disappointment. He'd hoped that it would be just him and Dacey.

After each grabbing a bagel from the hotel offering, they headed for the parking lot, eating as they walked. As they walked, Gideon couldn't help but notice how easily they fell into step together, matching each other's stride without thinking. This was their first real case working together, and he hoped it would go well enough that they'd be assigned more investigations as partners.

CHAPTER 8

Dacey pulled the car into the driveway of a modern-looking house on the opposite side of town from Millhaven's historic district. As they'd driven away from the marina and downtown area, Gideon had watched the scenery change to run-down neighborhoods where poverty was evident in the peeling paint and sagging porches, then transitioning into this newer development. The houses here all shared the same stucco exterior and modern farmhouse aesthetic as if they'd been stamped from the same mold.

While they waited for Detective Voss to arrive, Gideon pulled out Marcus Chauvin's case file, flipping through the pages. "Says here he was single?"

"Yeah, why?" Dacey glanced over at him.

"Did he have any roommates?"

Dacey shook her head, raising an eyebrow at him.

Gideon gestured at the house. "Maybe his parents are rich? It seems like a pretty nice place for a tattoo artist. Was he really that in demand?"

"Ah." Dacey smiled. "I sometimes forget that you're not familiar with our world yet. Chauvin wasn't just any tattoo artist – he specialized in Fae sigil tattoos. Those practitioners can charge astronomical fees for their work. Getting a magically-infused tattoo is expensive, but it's also highly sought after."

A police cruiser pulled up beside them, and Detective Voss stepped out. After exchanging greetings, he unlocked the front door.

The only hint of what lay beyond the pristine exterior was a large, overflowing ashtray on a small table by the front door. Once inside, the house told a different story entirely. The interior was a stark contrast to the well-maintained facade – pure bachelor pad chaos. A massive leather sectional dominated the living room, facing an equally oversized flatscreen TV. Several gaming consoles sat in an entertainment center below, their cables tangled in a black web. The kitchen wasn't much better – dishes filled the sink, and Gideon caught a whiff of something that had been sitting too long.

Marcus's Fae magic permeated the space, similar to how Willa's witch magic had suffused her home. It clung to the walls and furniture like a light mist. A collection of framed photographs of tattoos hanging in the living room caught Gideon's eye – they were the only splashes of color in the otherwise monochromatic black, white, and gray interior. Gideon admired the intricate Celtic knotwork where the artist had skillfully woven wolves and ravens into the flowing patterns of spirals and knots.

They continued their sweep of the house, finding more evidence of Marcus's profession scattered throughout – sketchbooks filled with intricate designs, boxes of supplies, and rows of ink bottles. Gideon noticed that the Fae magic concentrated most heavily around the inks, making them shimmer with an otherworldly glow to his eyes.

Gideon picked up one of the bottles, wanting to take a closer look.

When Voss moved to examine something in another room, Gideon quietly drew closer to Dacey. "I can sense a ton of Marcus's magic in the ink," he whispered, not wanting the detective to overhear them. "Is that the stuff he would've used for the sigil tattoos?"

She nodded slightly. "Specially created to hold Fae enchantments."

They made their way upstairs, investigating room by room. In Marcus's bedroom, Gideon paused, eyes closed in concentration. "No void here like at Willa's," he told Dacey quietly.

"That matches with a theory I have," she replied. "I think that the void only appears where death occurred. And Marcus didn't die here."

"That makes sense. We should go to where he died and see."

"That would be at the hospital. I want to talk to his co-workers first, but then we should check out the hospital and see if we can talk to anyone there who worked on him when he was admitted. Also, I want to check the bar where he was found unconscious."

The two-car garage was their final stop. A Tesla Cybertruck and a top-of-the-line Range Rover sat inside, both spotless despite the disarray in the house. Gideon whistled. "Sigil tattoos really *do* pay well."

"Sense anything unusual?" Dacey asked as he held his hands over the vehicles.

Gideon shook his head. "Nothing out of the ordinary. No void. Just traces of Fae magic, not quite as strong as it is around his tattooing supplies."

"Then I think we're done here. Let's check out his workplace next."

As they headed back to the car, Gideon felt the weight of his inexperience as an auramancer. The July sun beat down mercilessly, the humid Florida air already thick and stifling despite the early hour. The cookie-cutter houses looked almost cheerful in the daylight with their matching white paint and gray trim. But somewhere in this pleasant suburban setting, an unknown force was killing people, and Gideon worried his limited skills would fail Dacey when she needed them most.

He climbed into the passenger seat beside Dacey, pulling out his phone to check the address of their next stop, the tattoo parlor. He couldn't help glancing back at Chauvin's house as she backed out of the driveway. It looked perfectly normal from the outside – just another upper-middle-class home in an upscale development.

"What are you thinking?" Dacey asked, catching his troubled expression.

"I think that whoever or whatever did this isn't like anything in Vena's books." He turned back to face forward, his jaw set. "We're dealing with something I've never heard of."

Dacey nodded grimly as she turned onto the main road. “Don’t worry, Giddy. This is how all my cases feel. They don’t bring me in unless it’s confusing as shit and twice as hard to solve.”

“Oh goody,” Gideon deadpanned, earning a giggle from the bennu shifter.

CHAPTER 9

Wild Court Tattoos occupied a small standalone building on a busy commercial street. The industrial brick structure with large factory windows and exposed steel beams stood out among the other historic storefronts, its metal sign with riveted edges displaying bold, stenciled lettering against a black background.

Dacey pulled into one of the angled parking spots out front, cutting the engine.

Inside, the shop's reception area was cool and dim. It was decorated with framed artwork showcasing intricate tattoo designs. A young woman with multiple facial piercings looked up from her phone as they entered.

Dacey flashed her badge. "Is the owner available?"

"I'm the owner." A tall, lean figure emerged from a hallway behind the reception desk. A close-cropped pixie cut accentuated the woman's androgynous features; the tips of her hair dyed a deep burgundy red. Brilliant koi fish in orange, blue, and green twined up and down both arms, the fish's scales catching and dancing in the shop's lighting. "Can I help you?"

Gideon's senses immediately prickled. Behind the owner's carefully maintained human glamour, he could detect the unmistakable essence of an imp – that particular blend of chaos and mischief that no amount of concealment could fully mask. He kept his expression neutral, giving nothing away.

"Yes, if you have a moment." Dacey's tone was professional but gentle. "We'd like to ask you a few questions about Marcus Chauvin."

"Sure," she said, offering her hand to Dacey and Gideon. "Violet DuBonne."

"It's nice to meet you. I'm Agent Nash," Gideon murmured, clasping her hand briefly. The contact confirmed his suspicions – a subtle heat signature that no human would possess. His eyes met hers for just a fraction longer than necessary, wondering if she knew he could see through her disguise.

Violet led them to a small office cluttered with artwork, stacks of papers, and supply catalogs. She perched on the edge of her desk while Dacey and Gideon took the chairs across from her.

"How long did Marcus work here?" Dacey began.

"Five years, give or take."

"Was he a good employee?"

Violet shrugged one shoulder. "He was fine. Good tattoo artist; did quality work."

"I'm sensing some hesitation," Dacey prodded. "You didn't like him much?"

"Look, he was talented. His sigil tattoos were always in demand. But he was full of himself, sometimes a real jerk. Didn't work well with the rest of the team." Violet's expression hardened slightly. "He was cocky and condescending."

"Did he have any enemies that you know of?"

"I'm not totally shocked that he got into a bar fight. But he didn't have any enemies that I'm aware of. Not anyone who would want him dead." Violet paused. "At least, I wouldn't think so."

"So you heard about the bar fight?" The coroner had listed Marcus's official cause of death as injuries from that fight. Dacey watched Violet's reaction carefully. "Did he frequent bars? Get into fights often?"

"I couldn't say." Violet's eyebrows drew together, creating a sharp line between them. "He never came in with any visible injuries, and I never heard about any fights before this one."

Dacey handed over her business card. "Would it be alright if we look around, maybe talk to your other employees?"

"Sure." Violet stood, smoothing her black tank top. "We don't have any clients coming in for an hour, so you won't be interrupting anything. Most of our clients aren't exactly early birds," Violet said with a grin. "I'll show you Marcus's station."

She led them through the shop to a workspace near the back. Like the office, it was cluttered but organized, with sketchbooks and supplies neatly arranged on shelves. Gideon moved around the space slowly while Dacey and Violet watched. He subtly shook his head at his partner – no void signature here.

As he examined Marcus's tattooing supplies, he felt that same distinctive Fae magic emanating from his workspace. He glanced around at the other stations but sensed nothing – only at Marcus's workspace did he detect the telltale aura of Fae energy. The rest of the employees seemed entirely human.

Gideon opened the upper storage compartments and discovered all of Marcus's supplies, all neatly organized in neat rows. As he passed his hand over them, he could feel the unmistakable Fae magical signature – identical to the one he'd detected in Marcus's home.

"Is this all of his supplies, or does he have a storage space or locker somewhere?"

"Everyone keeps their stuff at their station," Violet replied before excusing herself. She paused, turning back. "Finding someone to replace Marcus is going to be tough. He was my only sigil tattoo artist – he had a real gift for it. The clients loved his work."

Their next interview was with Danny Bowley, a heavily tattooed man who worked the station next to Marcus's.

"How long did you work alongside Marcus?" Dacey asked, leaning against the counter.

Danny ran a hand through his short, spiked hair. "Almost three years now. Started a few years after he did. Guy was an amazing artist– had this way of making his art feel alive somehow."

Gideon nodded, watching Danny's face carefully. "Did you notice anything unusual about his behavior recently?"

Before Danny could answer, a woman with curly blonde hair spilling out from beneath a beanie appeared in the doorway as they spoke.

"Hey Danny, can I borrow some transfer paper? The new stuff I got isn't holding ink well – must be cheap."

Danny sighed but reached for his supplies. "Again, Jordan? You know we have to supply our own materials."

"I know, I know. I'll pay you back," Jordan said. "I tried this new brand, but it's not working like I hoped."

Danny gestured toward Dacey and Gideon. "Jordan, these officers are here about Marcus."

"Oh," the woman said, her expression shifting to something more serious as she turned to face them. "I'm Jordan Wellmer. I work here, too."

"Actually, Ms. Wellmer," Dacey said, "we were hoping to speak with everyone who worked with Marcus. Do you have a moment?"

"Sure, why not?" Jordan shrugged, leaning against a nearby counter.

Dacey repeated her earlier questions. Jordan's answers closely echoed her boss's assessment – Marcus had been talented but difficult to work with.

"He didn't have many friends that I knew of," Jordan added. "He was always bragging about money, about how much he was making. And so secretive about his work and clients – always worried someone was trying to steal them."

"Any girlfriends?" Dacey asked.

"None that stuck around long."

After Jordan left, Danny's assessment of his former coworker matched the others', but he offered one new detail.

"He'd been going on about some new technique lately," Danny said, absently adjusting one of his gauged earlobes. "Said it was going to make him famous."

Dacey leaned forward slightly. "Did he say exactly what he was working on?"

Danny shook his head. "Nah, he was all talk most of the time. Just liked to brag about how innovative he was, you know?"

After thanking everyone for their time, Dacey and Gideon headed for the exit. As they stepped into the humid air outside, Gideon squinted against the bright sunlight, his mind already working through this new information.

"Food for thought," Dacey said as they climbed back into her car. "Everyone we talked to described him the same way – talented but arrogant. And now we know he was working on something new, something he thought would be revolutionary."

"You think that's connected to what happened to him?"

"I think any time someone claims they're about to change the game, we should pay attention to who might not want the game changed." She started the engine, cranking up the A/C against the oppressive heat. "Let's head to the hospital next – see what we can learn about his final hours."

Gideon nodded, his thoughts turning to the void he'd felt at Willa's house. Would they find the same magical emptiness in Marcus's hospital room?

CHAPTER 10

As Dacey drove, she glanced over at Gideon. "Hey Giddy, can you find the number for that bar where Marcus got into the fight? First Street Social, I think it was called."

Gideon nodded, pulling out his phone and searched. "Got it." He dialed the number and set his phone in the console between them, activating the speaker.

"First Street," a woman's voice answered over the din of glasses clinking.

"This is Special Agent Nash. I'm following up on the attack on Marcus Chauvin in your parking lot last month."

The background noise dimmed as the woman presumably moved somewhere quieter. "Oh, yes. Terrible thing. What can I do for you?"

"I'd like to speak with the manager or owner."

"That's me; I'm the manager. My name's Teresa Suez."

"Were you at the bar the night that Mr. Chauvin died?"

"Yes, I was."

"Excellent. I would like to come in and talk to you and any staff members who were working that night," Dacey said.

"Most of them will be here tonight by six for the evening shift."

"Perfect. My partner and I will stop by around then." Dacey ended the call.

Gideon tried to ignore the flutter in his pulse at being called her partner so casually. While they waited at a stoplight, he watched Dacey send a quick text to Detective Voss requesting the name of Marcus's attending physician from the hospital.

The response came quickly. "Dr. Mizrahi," Dacey read. "Can you call the hospital?"

After being transferred twice, Gideon learned that Dr. Mizrahi worked nights in the ER. "He'll be in around nine," the HR representative told him. He disconnected and turned his attention to Dacey, who was still on her phone.

"Thanks, we'll see you soon," she said before hanging up. She turned to Gideon. "I asked Voss to get us to see Brandon Cho's body, but he has to clear it with Lake Mary PD first, but he can get us into Eleanor Preston's house now."

Following the GPS's directions to Eleanor's house, they found themselves driving along the main road that hugged Lake Monroe's shoreline. Gideon suddenly pointed to a sign. "Look – the Royal Palmetto Hotel."

The cream-colored sign, with its arched top adorned with a gold-leaf crown, read "The Royal Palmetto Hotel" in crisp black lettering, with crossed palm fronds below. A smaller sign hung underneath, announcing "Restoration Coming Soon."

Dacey whipped the car over and stared up at the building. "That's the place the mayor and Eleanor Preston were trying to preserve?"

Gideon leaned forward in the passenger seat, studying the abandoned Royal Palmetto through the car's window. The old hotel loomed three stories high, its U-shaped structure forming a once-grand courtyard entrance. The cream-colored façade with terracotta accents was a testament to faded glamour, overlooking Lake Monroe beyond its neglected, overgrown lawns.

Half the arched windows were covered in weather-stained plywood, while others were smashed, with jagged shards of glass jutting from their frames like broken teeth. Once-elegant terra cotta details and cornices now crumbled in places. Weeds pushed through sidewalk cracks, reaching up the stained stucco walls like grasping fingers. He could almost picture it in its heyday – when stars of the silent screen and well-dressed guests strolled through the grand entrance. Now, it stood as a hollow shell, waiting.

"Yep, that's the place," Gideon confirmed.

Dacey put the car in park and turned off the engine. "Let's check it out before we head to Eleanor's. We have time."

They walked the overgrown grounds, where crumbling fountains stood dry and empty. Weeds had forced their way between the old pavers, tilting them at odd angles and lifting them from their beds, creating a treacherous, uneven path.

They approached a side door secured with a heavy padlock. Dacey knelt before it, cupping the metal between her palms. Her brow furrowed in concentration as flames rose from her hands, dancing around her fingers. The padlock slowly turned red, then orange. With a soft metallic groan, the mechanism inside surrendered to the heat and snapped.

"Should we be doing this?" Gideon asked as she removed the broken lock and set it aside.

"Such a good, upstanding citizen," she teased, slipping inside.

"Wait—" Gideon started to say, but Dacey disappeared through the door. With a sigh, he followed.

The once-grand lobby stretched before them, its check-in desk a sprawling curved mahogany counter now warped and split from water damage. Behind it, rows of brass room keys still hung on their hooks, green with tarnish. Black and green mold crept up walls where moisture had peeled away the original paper in long, curling strips.

Their footsteps squelched in the sodden carpet, and the foul, musty smell made Gideon's nose wrinkle. "I don't like this."

"You're not having fun?" Dacey's eyes sparkled with mischief. "I am. I feel like one of those urban explorers on YouTube." She grabbed his hand, tugging him toward a set of ornate doors hanging askew on their hinges. The doors creaked open at her touch, and Gideon couldn't help but smile. Dacey was like a cat, he thought, impossible to predict – one moment all warmth and playful affection, the next moment distant and sharp-edged.

Through a set of double doors, they glimpsed the ballroom, its parquet floor buckled from moisture, creating waves in the wooden surface. Tattered curtains hung in shreds from tall windows, and chunks of ornate plasterwork littered the floor beneath a massive cobweb-covered chandelier.

"You sensing anything?"

"Nothing. I'm not picking up any magic, but I'm also not sensing a void. And those stairs don't look safe." He gestured to a grand staircase across from the ballroom, its marble treads slick with algae and crumbling at the edges.

They moved on to what had been the hotel restaurant, where overturned tables lay scattered like fallen dominoes. Bits of broken glass and grit crunched beneath their feet as they picked their way through.

A movement in the shadows behind an old service station made Gideon grab Dacey's arm, pulling her back. A snake slithered past, disappearing into a hole in the baseboards. The encounter reminded him of Detective Voss. "When are we supposed to meet Voss?"

Dacey pulled out her phone, grimacing at the screen. "Now, actually. We should go."

They retraced their steps through the moldering spaces, careful not to disturb anything. Outside, Dacey placed the heat-damaged padlock back onto the side door's rusty latch. The broken mechanism hung uselessly on the loop, unable to secure but preserving the appearance that the building remained untouched.

Back in the car, they pulled away from the curb, leaving the Royal Palmetto to its slow decay.

They found Eleanor's house only a few blocks away, a stately antebellum mansion complete with towering Corinthian columns flanking the entrance. Detective Voss was waiting by the front door.

"Didn't mean to keep you standing out here in the heat," Dacey said.

"Just got here myself." Voss glanced between them. "How's the investigation going so far?"

"Too early to tell," Dacey replied. "Still piecing things together."

Voss turned to Gideon. "What's your take?"

Gideon shrugged. "What she said."

Voss's gaze lingered on him. "You don't talk much, do you?"

"Only when I have something worth saying."

Voss smirked. "I appreciate a person who doesn't just jabber to hear their own voice."

Gideon dipped his chin in acknowledgment but didn't comment further.

Voss knocked on the door, and after a moment, it opened to reveal an older woman with silver-streaked dark hair, wearing a simple dark dress with an apron.

"This is Mrs. Dolores Ortiz," Victor explained. "She worked for Eleanor Preston for many years."

"I'm Agent Nash," he said with a polite nod. "And this is Agent Santiago."

"We'd like to speak with you briefly once we've finished looking around, if that's alright," Dacey added with a gentle smile.

Mrs. Ortiz nodded, stepping aside to let them enter.

The house was silent as they moved inside. Gideon sensed only faint traces of human aura, presumably Eleanor's and the maid's. "She was human?" he confirmed with Voss.

"Yes."

"Any children?" Dacey asked as they explored.

"Two sons, both out of state."

"Have they been cleared as suspects?" Dacey asked.

Voss shook his head. "They inherit all this, but they're wealthy already. They don't need it. Plus, they both had solid alibis."

"We'd like to see where Eleanor's body was found first," Dacey said. "Before we check the rest of the house."

Voss nodded and led them through the marble-floored entry. "Anyone else still in the house besides the maid?" Dacey asked as they climbed the grand staircase.

"From what I've been told, only Mrs. Ortiz. She will be maintaining the house until everything's settled with the estate. Everyone else has been sent home."

Generations of the same family lined the stairwell in portraits, their stern faces and fine clothes chronicling a lineage of wealth and power stretching back to before the turn of the century. Gideon studied each painting as they ascended, the subjects' eyes seeming to track their every step.

At the top of the stairs, before Voss could direct them, Gideon's head snapped toward a door halfway down the lushly carpeted hallway. He strode toward it, drawn by the emptiness he sensed behind the heavy oak panel.

"This is where they found her?"

"Yes." Voss gave Gideon a strange look as he opened the door. Gideon realized his behavior must seem suspicious – heading directly for the victim's bedroom without any direction from Voss. But he couldn't resist the pull of the void.

The bed was still unmade, covers thrown back where Eleanor had lain. "Mrs. Ortiz found her when she missed breakfast. In her statement, she said Eleanor went to bed after having dinner at the country club with some friends."

"Get me a list of her dinner companions?" Dacey asked. "I want to cross-reference it with the Heritage Foundation meeting attendance at Edelweiss Hall with Willa Wagner."

Voss raised an intrigued eyebrow but didn't ask any questions. "That shouldn't be too hard to get my hands on."

Gideon stood motionless by the bed, eyes closed, hands loose at his sides. The void was identical to the others – that same unsettling emptiness where life should be.

They searched the rest of the mansion methodically – the other bedrooms, sitting rooms, library, and study. The formal dining room where elaborate place settings waited for guests who would never come. But there was nothing to find. Only human traces lingered in the spaces. If Eleanor had dealings with Mythicals, she'd kept them far from her home.

They found Mrs. Ortiz in the kitchen, methodically scrubbing the marble island. She was an older woman with sad eyes.

"Mrs. Ortiz," Dacey said gently, "did you notice anything unusual about Mrs. Preston the night she died?"

"No, nothing at all strange." The maid twisted her washing cloth between her fingers. "She was in good spirits when she left for dinner with her friends. She said she was exhausted when she came home, but that wasn't unusual after an evening out."

"Did Mrs. Preston have any enemies?"

"Oh no," Mrs. Ortiz shook her head emphatically. "Miss Eleanor could be stern, but she was very kind to her friends. An excellent employer." She wrung the cloth harder. "Is… is something wrong? Why are you asking about that night?"

"Nothing's wrong," Dacey assured her. "Sometimes, with estates this size, we take extra precautions. You have nothing to worry about."

"Did you notice anything unusual about that night or anything strange happening recently? Was Mrs. Preston stressed or complained about any problems?"

"No," Mrs. Ortiz responded slowly. "Most of Mrs. Preston's time was spent with her friends or working with the Heritage Foundation. She hadn't mentioned any troubles, but I'm just the help. She wouldn't have confided in me."

Dacey gave the woman a sly smile. "Sure, but everyone underestimates their staff. I bet you knew everything going on in Eleanor's life."

"Oh no." Mrs. Ortiz straightened, indignant. "I do my job, that's all. Other people's personal lives are not my business."

"I meant no offense. I'm sure you are excellent at your job," Dacey said, quickly backtracking. "I can't think of anything else I need to ask. Thank you for your time, Mrs. Ortiz. If you think of anything else, please give Detective Voss here a call."

Dacey shook the woman's hand, and Gideon nodded his thanks.

Mrs. Ortiz followed them to the front door, the lock clicking into place behind them loud in the quiet.

"Find anything relevant?" Voss asked, pausing next to them on the stone-paved steps of the porch.

"Not really," Gideon said.

"Well, as soon as my contact in Lake Mary PD gets back to me, I'll give you a call about getting into the morgue and Brandon Cho's apartment."

"Okay, sounds good. Thanks for being so flexible with your time," Dacey said.

Voss shrugged. "The mayor told me to be at your beck and call. So here I am."

"Well, either way, we appreciate it."

Voss dipped his head in acknowledgment and then strode away toward his car. They watched him drive away before Dacey turned to Gideon. "Well… what did you feel?"

"The void was strong in her bedroom. I didn't feel anything else. And no magic – Eleanor Preston and everything in her house were entirely human. As far as the void goes… My theory is it forms when the victim dies – which explains why we didn't feel it at Chauvin's house. He died at the hospital."

"Okay… so what do we know?" Dacey asked, biting her nail as she thought. Her stomach gave a loud growl, reminding them both that it was approaching lunchtime.

"We know all the victims were single, with no apparent cause of death. The only indication of foul play is the void I've detected on each body. All victims were local except Brandon Cho – but he worked locally. So far, we've found just one connection – Eleanor and Willa belonged to the same philanthropist social club. Otherwise, there's nothing linking all the victims together."

"Alright, so what do we suspect, Giddy?"

Gideon felt like he was being quizzed by his teacher.

"I suspect that whatever is killing these people only activates once they are sleeping. If I had to guess, I would also say that whatever happened to these people makes them tired first. It makes them feel exhausted and want to go to bed. Remember? That's what the mayor said about her sister. That she teased her for being tired and told her to try being mayor sometime."

"Yes! The maid says Eleanor left that night in high spirits but was tired when she got home. Perhaps it was a normal amount of tiredness, but considering she went to bed and never woke up, I'd like to find out more. I need to talk to those socialites and see if anything strange happened at either the meeting or the dinner Eleanor attended." Dacey pulled out the mayor's card and dialed, putting it on speaker.

"This is Mayor Thorne," a crisp voice answered.

"Mayor, this is Dacey."

"Oh, Dacey! Any progress?" Mayor Thorne asked.

"Too soon to tell. We want to speak with the Heritage Foundation members who were with Willa or Eleanor before they died."

"I think we can make that happen. We're having an emergency meeting tomorrow. We've lost two key members in such a short period, and we can't afford to lose momentum right before the Independence Day celebrations. You could come as reporters doing a piece on the foundation and our recent losses."

"That would be perfect, Mayor Thorne. Thank you."

"Of course, dear. Just let me know what else you need. And please... call me Winnie."

Dacey ended the call after thanking Winnie. "Let's get a bite to eat before we check where they found Joe's body next. I think I know just the place I wanna eat, too."

The hunt was taking shape, Gideon thought, but he couldn't shake the feeling they were still missing something vital. Something that connected a homeless man, a nurse, a tattoo artist, and two wealthy philanthropists in death – beyond the void signature he'd felt at each scene. He just hoped they'd figure it out before anyone else died.

CHAPTER 11

The interior of Edelweiss Hall transported Gideon to another world. Blonde wood paneling and exposed beams lined the walls and ceiling, while iron chandeliers cast warm light over long communal tables. Hand-painted murals of Alpine scenes, depicting lederhosen-clad characters and snow-capped mountains, wrapped around the dining room.

"I haven't had real German food in ages," Dacey said, sliding onto a padded bench. They were seated at a table next to a large window overlooking a brick-paved pedestrian plaza, where workers were busy setting up for the Fourth of July celebration.

Their server, dressed in a traditional dirndl, handed them thick menus bound in leather.

"Excuse me," Dacey said, catching the server's attention. "Did you happen to work last week when the Heritage Foundation had their meeting here?"

The server shook her head. "Sorry, I only work days."

"No worries, I was just trying to figure out if my aunt attended the meeting." The server gave a slight shrug and walked away.

"Quick thinking," Gideon said with an appreciative nod.

"Worth a shot."

Gideon observed Dacey as she scanned the restaurant, methodically noting exits while discreetly studying other patrons. Her perpetual vigilance and calculating gaze impressed him – it all seemed so second nature to her. He hoped to be as good an agent as her someday.

Gideon forced himself to turn back to the menu, eyes widening at the extensive beer list. "Too bad we're on duty. Some of these beers sound interesting."

"Hmm, maybe we'll return once we've solved this case and treat ourselves. I think I want the schnitzel sandwich," Dacey said after quickly perusing her menu.

The bagels they grabbed on the way out of the hotel that morning felt ages ago, and Gideon wanted something hearty. Who knew when they'd next get a chance to eat? After scrolling through the menu twice, Gideon made his choice. "I'm getting the sauerbraten."

When their food arrived, the portions were enormous. Dacey's schnitzel spilled over the edges of the bun, surrounded by a mountain of crispy fries, while Gideon's sauerbraten came with spätzle and a sweet-vinegary red cabbage. The rich aroma of gravy, caramelized onions, and warm spices wafted up from their plates, making Gideon's stomach growl audibly.

As they ate, accordion music played softly through hidden speakers, mixing with the cheerful din of conversation and clinking steins. Halfway through demolishing her sandwich, Dacey suddenly stopped eating. She nudged Gideon with her elbow and pointed discreetly toward the corner of the ceiling.

A security camera.

Dacey pulled out her phone, a small smile on her lips. "I know someone who might be able to help us," she said, dialing a number and holding the phone to her ear.

"Leonhard! How's my favorite numerai?" She paused, listening. "True – you're the only numerai I know. But it doesn't make it less true! I've got a challenge for you. There's a security camera at Edelweiss Hall here in Millhaven that might have caught some interesting footage from the Heritage Foundation meeting earlier this week. Any chance you could get access to it?" Another pause. "Perfect, I'll wait."

Gideon watched her face as she listened. After a minute, she broke into a wide grin and pumped her fist, then blew a kiss at the camera. "You're the best! While you're in there, can you check all the footage from that night? Inside and outside the building? We're trying to figure out what happened to Willa Wagner."

She nodded at whatever Leonhard was saying. "Exactly. If anything weird happened near a camera that night, we need to know. I want to know if anyone interacted with her or if anything strange occurred. Awesome – we'll be waiting to see what you find." Another pause. "Thanks, you're amazing."

She hung up, looking pleased. "If there's anything to find, Leonhard will find it."

They were settling their bill when a woman began shouting out in the plaza. Her stringy blonde hair hung in tangled knots around her face, and despite the summer heat, she wore two ragged jackets over her dirty clothes. She was bony and thin, with prominent cheekbones that jutted sharply beneath her wild eyes.

Crude tattoos covered nearly every visible inch of skin – geometric patterns and interwoven knots that looked like they'd been done by hand. The inked designs snaked up her neck and disappeared into her hairline, reappearing on her weathered face in jagged, parallel tattooed lines across her cheeks.

"It's almost time!" she yelled, waving her arms. "Soon now. Valhalla is waiting!"

One of the workers setting up the stage outside the restaurant approached the woman. "Ma'am, you need to leave," he said firmly.

The woman huffed loudly. "I'm already gone! I'm nothing but a ghost."

She shuffled across the plaza to a bench, where she sat glaring at the worker.

Gideon stared through the window at her. "I don't think she's human."

"Mythical?" Dacey asked.

"I think so. Too far away to tell for sure, though."

"Who's that?" Dacey asked their server as she processed their payment.

"Oh, that's just Astrid," she said. "She's around all the time. Poor woman – she's loud but harmless."

"Do you get many homeless people around here?"

She shrugged. "Some. Not as bad as the eighties, but yeah. Millhaven's pretty good to them, though. Lots of programs to help out."

"Oh?" Dacey's eyebrows rose with interest.

"Yeah, there's a food bank, a soup kitchen, and even a local shelter. Plus, Metro Diner down the street feeds them breakfast before they open every morning. Stuff like that."

"That's nice of them," Dacey said as she gathered her things and stood.

"Have a nice day," the server said before returning to the kitchen.

As they left the restaurant, they had to walk past where Astrid sat on her bench. Gideon couldn't help glancing her way and instantly felt it – magic radiating from the woman in chaotic waves. His senses tingled as he instinctively reached out with his awareness.

The magical signature hit him like a discordant symphony. It was fragmented and disjointed, like a broken mirror scattered in a thousand pieces. Each shard still reflected power, but nothing connected properly. It reminded Gideon of a seer's divination crystal that he'd examined last week, except there was a quality to this woman's magic that felt unstable – fragmented and overwhelming in its intensity. The power seemed to leak from her in unpredictable pulses, lacking the controlled precision most magical practitioners maintained.

Astrid's head snapped toward them. "What are you looking at?" she shrieked. "You think you're better than me! You can't judge me, I'm going to Valhalla! You goody-two-shoes are blind fools. It's almost time!"

"Excuse me," Dacey said softly, carefully stepping closer. "We were wondering if you knew a man named Joe?"

Astrid scrambled backward, her eyes darting around wildly. "Leave me alone! You're not supposed to be here yet!" She jabbed a finger at Gideon, her chipped nail polish catching the light. "You're in for quite the surprise, mama's boy." Her gaze swung to Dacey, and a twisted smile spread across her face. She pointed one bony finger at Dacey. "And you... you're going to burn."

What the hell? 'Burn' was too specific to be a random threat. The hair on his arms stood on end as his mind raced through the possibilities.

"Please," Dacey held up her hands placatingly. "We just want to talk—"

"She's too agitated right now," Gideon whispered, leaning close to Dacey's ear. "And we're starting to draw attention." He subtly nodded toward the growing number of onlookers, pausing to watch the confrontation.

"I don't have to talk if I don't want to!" Astrid's voice rose to a fever pitch as she rocked back and forth. "I'm not really here anyway! It's almost time. Any day! Any day! Any day!"

"We're sorry," Gideon said, gently touching Dacey's elbow. "We'll leave you alone."

They backed away slowly until they were a safe distance from the agitated woman.

Once they were out of earshot, Dacey frowned thoughtfully. "She said I would burn... and technically, she's not wrong. Makes me wonder what kind of Mythical she is to know that about me."

"I think she has some kind of fortune-telling ability. She certainly pegged me as a mama's boy," Gideon said with a wry smile.

"Nothing wrong with loving your mom," Dacey teased.

Gideon glanced back to where Astrid had been and saw that she had disappeared. "I feel bad for her. It seems like her magic made her crazy, and now she's homeless."

Dacey nodded but then shrugged in a what-can-you-do kind of way. "Speaking of homeless people. Let's check out where Joe died, then maybe talk to the Metro Diner folks. See if they noticed anyone strange hanging around."

Outside, the sidewalks bustled with activity. Workers were setting up for the upcoming festivities, installing a temporary bandstand in the pedestrian plaza. American flags appeared on every lamppost, and porta-potties were being delivered to strategic locations.

They walked several blocks to a more residential area while Dacey consulted her phone, then led them behind a thrift store to a parking lot that backed up to a wooded area. "They found Joe's body back there," she said, pointing to where scrubby trees gave way to denser forest.

As they pushed through the undergrowth, Gideon grimaced. "This reminds me of when we first met, and we were trekking through the woods trying to track down where you were murdered."

"Ah, the good old days." Dacey ducked under a low-hanging branch.

"We never have good luck in the woods," Gideon said, absently running his fingers over the spiderweb-thin scars that marked his arms, vivid reminders of that day in Blackwater River State Forest when he had rolled himself and Dacey's blood-soaked body into a bonfire.

They found Joe's camp quickly enough – a cleared area littered with the detritus of desperate living. An old sleeping bag, stained and moldering, lay crumpled against a fallen log.

Gideon stopped abruptly. "The void's here, but there's something else. It's Astrid's magic alongside the void. It's layered on top like she's been here since he died." His face tightened with concentration. "It's like oracle magic I've tested, but... wrong. Crazed. Like a maelstrom of time flowing backward and forward at once. I'm seeing fragments, spider-web strands of images and time. Everything feels sharp, discordant, fragile." He pulled out his phone. "I want Vena's take on this."

He put the call on speaker. Vena answered quickly.

Vena hummed thoughtfully after Gideon described what he was sensing and describing Astrid. "She could be an oracle or one of Morrigan's priestesses, but it is most likely a Völva – especially going on the description of her tattoos. They're Norse seers, powerful women who can walk the threads of time. They're quite rare – I've only ever met one. However, my research says that many of them lose themselves in the visions – too many branching timelines, too many possible futures. They lose their grip on the present."

"That sounds like the woman we met," Gideon said. "Thanks for the help, Vena." He ended the call and pulled out his notebook, quickly jotting down notes about the magic he'd sensed. Walking the campsite's perimeter, he mapped the boundaries of the void and the Völva's magic.

"There's something else too," he said finally. "A faint trace of Fae magic, but it's mostly lost under the void and all this crazed seer magic."

Dacey watched as he sifted through the debris with his foot – dirty clothes, food wrappers, needles and drug paraphernalia, torn papers. "Can you pinpoint it?"

"No, it's too weak. But it's here."

Dacey pulled out her phone again. "Voss? I'm sending you a pin. We need everything at this location bagged and sent to the Savannah Conclave for analysis." She paused. "Yes, everything. Thanks."

They stood for a moment, studying the sad little camp where Joe had died. A breeze rustled through the trees, carrying the distant sounds of construction from downtown – the city preparing to celebrate while the dead accumulated in their quiet corners.

CHAPTER 12

Metro Diner occupied the prominent corner of a series of connected brick buildings in the downtown district. The two-story building had started life as a Woolworth's in the 1950s. A weathered metal sign with raised letters spelled out the diner's name, but the faint outline of the original Woolworth's lettering could still be seen in the brick underneath, a ghost of red and gold paint stubbornly refusing to fade completely. Large plate glass windows lined the front, giving passersby a view of chrome-edged tables and framed vintage posters.

Inside, ceiling fans spun overhead, doing little to dispel the heat that seeped in every time the front door opened. The worn linoleum floor showed decades of foot traffic, and the vinyl booths bore patches where countless customers had slid in and out. Despite its age, the counters and tables gleamed from thorough cleaning, and the whole place carried the comforting aroma of coffee and home cooking.

Dacey approached the teenager at the hostess station, badge already in hand. "We need to speak with the owner or manager."

The girl's eyes widened at the sight of the badge. She hurried toward the kitchen, returning with an older black woman moments later. Despite the heat, the woman's burgundy Metro Diner polo remained crisp and neat, covered by a black apron without a single stain.

"I'm Renee Thompson," she said, studying them with shrewd eyes. "What can I do for you?"

"Could we speak somewhere private?" Dacey asked.

Renee nodded and led them to an empty booth in the back corner. "Can I get you something to drink? You both look like you could use it."

Gideon realized his shirt was sticking to his back from their walk in the oppressive heat. "Water would be great, thanks."

"Same here," Dacey said.

Renee returned quickly with two tall glasses of ice water. "Now, what's this about?"

"We understand you feed the homeless here in the mornings," Dacey said.

"That's not a crime." Renee's chin lifted slightly.

"No, no," Dacey said quickly. "We're not here about that. We're following up on a homeless man who died recently – Joe?"

Renee's face softened. "Ah, Joe. That was a shame, what happened to him." She settled into the booth across from them. "Yes, we feed anyone who shows up at the back door at six. My only rule is they need to clear out by seven when we open and not cause any trouble with our paying customers. Been doing it for years."

"Do people have problems with that?" Gideon asked.

Renee shrugged. "Always gonna be somebody complaining. Usually, some rich snob who's never suffered a day in their life. But these people aren't hurting anyone – they just need help. Most can't function in regular society, whether it's drugs or mental problems, but they're generally harmless. I don't put up with troublemakers."

"Were you familiar with Joe?" Dacey asked.

"Known him a few years. He was pretty regular, but sometimes he'd disappear for weeks, then show up again looking worse for wear."

"Did you know his full name? Where he was from?"

"No idea on the name – I only ever knew him by Joe. But once, when I was complaining about the Florida heat, he said it was better than a Minnesota winter any day. Think he might've been from there, but that's all I know."

"What about Astrid?" Gideon asked, thinking of the woman from earlier. "Does she come around? Spend time with Joe?"

"Astrid's here almost every morning like clockwork. Yeah, she and Joe hung together quite a bit. Pretty sure they used together." Renee shook her head. "Poor woman needs to be in a mental health facility. She always says she can see the future, but most of what comes out of her mouth is gibberish. Won't go near a facility though – claims the government will kidnap her and use her for her visions, make her spy for them."

"Did Joe spend time with any other regulars?" Dacey asked.

"They all generally stick to the same areas, but I don't know much about what goes on outside breakfast here."

"Has anyone been acting strange lately? Anything seem off with Joe or the others?"

Another shrug. "Seem about the same as usual to me."

"Would it be alright if we came by tomorrow to talk to some of them? We won't cause any trouble."

"You can try, but they're pretty insular. Probably won't talk to you." Renee adjusted her polo. "I'll ask around, but I doubt they'll have anything to add. Most are saying Joe OD'd."

Dacey's phone rang. Gideon glimpsed Detective Voss's name on the screen.

"I need to take this," Dacey said, rising. "Thank you for your time and the water."

As they stepped back into the sweltering heat outside, Gideon's mind churned with new questions. A homeless man from Minnesota. A woman who claimed to see the future. And somewhere in the tangle of it all, five dead bodies and voids where there should have been auras and magic.

Dacey answered her phone as they walked. "Hey, Victor. What have you got for me?"

Dacey listened to whatever Detective Voss had to say before

turning to Gideon with a small smile and a thumbs up. "That's good news. We'll head that way shortly. See you soon."

She hung up and turned to Gideon. "Victor got us access to Brandon's apartment – and he confirmed that the roommate would be there to talk to us. He also arranged for us to examine Brandon's body at the Lake Mary morgue afterward."

"Victor, huh? You guys friends now?"

Dacey rolled her eyes. "Just because you don't like snakes doesn't make Voss an enemy."

"I know, I'm just teasing. You're too easy to fluster," Gideon joked, noting how quickly she'd defended Voss. He decided not to dwell too much on that thought. Dacey was working with him, not Voss, and that was what mattered.

* * *

THE SLEEK APARTMENT complex soared above Gideon, capturing Lake Mary's metropolitan essence. While Millhaven clung to its historic charm, Lake Mary was all glass and steel modernity. The apartment's facade gleamed in the afternoon sun, with manicured landscaping and paved walkways leading to each building's entrance. Between the buildings, a massive courtyard featured an expansive pool area, complete with cabanas and lounge chairs.

"Is it necessary for Voss to tag along?" Gideon muttered, watching the man in question's sedan pull into the parking lot.

Dacey shrugged. "He's getting us access. It'd be weird to tell him to stay away."

"He's probably spying for the mayor. With the amount of the mayor's magic lingering on Voss, they must spend a lot of time together," Gideon added. "Winnie's getting a full report of everything we say and do – I'd put money on it."

A knowing grin spread across Dacey's face. "Oh, almost certainly."

Detective Voss strode toward them, his pressed suit immaculate despite the heat and humidity.

They took the elevator to the third floor, its glass wall offering a view of the courtyard below. Only a handful of people lounged by the pool, though Gideon suspected it would be packed come Saturday. Despite the Fourth of July falling on a Wednesday this year, most people would be saving their celebrations for the weekend. Including his mother. Gideon hoped this case would be solved well before then – he hated to let his mother down and miss the festivities she'd planned. She was so excited to throw a neighborhood get-together.

Gideon grimaced and silently admitted that he was losing faith that they'd figure this all out before the weekend came. They'd been in town almost 24 hours now and had turned up nothing so far.

Voss hung back as Dacey knocked on apartment 312. The door opened to reveal a man in his late twenties, dirty blonde hair falling across his forehead. His Gator's Dockside restaurant uniform suggested he'd just finished or was about to start a shift.

They flashed their badges. Though the man's nervousness was evident, Gideon couldn't blame him – badges at your door rarely meant good news.

"I'm Agent Santiago; this is Agent Nash. May we come in?"

"Jason," he offered, stepping aside. "Jason O'Sullivan."

"Your roommate was Brandon Cho, yes?" When the man nodded, Dacey continued. "Can you tell us what happened to him?"

Jason swallowed hard, shoulders tensing, waving them inside the apartment. "His alarm woke me up that morning. It kept going and going, which wasn't like him. I banged on his door, but he didn't answer. Figured maybe he'd already left for work and forgotten to turn it off." He drew a shaky breath. "When I went in to turn it off, I found him there. For a minute, I thought he was sleeping, but when I shook him…." Jason shivered. "He was cold."

"I'm sorry you had to experience that," Dacey said softly.

"Anything unusual happen the night before?" Gideon asked.

Jason shook his head. "I worked late at the restaurant." He pointed to the logo on his shirt. "His door was closed when I got home, but that was normal. He worked early shifts at the nursing home."

"You didn't notice anything off? Something out of place in the apartment?"

Jason looked around the living room as if to check and then shook his head.

"Did he have any enemies? Problems with friends or family? Was he dating someone?"

"We weren't close – matched on an apartment finder site. Different schedules, you know?" Jason paused. "Though he did mention feeling sick the morning before.... Said he was feeling rundown and complained that he didn't have time to get sick."

Dacey shot Gideon a look. "The day before he died?"

"Yeah. He said it was bad timing, too, 'cause he wanted to start looking for another job. Hated working at Serenity Living."

"Why is that?" Gideon pressed.

"He said they were understaffed and management didn't care about the residents. There was lots of negligence, but he could do nothing about it. He said that all his complaints to upper management fell on deaf ears; that they didn't give a shit about their employees or the residents, just the money they brought it."

"Thanks for taking the time to speak with us," Dacey said. "I know it can't be easy to talk about what happened."

Jason shrugged as if it was no big deal, but the hunch of his shoulders and the look on his face said he wasn't as unaffected as he pretended.

Dacey handed Jason her card. "Call if you think of anything else. We're just going to take a look at his bedroom, and then we'll be out of your hair."

"Did... did something happen to him? I was told that he had an aneurysm, so I'm confused why you guys are here."

"We're just being thorough. Young, healthy people don't usually die suddenly. This is just a formality," Dacey assured the nervous man, who seemed relieved by her explanation.

Jason pointed them to Brandon's room. The bedroom was empty except for a bed and dresser. The space felt hollow and abandoned. "His parents came and took everything else earlier this week," Jason explained. "Guess I need to find another roommate now. Honestly, though, I'm thinking of switching to a single-bedroom apartment. It's... uncomfortable, being here after...."

Gideon approached the bed, tuning out Jason's voice. The void was strong here, with traces of shifter magic throughout the room and apartment. It felt similar to bear shifter magic he'd encountered before, yet remained distinct – likely unique to sun bears. Having analyzed black bear and grizzly signatures recently, he knew each species carried its own magical fingerprint.

Dacey joined him, raising an eyebrow and nodding toward the bed. Gideon gave a subtle nod, confirming the void's presence while Voss watched from the doorway.

Finding nothing else of interest in the empty room, they thanked Jason and left. In the parking lot, Voss announced he'd text them the morgue address and meet them there.

As they drove to the morgue, Gideon mentally prepared himself for what was to come. The corpse would likely reveal the same mystifying lack of cause as the others, but he needed to see for himself.

CHAPTER 13

An hour later, they stepped out of the morgue. As Gideon had expected, Brandon's body revealed nothing they hadn't already seen with the other victims – just another inexplicable death with no visible cause. The July heat hit like a physical wall after the building's frigid air conditioning. He tugged at his collar, trying to peel the fabric off his now-sweaty neck.

"Thanks for escorting us," Dacey said to Voss, who looked irritatingly unruffled by the heat.

"Find anything after looking at the body?" Voss asked, his viper gaze studying them intently.

Gideon shrugged. "Not really. Brandon's corpse was just like the others as far as I could tell – no sign of death, no trauma."

"It's weird," Voss said, frowning.

"I agree," Dacey nodded, "but we're gonna figure it out."

"Need me for anything else?"

They shook their heads. "Thanks for all your help," Dacey said.

They watched Voss's vehicle pull away before climbing into their car. The leather seats were scorching even through Gideon's clothes.

Dacey turned to him. "I assume Brandon was just like the others?"

"Yep. Almost all traces of his shifter magic were gone – just a shell left behind." Gideon rolled down his window, hoping for a breeze while the A/C struggled to catch up.

Glancing at the clock on the dash, Dacey said, "We've got some time before we need to get to First Street Social to talk to the bar employees. Want to grab some drive-through and head to Serenity Living? I want to talk to Brandon's co-workers and see if they noticed anything strange before he died."

Twenty minutes and some questionable fast food later, they pulled into Serenity Living's parking lot. The sprawling three-story building was nestled into a wooded area, its painted-stucco façade softened by carefully maintained landscaping. To one side, a garden area spread out with paved walkways winding between raised flower beds. A man wearing scrubs wheeled an elderly woman along one of the paths, seeking shade under the scattered oak trees.

Inside, Gideon wrinkled his nose at the smell – antiseptic with an underlying mustiness that even aggressive cleaning couldn't quite mask. Despite the institutional scent, the lobby resembled an upscale doctor's waiting room, with plush chairs and tasteful artwork on the walls. If there was the kind of neglect Jason had mentioned Brandon complaining about, it certainly wasn't evident from this carefully curated front-facing space.

They approached the front desk, where a woman about Gideon's age sat. Her name tag identified her as Sara. Dacey flashed her badge. Sara's eyes lit up with startling enthusiasm. "Oh! Are you here to arrest someone?"

"Uh, no," Gideon managed, taken aback.

Sara turned her avid attention toward him, her eager expression making him blush – as if she were hoping he'd personally slap the cuffs on her.

"No arrests," Dacey said. "We just need to speak with whoever's in charge."

"Hold on." Sara picked up her phone, shooting another glance at Gideon as she dialed. "Hi, there are some police officers here who want to talk to whoever's in charge." She listened briefly. "Okay, thanks." Hanging up, she smiled at them. "Bob will be right out."

A few minutes later, a man in his fifties appeared – average height and build, with thick glasses perched on his nose. "Bob Stibbons," he introduced himself, gesturing them away from Sara's obviously eavesdropping presence.

"Agent Santiago, and this is Agent Nash," Dacey said. "We're following up on Brandon Cho's death. We'd like to speak with you and some of the people who worked with Brandon around the time he died."

Bob held up a hand. "Let me stop you right there. This is a private facility. Our patients pay good money for their safety and privacy. I can't have people wandering around questioning my staff." He adjusted his glasses. "Unless you have a warrant, I'm going to have to ask you to leave. Mr. Cho's death was tragic, but I won't have you disturbing our employees and residents. It's nothing personal – just corporate policy." He gestured toward the door. "Come back with a warrant, and I'll happily accommodate you. Have a good day."

"Sure, we'll do that. Thanks for your help," Dacey said through gritted teeth as Bob herded them out.

Once outside, she turned to Gideon. "Feel anything in there?"

"Not really. Some old Mythical imprints, but nothing like what we're looking for. Would need to get past the lobby to find anything more concrete."

They headed back to the car and slid inside, positioning themselves with a clear view of the entrance. Dacey drummed her fingers on the steering wheel, staring at the building. "What time do visiting hours end?"

Gideon pulled out his phone. "Website says five."

"What are you thinking?" Gideon asked, not liking the evil grin spreading across Dacey's face.

"That receptionist seemed pretty interested in you. I'm betting she gets off work any minute now. Let's wait a bit and see if she comes out... perhaps you can talk to her. I bet she'd be willing to talk to you without Bob present. You'll need to turn on the charm, Giddy."

"You want me to flirt with Sara and see if she'll tell us about Brandon?"

"Oh, so you noticed her name?" Dacey's grin widened.

Gideon rolled his eyes. "Yes, I noticed her tag. And I know you did, too."

"Is she not your type, Giddy?"

"No, she's not, *Candy*," he said shortly. Gideon thought he detected a flash of relief in Dacey's eyes. Her shoulders seemed to relax, the corner of her mouth twitching upward ever so slightly. But he couldn't trust his own perception – not when his mind was so eager to find what it wanted to see.

"Well, try flirting anyway. What's the harm?"

"I'm not good at flirting. I've got zero game."

"You have game, Gideon," Dacey scoffed. "Besides, with how she was drooling over you, you'll hardly have to work for it."

"Jealous?" he teased, hoping the answer was yes.

"You wish." She pointed over his shoulder. "There she is. Let's see what you've got. Go get your girl, Giddy!"

"You're not as funny as you think."

"I'm hysterical. Now go flirt."

"Fine, but if I fall flat on my face, you'll need to soothe my wounded pride." Gideon climbed out of the car to the sound of Dacey's laughter.

"Miss?" he called out, jogging over to the receptionist as she unlocked her vehicle. "Sorry to approach you like this, but I hoped we could talk."

She blushed, tucking a strand of blonde-streaked hair behind her ear. Under different circumstances, he might have found her cute, but his attention was thoroughly captured by a certain snarky bennu shifter who didn't return his feelings.

"Sara, right?"

"That's right." She said, smiling at him and looking up at him through her lashes.

"I'm Gideon." He held out his hand. When she shook it, he confirmed what he'd sensed earlier – completely human, without a trace of magic. "I was hoping to ask a couple of questions, but your boss hustled us out of there before I got a chance to talk to you."

Sara's eyes lit up, and she leaned slightly closer to Gideon. "I'd be more than happy to help." Her gaze flitted over his clothes before returning to his face with an eager smile. "I always do what I can to assist an officer of the law. Bob can be... stubborn," she lowered her voice, "but I understand you have a job to do."

"Thank you for your understanding, Sara. Have you worked here long?"

"Only a few months."

"Nice place to work?"

Sara shrugged. "It's a job. Pays the bills."

"Did you know Brandon Cho?"

"Not well. He kept to himself. He wasn't as social as the other nurses. Such a shame – he was so young. Here one minute, gone the next." She gave him a flirtatious look. "Makes you not want to waste time in life, you know?"

Gideon pretended not to notice the invitation in her tone. "Notice anything strange happening at work lately?"

Another shrug. "Not really, but like I said, I haven't been here that long."

He handed her one of his cards. "If you think of anything, give me a call or text?"

Sara studied the card. "I will."

"Thanks. I should go."

"Bye, Gideon." She gave him a little finger wave.

Back in the car, Dacey pounced. "How'd it go?"

He decided to mess with her and said, "Got a date."

Dacey's face went slack before he cracked up. "She had nothing useful to add, but I gave her my card in case she thinks of something relevant."

Dacey huffed. "You're not funny."

"Your face says otherwise." He grinned, enjoying the way she scowled at him. "First Street Social?"

"Yeah." She started the car. "Wipe that smirk off your face before I do it for you."

The threat only made him smile wider. He'd take Dacey's annoyance over Sara's flirtation any day.

* * *

First Street Social occupied what had once been an auto repair shop. The original roll-up garage doors were replaced with floor-to-ceiling windows, and their metal frames still had the tracks where the doors used to rise. The industrial building's metal siding was partially covered with neon beer signs that were flickering to life in the early evening sun. The bar's name was painted in graceful black script on the beige-painted brick building. Promotional posters for upcoming bands plastered the converted garage bay windows. A collection of motorcycles lined one side of the building, their chrome glinting in the fading sunlight.

"Charming," Dacey said as they climbed out of the car. The asphalt still radiated heat, making Gideon wish they could have stayed in the air-conditioned vehicle a little longer.

Inside, the aroma of stale beer mingled with pine-scented cleaner – the unmistakable perfume of a seasoned bar. Wood paneling lined the walls, punctuated by TVs silently broadcasting various sports channels. A long bar dominated one wall, its surface bearing the scars of years of bottles and pint glasses. Behind it, mirrors reflected an impressive array of liquor bottles, while strings of multicolored Christmas lights hung above, promising to bathe the place in a dive bar glow once darkness fell.

A burly man with sleeve tattoos was wiping down the bar. He looked up as they approached, his expression neutral but watchful.

Dacey pulled out her badge. "We're looking for Teresa Suez."

"You the cops that called earlier?" a woman's voice called from the far end of the bar. She approached with the confident stride of someone who ran a tight ship, her dark hair pulled back in a practical ponytail.

"That's right," Dacey confirmed.

Teresa nodded. "We can use my office. Follow me." She led them through a swinging door into the kitchen, past stainless steel prep tables and an industrial dishwasher, finally stopping at a small office tucked into the corner. Several monitors mounted on the wall displayed different areas of the bar.

The office was organized chaos – invoices and schedules pinned to a corkboard, stacks of papers on the desk, and an ancient computer humming on the corner of the desk. Two chairs faced the desk, and Gideon was hyperaware of Dacey as she settled into the one beside him.

Teresa dropped into her chair. "What can I do for you?"

"You were working the night Marcus Chauvin died?" Dacey asked.

"Yeah, I was here. I'm here pretty much every night." Teresa leaned back, her expression resigned.

"Could you walk us through what happened that night?"

"It was crazy busy – Saturday night with live music always is. I didn't see Marcus, but Savanna, one of our servers, remembers serving him. She said he got a bit tipsy but not so drunk that we needed to cut him off." Teresa shrugged. "We didn't even know he was in the parking lot until after closing. Rocco – he's one of our bartenders – found him behind the dumpster when he went for a smoke break."

"What time was that?" Dacey's pen hovered over her notepad.

"We hadn't been closed long, so it must've been around 2:30." Teresa gestured at the monitors. "I figured you'd want to see the security footage, though I already gave copies to the police."

"Yes, please. We'd appreciate it," Dacey said.

"Not much to see, honestly." Teresa typed something on her keyboard, and the footage appeared on one of the monitors. A Tesla truck pulled into view, parking near a fence-enclosed dumpster. Marcus emerged, looking perfectly fine as he headed for the entrance.

Teresa switched cameras, showing Marcus entering and making his way to the bar. He claimed the last empty stool and ordered a drink.

"What time was this?" Dacey asked.

Teresa leaned closer to the monitor and pointed to the bottom corner, where the time and date were displayed in small white letters. "Looks like it was about 8. The band was scheduled for 9, so it was just starting to get busy."

Dacey and Gideon leaned closer to the monitor and watched Marcus waving to the bartender and ordering a drink.

"He just sat there drinking for a couple of hours," Teresa said. "Want me to fast forward?"

At Dacey's nod, Teresa sped through the footage. The bar filled steadily as the night progressed, bodies packing the space between tables until it was standing room only. Despite the growing crowd that periodically blocked their view, the camera angle kept Marcus visible at his post at the bar. Gideon watched intently, but nothing seemed out of place. Even as other patrons jostled for drink orders around him, no one approached Marcus except the bartenders until after a few hours, Marcus waved over a bartender and paid his tab. They watched as Marcus walked toward the exit.

The footage switched back to the parking lot as Marcus approached his truck. He had his phone out, the screen lighting up his face, when something suddenly made him straighten. He turned and walked toward the dumpster area, clearly speaking to someone behind the enclosure.

Gideon felt Dacey tense beside him as Marcus walked around the fence-enclosed dumpster, moving behind it and out of the camera's view. For a moment, nothing happened. Then Marcus stumbled partially into view, his movements desperate and jerky before he was yanked back out of sight.

"Can you rewind that?" Dacey asked, leaning forward. "Pause it."

Frame by frame, they watched Marcus get pulled back. Dacey huffed in frustration. "All you can see is a gloved hand. It tells us nothing." She turned to Teresa. "Is there anything more?"

Teresa shook her head and fast-forwarded the footage. A large man with tattoos – the same one who first greeted them when they arrived at the bar – exited the back door with a trash bag. "That's Rocco, the guy who found the body," Teresa explained.

Once Rocco threw the trash in the dumpster, he pulled out a

cigarette and walked around to the back of the enclosure. The moment he spotted Marcus's body, he dropped the cigarette and ran back inside. Less than a minute later, he returned with Teresa and another man, gesturing wildly toward the dumpster. Rocco hung back while Teresa and the other man investigated, both emerging looking shaken. They watched as Teresa said something to the men, then turned on her heel and jogged back into the bar.

"I told Rocco and Felix to guard the spot while I called the police," Teresa explained.

"Did you know Marcus well?" Dacey asked, as they watched an ambulance arrive and load Marcus into the vehicle.

"In passing. He was a regular, but I didn't know him personally."

"What was your opinion of him?"

Teresa shrugged. "He was fine. Not a great tipper, but he never caused real trouble. He sometimes got too flirty or rude with the staff when he'd had a few but never crossed any serious lines."

"Did he ever meet anyone here? Any regular friends or drinking buddies?" Dacey asked.

"Not that I noticed. Sometimes he'd bring a date – different women, you know how it goes. Rarely the same woman twice, as far as I could tell. I never noticed him hanging out with anyone regularly. He mostly kept to himself at the bar."

"Could we get a copy of all that footage?"

Teresa pulled a flash drive from her desk drawer. "Already made a copy for you. Figured you'd want it."

"Thanks." Dacey pocketed the disc. "Would it be possible to use this office to talk to the staff that worked that night?"

One by one, the employees filed in. Their stories were consistent – Marcus was cocky, sometimes rude, and occasionally flirted with the staff. He was a mediocre tipper but wasn't the worst. According to the staff, the man was a blowhard and a braggart but ultimately harmless.

As the last server left, Gideon caught Dacey's eye. They both knew what the other was thinking – somehow, that "harmless" man had ended up dead behind a dumpster, his magic drained just like the others.

Several hours had passed during their interviews, and the bar had filled impressively when they emerged from the office. The converted garage windows now reflected the neon beer signs inside rather than the fading daylight outside. Gideon was surprised to see such a crowd on a weeknight – bodies packed around the bar while others clustered around the high-top tables, the buzz of conversation competing with the music playing overhead.

"I'm going to get the video files to Wiz and see if she can spot the killer."

Gideon rubbed his eyes. "What's next?"

"Let's head to the hospital," Dacey said, rolling her shoulders to work out the stiffness. "See if we can get Dr. Mizrahi to talk to us. Maybe he noticed something about Marcus we missed. After that, let's get some sleep. I want to hit Metro Diner first thing tomorrow to talk to Astrid and the others."

They headed for the exit, the press of the crowd forcing them to weave between tables. The noise faded as the door swung shut behind them, leaving them in the relative quiet of the parking lot.

CHAPTER 14

The automatic doors of the hospital's main entrance slid open with a soft whoosh. Gideon suppressed a yawn as they walked into the antiseptic brightness. They'd parked next to the coroner's office they'd visited the day before – though it felt like a week had passed.

The harsh institutional lights buzzed overhead as they approached the front desk. Dacey pulled out her badge, and Gideon followed suit. "We need to speak with Dr. Mizrahi."

The receptionist, a woman with the unflappable stare of someone who had seen it all, nodded and picked up her phone. After a brief conversation, she gestured to the waiting area. "The doctor will be with you as soon as he's finished with his current patient."

The next twenty minutes crawled by. Gideon fought against his heavy eyelids, shifting in the uncomfortable plastic chair. To keep himself awake, he turned to Dacey. "Got any theories about our killer? Why these specific victims? What the void is, and how it's killing them?"

Dacey tapped her lip thoughtfully, a gesture that drew Gideon's attention to her mouth. "I've got three vague theories I'm working with." She held up her fingers, ticking them off one by one. "First, it could be connected to the Royal Palmetto restoration project. Second, someone might be trying to derail the mayor's reputation in order to destroy her chances at the governor's seat. Or third, we've got someone local experimenting with some new type of magic to steal power or life force, and these victims are just… convenient."

"All three seem possible," Gideon mused. "The Royal Palmetto angle would explain why two of our victims are tied to the project. It might even explain Joe – wanting to get rid of the homeless. But it doesn't explain the tattoo artist or the nurse. The political angle tracks with the timing of the murders coinciding with the mayor's campaign ramp-up. I like the experimental magic theory the most…." He shrugged. "It would explain how even Vena has never heard of it." He paused, a new thought occurring to him. "You know, we might be looking at this wrong. Maybe it's not even a person we're dealing with. What if there's something in the city – some magical anomaly or artifact these people are stumbling across? That would explain why the victims seem so random, why we can't find any real connection between them."

"I mean… that theory is as good as anything else I can think of. Nothing makes sense yet. Too many missing pieces still," Dacey sighed, running a hand through her hair. "Not enough solid evidence for any of them. I'm worried, Giddy. What if we can't figure this out before someone else dies?"

Gideon reached over and gripped her hand. "Hey, we're doing everything we can. We'll keep working until we solve this. Together."

The smile Dacey gave him made his heart thump against his ribs. He'd move mountains to keep having her look at him like that.

Her expression shifted suddenly, attention caught by something over his shoulder. She started to rise, and Gideon followed suit, turning to see a man in a white lab coat with black hair, a trimmed beard and mustache, and deeply tanned skin approaching the receptionist's desk.

The receptionist pointed in their direction, and the man turned toward them. "I'm Dr. Mizrahi. You asked to speak with me?"

"Yes." Dacey held up her badge again. "I'm Agent Santiago, and this is Agent Nash."

While Dacey spoke, Gideon assessed the doctor. He was definitely all human, though faint traces of Mythical energy clung to him – not unusual for someone who probably came into contact with dozens of people every day, some of them bound to be Mythical.

"We're investigating a death from several weeks ago," Dacey explained. "A patient of yours."

Dr. Mizrahi's expression turned frosty. "I see so many patients. I'm not sure how much help I can be after that much time."

Dacey pulled out Marcus's autopsy photo. "This man came in unconscious after an assault. His injuries were superficial, but he never woke up. Do you remember him?"

The doctor studied the photo, brow furrowed. "Vaguely, yes. He had a very weak pulse when he came in. We tried several treatments. We were prepping to get him scanned for brain injury, but…." He shook his head. "He passed before we could get him into the machine."

"Doctor, did you notice anything else unusual about the patient?" Dacey asked.

"Not that I can recall," he replied, his tone growing exasperated. "If there had been anything strange, I would have noted it on the chart."

"Anything else you can remember?"

"I'm afraid not."

"Mr. Chauvin's medical charts show that nurses Emma Kim, Serena Robberts, and Ernesto Garcia attended the man," Dacey said, consulting her file on the victim. "Did any of the nurses notice anything unusual?"

He pinched the bridge of his nose, looking annoyed by the questions. "It was weeks ago – I don't remember what I ate for dinner today, much less who was working that night or if they said anything about the patient. If there was something strange, they should have noted it in the man's chart. I can't speak for the nurses, you should talk to them yourself. The receptionist can get you their information." He glanced at his watch. "If that is all, I need to return to my patients."

They shook hands, Gideon assuring him they appreciated his time as the doctor hurried off.

Back at the reception desk, Dacey checked to see if any of the three nurses who'd worked that shift were on duty. Two of them, Serena and Ernesto, were currently working in the ICU on the third floor.

In the elevator, Dacey flipped through the chart. "Says here he was in room 338."

The rest of the short elevator ride to the third floor was silent, both of them lost in thought. They found the room Chauvin had stayed in empty and stepped inside. Almost immediately, Gideon felt the void, though it was fainter than the others.

"It's here," he told Dacey quietly. "Not as strong as the other locations. Could be from the passage of time, or just how many people have been through here since."

A woman in her thirties appeared in the doorway. Her blue scrubs marked her as one of the floor nurses. Her ID badge read 'S. Robberts.' She eyed them suspiciously. "Can I help you?"

Dacey showed her badge. "We're looking for Serena Robberts and Ernesto Garcia. We have a couple of quick questions about a former patient."

"I'm Serena." She leaned out into the hallway. "Hey, Ernie!"

A muscular Asian man with a buzzed haircut joined them. Dacey showed them Marcus's photo. "Do either of you remember this patient? He died here a few weeks ago."

Serena shook her head, but Ernie squinted at the photo. "Maybe? I remember changing his fluids, but I didn't work with him much. Someone else was assigned to him primarily, but I can't remember who."

"Emma Kim?" Gideon suggested.

Ernie shrugged. "Could be."

They handed out their cards and asked the nurses to call if they remembered anything unusual from that night. After the nurses left, Gideon made one more circuit of the room before they walked the rest of the floor. Nothing else felt off.

Back at the front desk, they left a card for Emma Kim with

instructions to call them. The walk to the car felt longer than it should have, exhaustion weighing down their steps.

"Hotel?" Gideon asked hopefully as they climbed in.

"Hotel," Dacey confirmed, starting the engine. "But first thing tomorrow morning—"

"Metro Diner to talk to Astrid," Gideon finished. "I remember. And then we get to attend our first meeting with the Heritage Foundation. Do you think they'll kick us out if I use the wrong fork? Because I definitely can't tell a salad fork from a dessert fork."

"Probably. And I forgot to pack my good pearls and white gloves," Dacey sighed dramatically. "The *country club contingent* might revoke my membership."

Gideon watched Dacey as she chuckled, her nose crinkling and her eyes sparkling in the dashboard lights. Even exhausted, she was beautiful. The moment felt fragile, precious – just the two of them sharing a joke, temporarily pushing aside the weight of their investigation.

Dacey pulled out of the parking lot, and the hospital's lights grew smaller in the rearview mirror. Tomorrow was another day, another chance to catch their killer – because Gideon was becoming increasingly sure that they were dealing with murders, not magical accidents. Gideon just hoped they'd catch them before anyone else ended up in that hospital, life force drained away to nothing but a void.

CHAPTER 15

The blare of an alarm shattered the pre-dawn silence. Gideon groaned, blinking in the darkness of his hotel room as he fumbled for his phone. The bright screen made him wince as he silenced the intrusive noise. He sat up on the mattress, cursing under his breath as exhaustion tugged at him like an insistent child. After the long day yesterday, his body was staging a protest against such an early start.

Shrugging off the temptation to fall back into the surprisingly comfortable hotel bed, Gideon forced himself up and into the shower. The hot water helped chase away some of the lingering fatigue, though he knew he'd need at least two cups of coffee before he'd feel properly human again.

Less than twenty minutes later, dressed and marginally more alert, Gideon knocked on Dacey's door.

"Door's unlocked!" Dacey's voice called out. "Come in, I'm almost ready. Just give me a sec!"

Gideon hesitated for a moment before turning the handle. The sound of a hair dryer greeted him as he stepped inside. Through the open bathroom door, he could see Dacey drying her long dark hair, already dressed for the day in dark slacks and a white button-up shirt.

The hair dryer clicked off, and Dacey emerged, running her fingers through her hair. "Sorry for running late. When I woke up, I swore my hair smelled like the hospital. Had to wash it."

Gideon raised his hands. "No worries. We've still got plenty of time."

Dacey glanced at her watch and grabbed her badge from the dresser. "Let's go, but I want to stop in the lobby for coffee. We're running a little behind from when I wanted to leave, but Renee said the homeless don't clear out until seven, so we should still have enough time." She patted her pockets, doing the familiar dance of keys-phone-badge. "I need something to help wake up my brain."

As they stepped into the elevator, Dacey leaned against the wall with a sigh. "I didn't sleep well. My brain wouldn't shut up about the case."

"Same here," Gideon admitted. "Come up with anything?"

Dacey blew out a raspberry, her expression grumpy. "No. You?"

Gideon shook his head.

After a quick stop for coffee and bagels from the hotel's breakfast bar, they drove to Metro Diner. They could see Renee inside through the front windows, prepping for the day. They knocked on the glass, waving when she spotted them.

The lock clicked, and Renee pulled open the door. "Morning."

"Has Astrid shown up this morning?" Gideon asked.

"Not yet, but if you want to wait for her, there are some benches and picnic tables around back." Renee glanced at the paper cups in their hands and wrinkled her nose. "Let me get you some real coffee first."

"You're officially my favorite person," Dacey declared.

Renee waved her away. "If I had a nickel.... I'll bring it out back in just a minute." She paused. "Fair warning though – the homeless might be wary around you. Might want to stay somewhat out of the way."

They thanked her and started walking around the building. As they reached the corner, Gideon noticed two men sitting behind the restaurant at a weathered picnic table. One was nursing a paper cup of coffee, his beard matted and clothes layered despite the heat, while the other sorted through an overstuffed backpack, its fabric worn thin at the seams. He was about to warn Dacey about their presence when movement from the side caught his eye. Detective Voss approached from around the corner. Voss did a double-take when he saw them.

"You're up early," he said with a grin.

"Good morning, Victor. We were hoping to talk to some of the homeless people, see if they knew Joe," Dacey explained.

Voss nodded. "Makes sense."

"What brings you here?" Gideon asked.

"My shift starts soon. I wanted to grab breakfast first. My fridge is pretty much empty at this point."

Dacey opened her mouth to respond, but something at the edge of the woods drew Gideon's attention. A figure emerged from the trees, stumbling around as if drunk – Astrid.

"There she is," he whispered, nudging Dacey.

"Who?" Voss started to turn.

Astrid's eyes locked onto them. She jabbed a finger at Gideon. "You!" Her voice rose to a shrill cry. "Valhalla awaits! The end of times – my time, everyone's time! Too late, too late! Fool! Murderer!"

Unlike their previous encounter, Astrid wasn't bundled in multiple layers of jackets. She wore only dirty, ripped sweatpants and a ratty tank top. The exposed skin of her arms, shoulders, and chest was covered in more crude tattoos – runes and strange symbols that seemed to shift and writhe in the early morning light. Dominating the collection was a large spiral-shaped seashell just above her sternum.

Dacey stepped forward, hands raised placatingly. "Astrid, we just want to talk—"

Moving with surprising speed, Astrid spun and sprinted back into the woods.

"Damn it!" Dacey broke into a run. "We just have some questions! We're not here to hurt you!"

Gideon plunged into the woods after Dacey, hearing Voss's footfalls behind him. The early morning light filtered weakly through the canopy, casting confusing shadows across the uneven ground. With each step, his boots sank into the mud, the earth still soft and treacherous from Florida's rainy season. His foot caught on a half-buried root, and he stumbled, but training sessions with Silas had transformed his stamina. He caught himself against a tree trunk, the rough bark biting into his palm as he pushed off and chased after Dacey.

Ahead, he could hear the crack of branches as she crashed through the undergrowth. Gideon pushed harder, pleased at how his endurance had grown. Just two months ago, this kind of chase would have left him winded. Now, he was gaining ground on Dacey. A low-hanging branch thwapped him across the face just as he caught up to her, sending a shower of morning dew over him.

A tangle of thorny vines grabbed at his pants leg. He yanked free with a curse, feeling the material tear. Glancing over, he saw Voss keeping pace beside him, the man seeming to glide through the undergrowth with an almost preternatural grace. While Gideon battled the thorns and branches, Voss moved like water through the obstacles, each step precise and fluid. Gideon's lungs burned as he pushed harder, trying not to feel envious of Voss's effortless navigation through the dense swamp-like forest.

They were both right on Dacey's heels as she burst into a small clearing. Dacey came to an abrupt halt, standing there, bent over with her hands on her knees, chest heaving. She straightened up, turning in circles with a bewildered expression.

"I lost her," she panted, wiping sweat from her forehead. "She outran me somehow. I thought I was right on her heels, but I lost her somewhere in the brush. She was right ahead of me, and then... nothing. Like she vanished into thin air."

"She lives in these woods. I'm sure she knows them like the back of her hands." Voss lifted his nose to the air, then flicked his tongue out. "This way."

At Gideon's questioning look, he explained, "I'm a basilisk shifter. I have a superior sense of smell."

They followed Voss through the dense underbrush, moving more carefully now. Gideon's pants were already muddy to the knee from their headlong chase, and thorns had left tiny tears in his clothes and itchy scratches all over his arms. The woods seemed different here – older somehow, the trees pressed closer together, their branches interweaving overhead to block out most of the growing daylight.

Finally, they emerged into another clearing – one Gideon recognized. Joe's former camp lay before them, now stripped bare of the man's belongings. Only the tamped-down earth and a few scraps of weather-beaten trash remained to show anyone had lived here. Voss turned in a slow circle, confusion evident as he tested the air again.

"The trail dies here," he said, frowning. "She might have backtracked to hide her trail. Smart move if she did."

"Do you think you can find her trail again?" Dacey asked.

"I'll try, but she's craftier than I expected."

They spent the next half hour tramping through the woods. As they walked, Gideon pushed out his senses, trying to sort through the magical signatures laid throughout the woods. Astrid's fractured magic dominated the area, scraping against his senses. A few fainter trails of other Mythicals threaded through her overwhelming presence, but her magic was unlike anything he'd encountered before – it seemed to fill every corner of the forest.

Following Voss, the trail spilled out onto First Street, the busiest part of the main drag. The detective looked agitated and slightly embarrassed.

"Sorry," he said. "Too many other scents here. I can't track her any further."

"That's okay," Dacey assured him. "We only had a few questions for her. We probably shouldn't have chased after her, but she ran."

When they returned to the back of the restaurant, the remaining homeless people were gone. Gideon figured they'd all scattered once they witnessed him and Dacey chasing after Astrid.

Voss cleared his throat. "You know, there's another spot where Millhaven's homeless population congregates. Down by the base of the bridge, along the edge of Lake Monroe. Astrid might head there, and the others might be more willing to talk about Joe."

Dacey's face brightened. "That's a great idea—" Her phone buzzed in her pocket, cutting her off. She pulled it out and glanced at the screen. "It's Dr. Blackwood from the morgue."

She answered, putting it on speaker. "Dr. Blackwood, good morning. You're on speaker – Gideon and Detective Voss are here with me."

"Another body just showed up in my morgue with the same symptoms as the others." Dr. Blackwood's voice was terse. "The victim is a man named Grant Vandermeer. He was in his early sixties and healthy as a horse. Except for the fact that he's dead."

Voss did a double-take at the name, his expression shocked.

"You know him?" Dacey asked.

"Yeah," Voss nodded grimly. "He's a well-known local real estate developer. Pretty big player in Millhaven."

Dacey pinched the bridge of her nose. "How long will you be at the morgue, Doctor?"

"Until around one. I have meetings scheduled for the rest of the day after that."

Dacey glanced at her watch and grimaced. "I want to visit that encampment, but I don't know if there is enough time before the Heritage Foundation meeting."

"Do you want to come examine the body, or should I just send you my notes?" The coroner offered.

"No, we need Gideon to examine him." From the corner of his eye, Gideon could see Voss staring at him. "We'll come as soon as possible," she assured Blackwood.

Once Dacey ended the call, Voss cleared his throat. "I guess we'll skip the homeless encampment then?"

Dacey looked torn, her gaze shifting between Voss and Gideon.

"Why don't you go to the encampment while I check out the morgue?" Gideon suggested. "I just need to examine the body and get the victim's information. We can meet up afterward."

"That could work," Dacey said, brightening. "Victor, would you be willing to take me to the homeless encampment so Gideon can take the car?"

"Of course."

"I'm going to shower first at the hotel, then head to the morgue," Gideon told Dacey, indicating his mud-caked pant legs. "I'll call you as soon as I'm done and let you know what I find out."

"Sounds good." Dacey tossed him the car keys.

Dacey turned to Voss. "Give me just a second to talk to Gideon. I'll be right there."

"Sure thing." Voss nodded and headed toward his parked vehicle.

Once he was out of earshot, Dacey turned back to Gideon. "Did you sense any magic or voids in the woods?"

Gideon shook his head. "I didn't sense any voids – other than the one in Joe's campsite. As far as magic… Astrid's magic is all over the area."

"Could we follow that to track her?"

Gideon shook his head. "Just like the scent trail Voss tried to follow, her magical signature is crisscrossing back and forth so many times it's impossible to trace. It's like she's been pacing these woods for weeks, maybe months."

"Well damn. It was worth asking. I'm going to head out with Voss and see what we can find. Call me the second you learn anything interesting." Her expression was serious. "A real estate developer makes me wonder if this *is* all tied back to the Royal Palmetto."

"I had the same thought," Gideon agreed quietly. "Be careful at the encampment."

They shared a quick nod before heading to their respective vehicles, the morning's plans completely reshaped by this new development.

Gideon stood by the car and watched Voss and Dacey drive off, waving as they drove past.

As he opened the driver's side door, the diner's front door opened, and Renee emerged with a to-go cup of coffee.

"I'm guessing from all the shouting earlier that your chat with Astrid didn't go well?"

"You could say that." Gideon sighed, accepting the cup gratefully. "Has she always been so…."

"Intense? Unstable?" Renee supplied. "More or less, though, I'd say that she's gotten worse lately. Used to be she'd at least come inside sometimes, let me give her a hot meal. Now she just prowls the woods, muttering to herself." She looked at his mud-splattered clothes and gave him a sympathetic smile. "Do you want to come inside? You deserve some hot food after tramping around those woods."

"I wish. Sadly, I have somewhere I need to be," Gideon replied.

CHAPTER 16

The same attendant sat at the morgue's front desk, hunched over a sudoku puzzle. He glanced up at Gideon's arrival, his expression a blend of boredom and irritation at the unwelcome interruption.

"Dr. Blackwood is expecting me," Gideon said, flashing his badge.

Almost immediately, a familiar voice called out from the back. "Send him in!"

The receptionist waved Gideon through absently, attention already back on his puzzle. "Through there."

Dr. Blackwood stood waiting in the hallway, running her hand over her buzzed hair in agitation. Her eyes darted past Gideon, searching the space behind him. "Your partner's not coming?"

"Dacey had to follow up on another lead," Gideon explained. "It'll just be me examining Mr. Vandermeer."

She nodded and led him to an autopsy room. Before they'd even crossed the threshold, Gideon felt it – the telltale void that had become all too familiar. In the center of the room lay a naked human man on the examination table. Despite Gideon's years of experience at the crematorium, the stark reality of an autopsy victim felt much different from the cleaned and prepared bodies he usually dealt with. It felt more raw, more real.

Dr. Blackwood handed him a copy of the autopsy report. Gideon set it aside for the moment, stepping closer to examine the body. Grant Vandermeer looked to be in his sixties, and something about him reminded Gideon of Thurston Howell from Gilligan's Island – a show he'd watched endless reruns of with his mom in the days before they could afford cable. The resemblance was striking, though somewhat marred by the fact that Grant was naked and bore the distinctive Y-incision of a completed autopsy.

Dr. Blackwood raised an eyebrow. "Well?"

"Shit," Gideon muttered. He turned to face her. "This is definitely related to the others. His aura's completely gone."

Blackwood nodded as if this confirmed her suspicions. She handed him the police report next.

Scanning the document, Gideon noted that Vandermeer had died at home – in bed next to his wife. He did a double-take at that detail. There went the theory that only single people were being targeted.

After thanking Dr. Blackwood, Gideon headed out to his car. He tried calling Dacey, but the call went straight to voicemail. Not surprising if she was interviewing potential witnesses.

Looking at the police report again, Gideon realized Vandermeer's house wasn't far away. He decided to check it out while waiting for Dacey to call back.

The drive was short, taking him to a modern upscale neighborhood near where Marcus Chauvin had lived. Vandermeer's house backed up to Lake Monroe, and Gideon could only imagine the price tag on the waterfront property. The driveway was packed with vehicles, forcing him to park on the street.

When he rang the doorbell, a woman in her thirties with blonde hair and red-rimmed eyes answered. Gideon showed his badge and gave her a sympathetic look. "Mrs. Vandermeer?"

"No," the woman replied, shaking her head. "I'm Claire, Mr. Vandermeer's niece."

"I'm sorry to intrude, but I need to speak with Mrs. Vandermeer for just a moment."

"Is this necessary right now?" the woman asked, her voice tight with frustration. "The police only left a few hours ago, and now you're back?"

"It will only take a minute," Gideon assured her apologetically.

She huffed but gave him a resigned look. "Wait here."

Gideon hadn't realized he'd been expecting someone who looked like Lovey Howell to match Thurston until the actual Mrs. Vandermeer appeared – a redhead who bore more resemblance to Ginger than to the dowdy, pearl-clutching widow he'd pictured. If it weren't for her puffy, tear-stained eyes and the crumpled tissue in her hand, she might have been headed to a charity luncheon.

"I'm Mrs. Vandermeer. How can I help you?"

"I apologize for the intrusion," Gideon said gently. "I just have a few questions about your husband. I know this is a difficult time, but could you spare a moment?"

Mrs. Vandermeer nodded, clutching her tissue tighter. "Of course. Please, what do you need to know?"

"Can you tell me about yesterday? The events leading up to…." Gideon let the sentence trail off delicately.

"Nothing strange happened," she said, dabbing at her eyes. "Grant came home from work, we had dinner, and he went to bed first while I stayed up to watch some television. When I went to bed later, everything seemed fine…." She took a shaky breath. "I woke up in the middle of the night and realized he wasn't breathing. I called 911, but they couldn't… they couldn't save him."

"Was Grant acting different?"

"Not really. He was in a bad mood from a meeting he'd had earlier, but that's not unusual."

"Do you know who he met with?"

Mrs. Vandermeer shrugged. "I have no idea. Probably just another real estate thing."

"Did he seem abnormally tired?"

She gave him a thoughtful look. "He did go to bed earlier than usual, now that you mention it."

"Can you describe what happened when you woke up?"

"I noticed right away that something was wrong because Grant usually snores. It was too quiet. When I shook him, he didn't...." Her voice cracked, and fresh tears welled up.

"I'm sorry to make you relive this," Gideon said quickly. "However, it's important that we confirm the sequence of events."

Mrs. Vandermeer nodded, seeming to accept this explanation.

"Do you remember what woke you?"

"I don't know. I must have sensed something was wrong," she said, wiping her eyes. "I'd taken an Ambien because Grant's snoring keeps me awake unless I go to bed first. I was pretty groggy, so I don't remember if anything specific woke me. I just... I must have sensed that he needed me. But I was too late...."

"I'm so sorry for your loss, Mrs. Vandermeer," Gideon said gently. "Thank you for walking me through this. I just have one last question, if you feel up to it – you mentioned Grant had a meeting. Would his office be able to tell me who he met with yesterday?"

"Frank might know," she said with a slight shrug.

"Who's Frank?"

"Frank Stoope was Grant's business partner at Atlas Builders."

Back in his car, Gideon looked up the address for Atlas Builders. The company had two partners listed: Grant Vandermeer and Frank Stoope. He sent Dacey a quick text updating her on what he'd learned, then headed for an office complex on the edge of Millhaven.

Atlas Builders occupied a suite on the fourth floor in a collection of matching office buildings. Once Gideon exited the elevator and found the suite that Atlas Builders occupied, he entered the company's lobby – all sleek chrome and glass with generic artwork on the walls. The receptionist looked up as he approached.

"I'm Special Agent Nash," he said, showing his badge. "I'm investigating Grant Vandermeer's death. Can I ask you a few questions?"

The receptionist straightened in her chair, her expression growing somber. "Of course."

"Did Mr. Vandermeer come into the office yesterday?"

"Yes, he did."

"Was he acting strange?"

"No, not that I noticed."

"Tired?"

The receptionist paused, her brow furrowing slightly as she considered the question. "No."

Gideon fixed her with his most serious expression. "Could you print me a copy of his schedule from the last few days?"

The receptionist hesitated only briefly before turning to her computer. A moment later, she handed him a printout.

"Is Frank Stoope available?"

"Yes, he's in his office," the receptionist said.

"I'd like to speak with him."

She picked up her phone and pressed an extension. "There's an officer here to ask about Grant," she said into the receiver.

A minute later, a harried-looking man in his late forties appeared. He shook Gideon's hand and started leading him back to his office. They passed a door with a nameplate reading "Grant Vandermeer."

"Was this Grant's office?" Gideon asked, already reaching for the handle.

"Yes."

The office was pristine, not a paper out of place. Gideon did a quick scan but sensed no trace of magic. After walking around the space and looking over Grant's desk and not finding anything, he followed Frank to his own office, which presented a stark contrast – papers scattered across every surface, a rumpled jacket thrown over one chair, and a stack of files occupying the other seat facing the desk.

"Sorry," Frank said, moving the files. "Everything's crazy right now. I'm trying to deal with the fallout from Grant's death. I can't even take a minute to mourn him – too many people are relying on me to pick up the slack."

Gideon ran through the same questions he'd asked Mrs. Vandermeer. Yes, Frank had seen Grant yesterday. No, he hadn't noticed anything unusual.

Looking at the schedule, Gideon pointed to the last entry. "Did you attend the Board of Zoning Appeals meeting with Grant?"

"No, I was with one of our general contractors at a job site most of yesterday."

"His wife mentioned he came home in a bad mood. Would any of these appointments have upset him?"

Frank studied the schedule. "Probably the Zoning Appeals meeting. Those are always the worst."

"Did you talk to him after the meeting?"

"No, I'd already left for the day."

On a hunch, Gideon asked, "Is your company involved with the Royal Palmetto restoration?"

Frank's expression darkened. "We'd been trying to buy that property for years. That building's a disaster waiting to happen – rotting floors, failing foundation, the works. The plan had been to tear it down and build something that would actually bring value to the area."

"I heard the Heritage Foundation has an initiative to preserve the hotel."

Frank snorted. "Those snobby old ladies did everything they could to block the purchase. And succeeded. Grant warned them that restoring that death trap would cost six times more than building new. They didn't care. Claimed it was 'historically significant'." He made air quotes with his fingers. "I wanted to purchase that hotel out from under the Heritage Foundation's nose, but Grant pulled rank as a co-owner. I was forced to give up on it. Frankly, I'm glad we're out of it now. It would've been a nightmare project with them breathing down our necks at every turn."

"Does Grant's death change things for you regarding the hotel?" Gideon asked.

Frank sat back and crossed his arms over his chest. "I hadn't thought about that yet. Everything is too fresh."

The defensive posture and averted gaze gave Gideon the impression that Frank was lying.

"So you're familiar with the Heritage Foundation and their members?"

"Oh yeah," Frank said in the same way that people discuss an overbearing mother-in-law.

"Have you done any projects with the foundation?"

"Not if I can help it. Those old biddies make even the simplest project difficult. We avoid them whenever possible. Historic preservation is generally outside the scope of work we offer anyway. All that fussy restoration work – having to match hundred-year-old crown molding and dealing with preservation boards.... We stick to new construction. Much cleaner and simpler."

Unable to think of any other questions, Gideon handed Frank his card. "Call me if you think of anything unusual that happened with Mr. Vandermeer."

Frank hesitated before taking it. "Isn't this a bit much? Grant died from a heart attack or something, right?"

Gideon fixed him with a flat look. "I'm not at liberty to say, but when a prominent member of society dies, we take it very seriously."

Frank nodded, leaning back in his chair.

"I appreciate your time," Gideon said, rising from his seat. "If you recall anything about the days before Grant's passing, please call me."

As Gideon exited the office suite, his phone rang. It was Dacey.

"Did you find Astrid?" he asked as he stepped into the elevator.

"Nope," Dacey sighed. "And the few homeless people willing to talk to us didn't have anything helpful to say about Joe or Astrid. It was pretty much a bust. You have any success while I was tramping through a homeless encampment?"

"Grant Vandermeer is definitely another victim, but other than that, I haven't found anything solid yet. I need you to ask Wiz to look into Grant's business partner's life – there's something off and suspicious about Frank Stoope. Let's meet, and I can catch you up on everything."

"I need to get back to the hotel and shower before we head to the Heritage Foundation meeting. I'll call Wiz on the way and tell her to tear apart Frank Stoope's life piece by piece. We'll nail him to the wall if he's behind all this. I'm honestly getting pissed that we haven't made more progress yet."

"Need a ride to the hotel?"

"No, Victor will drive me."

"Sounds good," Gideon said, even though it didn't really. "I'll meet you there."

CHAPTER 17

Gideon and Dacey exited the hotel's air-conditioned lobby into the late afternoon heat. The sun beat down mercilessly, turning the parking lot into a shimmering mirage. Before they could start walking to the car, Gideon's phone started ringing. His mother's smiling face lit up the screen.

"I need to take this," Gideon said with a grimace.

"Here, give me the keys," Dacey said. "I'll go cool down the car."

Gideon tossed her the keys and swiped to accept the call. "Hi, Ma."

"Giddy! How's everything going with that cremation job in Orlando?" Her voice carried that particular tone of forced casualness that meant she was trying not to sound worried.

"Good – nothing much happening." He squinted against the glare, watching Dacey walk across the parking lot.

"Nonsense! This is a wonderful opportunity. Helping out another crematorium will show your boss what a good team player you are. You're such a hard worker. You know how proud I am—" His mother paused. "Did you pack enough clean shirts? The humidity down there will have you sweating through them in no time."

"Yes, Ma," Gideon said, her reminder making him grab the collar of his polo shirt and fanning it, trying to get some air moving. His mom was entirely correct about the heat and humidity. It was brutal, even in the covered entrance. He didn't want to show up at the Heritage Foundation meeting already stinking of sweat.

"Are you sleeping okay? You sound tired. You know how you get when you don't—"

Gideon let his mother's voice fade into background chatter as he watched Dacey through the windshield. The car was already running, and she was bobbing her head to whatever song she'd put on, lost in her own little world. He could see her lips moving as she sang along, completely caught up in the music.

"Giddy? Are you listening to me?" His mother's voice cut through his distraction.

"Yes, Ma," he said, turning back to her.

"So... do you think you are going to make it back in time for the Fourth of July barbecue?"

"I'm not sure yet how much longer they'll need m—"

A car horn cut through the humid air, interrupting his response. Dacey pulled up to the curb before him, the car's engine humming. She rolled down the passenger window. "Come on, Giddy! We gotta get a move on, or we're gonna be late!"

"Who is that?" His mother's voice sharpened. "Is that... Dacey?"

Gideon winced. "Uh, yeah, Mom. She's working with me here in town."

"Working with you? At the crematorium?" His mom's tone let Gideon know she didn't believe that for a second. The worry and agitation in her voice ratcheted up several notches. "The last time you two *worked* together, you almost died. We all could have died! Is that woman putting you in danger again?"

Dacey gave him a concerned look through the open window and waved him toward the car. Gideon held up one finger and mouthed, 'Sorry, give me a moment' before turning away.

"No, Ma, there's no danger," he said, trying to keep his voice level. "This is a simple project. It's going to help with my job. It's no big deal."

"That's what you said last time." The fear in her voice made him feel guilty but also frustrated.

"Look, Mom," he said, unable to keep the aggravation out of his tone, "I'm an adult, and I know what I'm doing. I promise. I'm sorry I didn't tell you about working with Dacey again, but I knew you would worry for no reason. I swear to you, I am in no danger."

"I just don't want—"

"Ma, working with Dacey and her organization is going to do wonders for my career," he said, trying to keep his voice level. "This project is just the beginning."

"What? The beginning? With that Nexus company?" His mother's voice was sharp with worry. "You don't need that place. You have a good job at the crematorium. Why risk that working with Dacey?"

"The crematorium job is just that, Ma –a good job, but still just a job. Nexus Consulting is my chance at a real career." He fought to keep the aggravation out of his tone.

"That girl is bad for you, Gideon. She's already put you in danger once. I don't want—"

"Look, Mom," he said firmly but kindly, "Dacey is a great friend, and I want her in my life. You need to respect me enough to know I wouldn't have bad people as friends. Trust my judgment on this. You have to trust me, Ma. I have to go, but I promise you, I know what I'm doing. I'm going to be fine; I am in no danger. I'm sorry. I should have been honest and talked to you sooner, but I'm doing what is right for me. I love you, and I promise to be safe."

There was a long pause before his mother sighed. "Okay. I trust you. I love you too, Gideon." His mom let out a rough sigh. "Listen, if you want this woman in your life, then I accept that. Perhaps she'd like to come to the barbecue this weekend. It'll be a chance for us to start over."

"That's... that's kind of you. I'll see if she's interested."

After they said their goodbyes, Gideon slid into the passenger seat of the mercifully cool car.

"Everything okay?" Dacey asked as she pulled away from the curb.

"Yeah, just an aggravating call with my mom."

Dacey made an understanding sound in her throat. "I totally get it. My mom makes me crazy, too."

It surprised Gideon to hear this – Dacey had never talked about her home life before. It was hard to picture her having anything so mundane and normal as a mother and family.

"What's your mom like?" The question slipped out before Gideon could stop it, but he was genuinely curious. In all the time he'd known Dacey, she'd never once mentioned her family.

"Probably a lot like the women we're about to meet at the foundation – a snobby socialite." She flashed him a grin at his incredulous look. "I know, right? My mom is scandalized by what I do. She doesn't understand me at all."

They stopped at a red light, and Dacey's expression grew more serious. "At least you know your mom cares about you and not only her reputation."

"I'm sorry," Gideon said quietly. "That sucks."

Dacey's shoulders hunched forward as she picked at a loose thread on her sleeve. "Parents... What can you do?"

"Well, you could always fake your own death and move to Fiji," Gideon offered with a gentle smile. "I hear the weather's nice year-round."

"What? And leave this glamorous life behind?" Dacey waved her hand over the case files scattered across the back seat, gesturing to the collection of empty fast-food bags and wrinkled clothes that had colonized the car – evidence of a life lived more out of a suitcase than a home.

As Dacey drove, Gideon pulled out his phone to check his email. "Oh, hey! Vena finally sent me that list of energy-draining Mythicals she promised to put together."

He started scrolling through the detailed breakdown. "Let's see.... Succubi and incubi drain life force through physical contact, aka sex, leaving traces of lust magic and physical exhaustion. They rarely kill their victims, and even if they did, they wouldn't need to feed five times in a month. So it's not them. Alright, Mara – that's a Slavic spirit

– sits on sleeping victims' chests and drains energy while causing nightmares. Their magic leaves a cold, heavy residue."

He continued reading. "Pishacha are Hindu demons that feed on both life force and emotions. They leave behind a corrupted energy signature that feels like spoiled food. Lidérc, from Hungarian folklore, drains victims while they sleep but leaves burn marks from their fiery touch."

"None of them sound like our guy," Dacey agreed, taking a turn.

"Then there are vampires who leave fang marks, and I am very familiar with the feel of their magic. Then there's the Alp – a Germanic nightmare spirit that causes sleep paralysis while feeding. Victims report feeling like they're drowning in dark water. And Jiangshi…." He paused, squinting at the screen. "They're Chinese energy vampires that drain life force through breath and blood, leaving victims with bruised lips and a slimy magical signature that lingers for days after the attack."

Gideon lowered his phone with a frustrated sigh. "Vena's thorough – she's got pages more of these things. But none of them fit. Every single one leaves some kind of magical trace or signature behind after they feed, and many of them target specific types of victims that don't match one or more victims in our case. There's not a single mention of anything that leaves a void like what I've sensed."

"Well, then we know what it's not," Dacey replied. She reached over and gave his shoulder a gentle squeeze. "Hey, we'll figure this out. Sometimes knowing what you're *not* looking for is just as important as knowing what you *are* looking for."

Gideon relaxed slightly under her touch, grateful for the reminder that he wasn't facing this alone. A small smile tugged at his lips – Dacey knew how to put things in perspective.

They drove in comfortable silence for a few minutes before Dacey brightened. "We're here!"

The Millhaven Garden Club building rose before them. The two-story structure was painted a cheerful yellow with crisp white trim, its wooden siding weathered but well-maintained. A wraparound porch supported by classic white columns gave the building a genteel air, complete with several rocking chairs arranged in conversational groupings. Hanging baskets overflowing with vibrant flowers adorned the porch, their blooms providing splashes of purple and pink against the yellow backdrop.

The grounds were immaculately maintained, with neat beds of plants and dwarf palm trees creating a lush frame for the historic building. A brick pathway wound through the garden, leading to the broad front steps. Several expensive cars were already parked in the crushed shell parking area to the side of the building, their polished surfaces gleaming in the sunshine.

Dacey pulled into an empty spot, turning to Gideon with a smirk. "Ready to schmooze with Millhaven's elite?"

CHAPTER 18

Dacey twisted around and reached into the backseat, pulling a worn leather case onto her lap. She rifled through several manila folders inside, then extracted a piece of paper and a pen, handing both to him.

"Here's the list of everyone who was at Edelweiss Hall the night Willa Wagner died," she said. "And I highlighted the three women who had dinner with Eleanor Preston the night she died. Lucky for us, they're all foundation members, so I'm hoping they're here. I'll take point on the interviews if you keep track of who we've talked to. And obviously, keep an eye out for any magical signatures – especially void magic."

Gideon unfolded the paper, scanning the neat rows of names. "Got it. What's our cover story again?"

"We're reporters from Florida Today," Dacey explained, adjusting her blazer as she killed the engine. "We're 'writing' an article about the Heritage Foundation and doing memorial pieces for Willa and Eleanor. The mayor helped set this up, so everyone's expecting us."

As they climbed to the wraparound porch, the wooden steps creaked slightly under their feet. Before they could reach for the door, it swung open to reveal the mayor. Winnie's coral-colored dress looked perfectly pressed despite the heat and humidity, her sleek brown bob without a hair out of place. The moment she appeared, Gideon's magical senses were overwhelmed by her mountain witch aura – as powerful and ancient as the Appalachians themselves. Only Dacey's fiery magic cut through the mayor's dominating presence.

"Thank you both so much for coming," she said warmly, then glanced back over her shoulder before stepping onto the porch and lowering her voice. "Have you... made any progress? Found anything worth reporting about what happened to my sister?"

Before Gideon could respond, Dacey drew a deep breath. "Madam Mayor—" She caught the mayor's look and amended, "Winnie. I need to inform you that another victim turned up in the morgue this morning. Grant Vandermeer, a local real estate developer."

"Oh my god.... Grant?" Mayor Thorne's hand flew to her strand of pearls, clutching them as the color drained from her face. Gideon had heard of people clutching their pearls but had never expected to witness it in real life.

"You knew him?" Dacey asked quietly.

The mayor's fingers remained wrapped around her pearls as she composed herself. "Only professionally – he's been part of the chamber of commerce for years, so our paths crossed frequently at meetings and events. But I can't say I knew him personally." She shook her head. "This is devastating. So many deaths in such a short time...."

"Which is why I'm calling in a full Conclave investigative team once we're done with this meeting," Dacey said firmly. "We can't risk this situation getting out of hand and potentially exposing the existence of Mythicals."

The mayor's shoulders slumped slightly, though she maintained her dignified bearing. "Of course, I understand completely. It's just...." She glanced toward the window where patriotic bunting had been hung. "The Fourth of July celebration this week is one of our biggest fundraisers of the year. But obviously, public safety comes first."

Mayor Thorne gestured for them to follow her inside. As they crossed the threshold, Gideon leaned close to Dacey, his voice barely a whisper. "We're really calling in a team?"

Dacey gave a subtle nod, her eyes scanning the entrance hall. "Yes. As soon as we're done here, I'm calling Wiz."

Warm sunlight streamed through the tall windows of the main meeting room, highlighting the original heart pine floors that gleamed with years of careful maintenance. Crown molding framed the high ceiling, which supported three antique chandeliers. One wall featured built-in cabinets displaying horticultural awards and club memorabilia, while another held a gallery of framed photographs showing past presidents and notable events.

Winnie pointed to the man they'd met outside her office on their first day in town. The distinctive streak of white at his temple made him instantly recognizable to Gideon. The man hadn't noticed them enter as he stood near the refreshment table, organizing papers. "You remember my assistant Michael? If you need anything during your visit, please don't hesitate to let him know."

About two dozen people, primarily women with a few men scattered throughout, stood in small conversational clusters. The air was thick with expensive perfume and the murmur of voices. Gideon noticed that nearly every woman wore enough jewelry to fund a small country's GDP.

As Gideon discreetly scanned the room with his magical senses, the mayor's powerful witch magic and her assistant's tightly controlled sorcerer aura dominated the space. The only other magical signature he could detect was a subtle Fae presence emanating from one of the socialites, her otherworldly essence carefully concealed beneath layers of expensive perfume and Southern charm.

Winnie cleared her throat. "Everyone? May I have your attention, please?" The room quieted immediately. "I'd like to introduce Dacey Santiago and Gideon Nash from Florida Today. They're writing an article about our organization and preparing memorial pieces for our dear Eleanor and Willa." A ripple of appropriately sad expressions passed through the crowd.

For the next few hours, they worked their way through the interviews. Gideon couldn't help but notice how every woman seemed to have a cutesy nickname. There was Caroline "Cookie" Whitmore, Elizabeth "Boots" Sterling, who'd been on the foundation board, Philomena "Scrappy" Randolph in her Chanel suit, and Katherine "Kippy" St. Claire. Even the younger members had embraced the tradition – Patricia "Poppy" Whitaker couldn't have been more than thirty-five.

They started with 'Cookie' Whitmore – the Fae whose magic Gideon had detected earlier – whose diamond tennis bracelet caught the light with every animated gesture.

"Oh, it's just devastating about dear Willa. She and I were such good friends. I don't know what I'm going to do without her." Cookie dabbed at her eyes with a monogrammed handkerchief. "And the foundation has lost a piece of its heart. She was such a fixture at all our events."

"Were you at Edelweiss Hall the night she passed?" Dacey asked gently.

"Why yes, I was. Though I barely saw her that evening. We're on different committees for the Foundation, so we didn't get to work together as much as I would've liked."

"Did she seem different that night?"

Cookie tilted her head as she thought. "She seemed rather tired, poor dear. But with all the foundation work and the Fourth of July planning…." Cookie trailed off with a delicate shrug.

Dacey turned the conversation toward the Royal Palmetto project. "The mayor told me that your foundation's focus has been on restoring the Royal Palmetto to its former glory. Have you had much to do with that project?"

Cookie shook her head. "I've mostly just been involved in fundraising. And the gardening committee. I love flowers and plants and want to ensure our town is always in full bloom." She tittered at her own pun. Belatedly, Gideon chuckled for her benefit.

"However, I will say that the Meridian Hospitality Group's proposal is exactly what we need," Cookie announced with an arch look, clutching Dacey's upper arm for emphasis. "Their resources could save the hotel before it's too late. The building will collapse before work starts at the rate we're going. And then some developer will swoop in and build some modern monstrosity on the land that will destroy our lovely town."

"Cookie, I must disagree," interrupted a woman dripping in diamonds and old money confidence. "You must understand how vital it is to maintain local ownership of our historic properties. Outsiders simply don't grasp what it means to preserve our traditions and style. This is why keeping the hotel within our control is essential." She gave Dacey a pointed once-over, her gaze lingering on Dacey's blazer. "We can't have strangers coming in to ruin our lovely town. Standards of quality and elegance must be upheld." Her practiced smile didn't reach her eyes. "I'm sure you agree, don't you? Well, perhaps you don't, dear, but I assure you it's crucial to our community."

Gideon watched as amber fire rolled across Dacey's eyes, ghostly wings of flame rising from her back – invisible to everyone but him. He'd seen that look before. It never ended well for whoever had provoked it. As Dacey's temperature rose with her irritation, Gideon noticed that the slight serpentine magic still clinging to Dacey from her morning with Voss and the Fae essence from Cookie's brief touch seemed to intensify, releasing their magical signatures like spices releasing their flavors when heated.

The woman fluttered her hand with a set of gold bangles that probably cost more than most people's cars. "Goodness, it's so warm in here. The A/C isn't working properly at all."

"If you're so worried about Meridian," Cookie responded with an exasperated sigh, "you really should talk to Mayor Thorne. Winnie will explain everything and assure you how she'll personally make sure Meridian restores the hotel properly. They aren't just some outsider company – they genuinely care about Millhaven's heritage. The mayor wouldn't align herself with them otherwise."

The woman sniffed derisively but didn't argue further.

Gideon stepped closer to Dacey, letting his shoulder brush against hers. Part of him would have loved to see Dacey immolate this snob where she stood, but he couldn't let that happen. "I believe our next interview is waiting," he said smoothly, guiding Dacey away.

Dacey thanked Cookie for her time, ignoring the rude woman, and gave Gideon an appreciative look before turning to the next socialite waiting to speak with them.

Elizabeth 'Boots' Sterling, who'd been on the foundation board with Eleanor for fifteen years, was the next person they interviewed. "Ellie was tireless when it came to preserving Millhaven's history," she said, her perfectly manicured hand pressed against her heart. "Did you know she personally cataloged every historical document in our archives?"

"That's wonderful," Dacey said warmly. "I understand you had dinner with her at the country club the night she died?"

"Yes – it's been such a terrible shock. She'd left early, saying she needed rest. I wish I'd realized…." Boots attempted to frown, but only her lower face complied – her forehead remained unnaturally smooth. "She'd seemed a bit distracted that entire evening, but I know how busy she'd been with the Royal Palmetto project."

They moved on to Scrappy, who spoke at length about both women's dedication to the foundation. When asked about Willa's final night, she mentioned seeing her in deep conversation with someone by the refreshment table, though she couldn't recall who.

Kippy St. Claire, another of Eleanor's dinner companions the evening she died, was particularly eager to share. "Eleanor barely touched her beef wellington that night," she confided, toying with an enormous diamond ring on her finger. "But you know how Ellie was about her figure – always watching what she ate."

The interviews continued, with each society matron more polished than the last. Sugar Alcott, Poppy Whitaker, and Sunny Covington all expressed shock over Eleanor and Willa's deaths, though none had noticed anything unusual that night at Edelweiss Hall. Last was Mimi Carrington, the third woman from Eleanor's final dinner, who'd also remembered Eleanor seemed distracted and tired during the meal – "Most unlike her, she was usually so present."

After speaking to most of the foundation members, a clear picture emerged of a deeply divided membership.

"The Meridian Hospitality Group would bring in some much-needed revenue and expertise," insisted Tinsley Woodbury, examining her manicured nails in the light. "Their offer to restore the Royal Palmetto while maintaining its historical character is more than generous."

Ten minutes later, Kitty Dunworthy passionately argued the opposite position. "That corporate monster would destroy everything unique about the Royal Palmetto! They'd turn it into another cookie-cutter hotel with a few token 'historic' touches."

Gideon leaned close to Dacey after that exchange. "I'm noting who's pro-chain and who's against – just in case it's relevant."

Finally, Mayor Thorne stepped to the front of the room, calling everyone to order. "Thank you, Dacey and Gideon, for attending our event and speaking with us. I know I can speak on behalf of everyone when I say that we are looking forward to your article." Her witch magic pulsed through the room as she gestured to her assistant. "Now… If we could all take our seats. Michael, could you please pass out today's agenda? With the Fourth of July tomorrow, we need to discuss some final details for the parade and auction."

Michael moved through the room with careful precision. His sorcerer magic remained tightly controlled, barely detectable even to Gideon's trained senses as he methodically placed each agenda at every seat.

As everyone settled into their chairs, Dacey touched Gideon's arm. "Let's stay for a bit," she whispered. "I want to see how they behave when they think we're not watching."

They claimed seats in the back corner, observing as the mayor began discussing parade routes and booth assignments. After fifteen minutes of watching the polite but pointed exchanges about table decorations and silent auction items, Dacey tipped her head toward the exit, signaling for them to leave, much to Gideon's relief. They quietly slipped out, leaving Millhaven's elite to their planning.

Gideon looked down at his list, now covered in neat annotations.

The conversations had been enlightening about the foundation's complex web of relationships and interests, but they hadn't uncovered any bombshells. While the pattern of deaths seemed increasingly tied to the Royal Palmetto's fate, that theory still couldn't explain the other seemingly random victims – Marcus Chauvin, Brandon Cho, and Joe the homeless man. He glanced back at the garden club, thinking about all these wealthy, influential people playing their parts in what felt increasingly like an elaborate performance.

However, he couldn't picture any of those women as the masterminds behind the strange series of deaths that they were investigating.

CHAPTER 19

Stepping out of the Garden Club's air conditioning, Gideon untucked his navy polo shirt which was already damp with sweat. At his side, Dacey peeled off her blazer, draping it over her arm as they descended the creaking wooden steps to their car. Once inside the vehicle, Dacey let out a theatrical groan and slumped against the steering wheel.

"I swear, if I have to hear one more story about how someone got their funny little nickname," she said, sitting up and mimicking one of the society matrons' affected drawls. "'Oh, darling, they call me Beebee because my precious baby sister couldn't say Barbara.' I thought I was going to scream."

Gideon chuckled. "Did you notice how many of them had that weird frozen expression? I couldn't tell if it was Botox or just resting disdain face."

"Both," Dacey said, starting the car. "What did you think about the interviews overall?"

Gideon shrugged, reviewing his notes. "Well, we learned plenty about the hotel restoration drama, but beyond that...." He trailed off, shaking his head. "Not sure how much we really got."

"My thoughts exactly." Dacey pulled out her phone and put it on speaker. "I feel like we're running out of time. Let's call Wiz and have her gather the troops."

The phone rang twice before their Conclave team coordinator answered. "Dacey, tell me you've got something."

"Sort of. We just finished interviewing the Heritage Foundation members." Dacey filled her in on the deaths, the hotel politics, the newest death, and the void magic traces. "I think we need a full investigative and containment team."

"From what you're describing, I agree."

"Is my usual team available?"

"Should be able to get everyone there tomorrow. I'll text you the details once I have them." There was a rustling of papers. "Oh, and Gideon? Vena examined the watch you sent. She says she's never experienced anything like it, but she agreed that it feels like a void – like the item's residual magic just disappeared and left a hole behind. She also confirmed there's no ward or glamour on the watch. She's doing more research. If she doesn't find anything in the next few days, we'll bring her on location too."

"Here's hoping we solve this before then," Dacey said, "but I'm starting to doubt it."

"Never known you to lose faith in yourself, Menet. Don't start now." Wiz's voice held a hint of amusement. "Besides, you and Gideon work well together. You were pushing to have him on the team as soon as possible – wanted to expedite his training, maybe even skip some parts."

Gideon turned to Dacey, eyebrows raised, flattered beyond measure. "That true?"

Dacey punched his arm lightly. "Of course. You're awesome to work with. We're one hell of a team."

"Yeah, when you're not setting him on fire," Wiz snorted.

"That only happened one time!" Dacey protested as Gideon laughed. "And if you think about it, he set *himself* on fire."

After hanging up, they debated their next move. "We still haven't heard back from that third hospital nurse who worked on Marcus," Gideon suggested.

"Oh yeah. What was her name?"

"Emma something or other…" Gideon responded, wracking his brain trying to remember.

Dacey shuffled through her notes. "It was Kim. Emma Kim. I also want to check out the country club where Eleanor had her final meal."

Gideon checked the time on his phone. "We've got time for both —" He broke off as a message notification popped up. Opening it, he frowned at the unfamiliar number.

"What is it?" Dacey asked.

"It's Sara, the receptionist from the Serenity Living nursing home. She's… asking me out."

Dacey snatched his phone, reading the message. "Says she gets off work in an hour." A slow grin spread across her face – the kind that usually meant trouble. "You should take her up on that offer."

"What?"

"Tell her you'll pick her up from work. Get there early…." Dacey waggled her eyebrows meaningfully. "Turn on the charm and then find an excuse to get away from her and look around the place."

"You know, you're starting to sound like my pimp," Gideon said dryly.

Dacey's eyes lit up. "Hey, with those baby blues and that jawline?" She gestured at him appreciatively. "I could retire to my own private island in just a few months if I put you to work properly. Even less if we got you some tighter shirts."

"Can we focus?" Gideon asked, feeling the heat of a blush rise up his neck. "This isn't exactly a dating service."

"No, it's an investigation," Dacey agreed, sobering slightly, handing Gideon back his phone. "And this might be our best shot at getting inside that facility without a warrant. We still haven't figured out how Brandon fits into this mess."

Gideon stared at his phone for a long moment, then typed a response, hoping this wouldn't blow up in their faces. "Once I get there, I could tell her I need to use the restroom, then find a way to slip into the facility, just to take a quick look around."

"Oh! I can create a distraction to keep her occupied." Dacey bounced in her seat in anticipation, making him nervous.

* * *

GIDEON WIPED his sweaty palms on his chinos as he approached Serenity Living's entrance. In his polo shirt and khakis, he felt like a missionary about to knock on doors. He glanced back at the car where Dacey waited, receiving an enthusiastic thumbs up and encouraging grin. He stuck his tongue out at her, pleased when she laughed.

Inside, he spotted Sara immediately at her desk, her blonde hair swaying as she looked up. Surprise flickered across her face before settling into a pleased smile.

"You're early," she said, checking the clock. "I don't clock out for another twenty minutes."

"Just thought I'd wait inside instead of in my car," Gideon replied with a friendly smile. "The air conditioning in here beats sitting in that heat."

Sara nodded, tucking a loose strand of hair behind her ear. "Well, I don't mind the company."

"Thanks. Hey, would you mind if I used the restroom?"

"Of course not," Sara said, gesturing down a short hallway that branched off the lobby. "First door on your left."

Gideon followed her directions, noting with frustration that the bathroom door was visible from Sara's desk. He knew he couldn't slip out of the bathroom and into the facility without her seeing him. Once inside the restroom, he texted Dacey his location and the issue. Pressing his ear against the door, he listened intently for Dacey's 'signal', growing more impatient with each passing second. His heart beat a rapid rhythm against his ribs as he waited.

Finally, he felt the surge of her fire magic, followed by shouting. He cracked the door open to find chaos in the lobby – a flaming trash can, Dacey yelling, and Sara rushing around her desk. The manager, Bob, came barreling out of his office, his eyes wild and shocked, and his thick glasses sitting askew on his nose.

Gideon eased the restroom door open, catching it before it could slam shut and letting it close with a soft click. He glanced down the hall, confirming everyone was occupied with the chaos in the lobby.

As he slunk toward the resident wing, he came to an abrupt halt, his breath catching – there, barely perceptible but unmistakable, was the distinct emptiness of a void.

Following the sensation about twenty feet down the hall, he pushed open a door to find what looked more like a hotel room than a resident's apartment. A flat-screen TV mounted on the wall played golf at low volume while framed photographs of smiling family members lined a cabinet. In a recliner by the window, a robust-looking man in his eighties dozed, a half-finished crossword puzzle in his lap.

Gideon moved silently through the tiny efficiency apartment. The only magic he detected in the room was the void centered on the bed – an otherwise unremarkable hospital bed with a navy comforter.

The void magic was weaker than the oppressive darkness he'd felt at the previous death scenes. Rather than a raw wound, this felt like an old scar – the void's edges softened and dulled with time, but the signature was unmistakable. This had a muted quality, like looking at a shadow through frosted glass. But despite its age, the magic still made his skin crawl with its wrongness. Gideon crept out silently.

Stepping out into the hallway, Gideon channeled Dacey – shoulders back, moving with calculated ease, like he owned the place. He nodded to a nurse pushing a medication cart, gave a pleasant "evening" to an elderly woman using a walker, and didn't break stride when a maintenance worker looked up from changing a light bulb. No one questioned his presence as he headed deeper into the building.

Moving methodically through the facility, Gideon found two more voids on the first floor – one in a shared room where both residents were watching TV, forcing him to pretend he was lost when he opened the door. The second void emanated from an empty apartment, and he felt relieved at not having to fabricate another excuse for his intrusion into someone's personal space.

The second floor yielded two voids, one emanating from a bed and the other from a recliner in the room's corner. On the third floor, Gideon found four more voids, but by then, worried that he was running out of time, he'd stopped bothering to go inside the rooms. He raced down the hallway, sensing the void signatures through the walls and typing the corresponding room numbers into his phone. He was certain now – the void only manifested in places where someone had fallen asleep and died.

Worried that one of the residents would soon complain about a strange man prowling the halls, Gideon entered the stairwell and headed back to the first floor.

He rushed back to the lobby, his heart pounding. Hazy smoke filled the air as the manager wielded a fire extinguisher. Dacey stood in the middle, loudly demanding answers about facility safety.

"A guest must've dropped a cigarette or something in the trash can," Bob assured Dacey, adjusting his glasses. "We run a good facility here."

"What is going on? I just went to the bathroom, and now there's all this smoke. What happened here?" Gideon asked, coughing.

"Found a trash can on fire when I came to get you."

"Came to get me?" Gideon asked, playing along.

"I know you were supposed to have the night off, but we have a lead," Dacey explained, giving a fake excuse for Gideon to cancel his 'date'.

"We need to go," Dacey announced.

Sara made a disappointed sound.

"I'm sorry, Sara, but it sounds like something urgent came up," Gideon said, running a hand through his hair. "I have to cancel."

"That's okay, I understand," Sara said, though her smile dimmed slightly. "Maybe we could do something after you're done?"

Gideon shifted uncomfortably. "I appreciate the offer, but I'm not sure how long this will take. Plus, I'm only in town for a couple more days at most." He left the implications hanging in the air.

"Oh." Sara's face fell for a moment before she recovered her composure. "Well, it was nice meeting you anyway."

"You too."

Outside, Dacey asked, "Not planning to date her while you're here?"

"Not my type," Gideon said dismissively.

"Did you find anything interesting in there? You were gone for so long I was starting to worry we'd get caught."

A smile spread across his face as they shifted topics. "Yeah, I found something interesting – nine voids in there, all faded – older than Marcus Chauvin's. This has been happening for a while."

"No way! Are you certain?"

"There is no doubt. Someone or something has killed at least nine other people before our 'first' victim."

"Hmm. I wonder... Maybe that's why Brandon Cho was targeted. He noticed something?"

"It would make sense."

Dacey pulled out her phone and dialed Wiz. "Hey, we've got something big. Gideon found nine more voids at Serenity Living. All older than Chauvin."

She listened for a moment. "Yeah, exactly. See if you can get us a warrant to search the nursing home. I want to pick that place apart.... No, Gideon is certain. The voids are there; they're faded, but they're definitely there.... I know it's late, but this can't wait.... Thanks, I owe you one."

She hung up and turned to Gideon. "Wiz thinks she can fast-track a search warrant. We should have that warrant ready by the time the rest of the team arrives tomorrow. Good work, Giddy. We're getting closer – I can feel it. Now we need to figure out what connects Serenity Living to the Royal Palmetto and the rest of our victims."

"What's next?" Gideon asked.

Dacey's stomach growled. "First, I'm craving some enchiladas. Then, I want to go over the case files again. We might spot something we missed before with what we know now."

CHAPTER 20

The waitress cleared their plates, and Gideon shook his head in amazement. "I will never get used to how much you can eat."

Dacey patted her flat stomach with satisfaction. "Bennu metabolism. Fire magic burns through calories like you wouldn't believe." She'd demolished an enchilada combo platter, chips and salsa, and still found room for fried ice cream. The small Mexican restaurant was mostly empty this late, which suited their purposes perfectly.

She pulled her laptop from her bag while Gideon spread the case files across their table.

"Okay," Dacey said, cracking her knuckles. "Let's start with what we know. We now believe that the first deaths happened at Serenity Living."

Gideon nodded, rifling through his notes. "Nine voids, all older than our other victims. Room numbers...." He rattled off the numbers he'd documented during his covert facility exploration.

"We need to find out who was placed in those rooms going back.... How long do you think we should check? Six months, a year, maybe?"

"Just to be safe, that sounds good to me."

Dacey's fingers flew across the keyboard. "I'm making a list of everything we need from Wiz and Leonhard. Complete ownership records for Serenity Living. Employee records – current and former. All residents, going back at least five years. All cross-referenced against our other victims."

"Hopefully, that will help us find our missing connection."

"Exactly." Dacey typed furiously. "The void signatures you found were weaker, right? Older?"

"Much older. Like scars rather than fresh wounds." Gideon shuffled through autopsy photos, arranging them chronologically. "The magic felt... muted. Less raw."

"So whatever's causing this has been active for a while. Why didn't anyone notice sooner?"

"Maybe because the victims seemed to die naturally?" Gideon suggested. "Elderly people in a nursing home – no one looks too closely."

"Until Brandon Cho noticed something." Dacey's eyes narrowed. "Which probably got him killed."

"And then they branched out. Got bolder." Gideon tapped Marcus Chauvin's photo. "Started targeting people outside the facility."

"But why? What changed?" Dacey finished typing and hit send on the email to Wiz and Leonhard. She closed her laptop with a sigh and ran her hands through her dark hair, leaving it slightly mussed.

Gideon noticed the shadows under her eyes and the slight slump in her usually perfect posture. He felt the weight of the case himself – the frustration of being so close yet still missing crucial pieces.

"How did you get into this?" he asked, wanting to distract her. "You mentioned your mother's a socialite. This seems... pretty far from that world."

Dacey's expression darkened. "Hunters murdered my college roommate."

"What?" Gideon's shock must have shown on his face because Dacey's lips twisted in a bitter smile.

"Michelle was a wolf shifter – a lone wolf, which is pretty rare. Most shifters are pack-bound, but Michelle...." Dacey smiled fondly at the memory. "She was special. Strong. Her alpha was a controlling jerk, but she found a way to break free. That took serious guts." Dacey traced patterns in the condensation left by her water glass. "God, she was so funny too. She had this way of seeing straight through people's bullshit and calling it out but without being mean. I really admired her." Her expression darkened. "One night, she went for a run in the nature preserve behind campus. Never came back."

She took a deep breath. "The police said it was a mugging gone wrong, but it didn't add up. She didn't have her wallet or even her phone on her. She was going for a run in her wolf form, so she left that all in the dorm. Nothing was taken. Plus, she was a shifter. It would've taken more than one guy to take her down."

"What happened?"

"I started digging. I skipped classes, barely slept. I finally discovered that the guy she'd been seeing casually figured out what she was. He turned her in to the local hunters' guild." Her voice hardened. "Self-righteous zealots who think it's their sacred duty to eliminate all Mythicals. They're nothing but murderers with a manifesto. Usually, they're just losers full of beer, hate, and hot air. And not much else. Blaming their crappy lives on magical beings. Either that, or they're the religious zealots – and those ones are much harder to deal with. They're quite willing to die for their cause."

Gideon stayed silent, watching emotions play across her face.

"I tracked them to their headquarters – this run-down warehouse on the edge of town." A spark of fire danced briefly in her eyes. "I burned it down. With most of them inside."

"The Conclave—"

"Oh, they were pissed." Dacey gave a harsh laugh. "They usually crack down hard on unauthorized hits like that. But they saw potential. Especially after learning I was a bennu shifter. Do you know how rare we are? A fire shifter who can be reborn from their own ashes? We're very, *very* hard to kill."

"Oh, I remember," Gideon teased. "I'll never forget the sight of you kicking open the oven door and scaring years off my life."

"Being naked probably caught your eye, too."

Gideon grinned, not stating how that had been seared into his mind. He tried not to dwell on that memory often – otherwise, he'd never get anything done.

"So... you went to work for the Conclave after that?" Gideon asked, changing the topic.

She grimaced. "They didn't give me much choice. Join the Conclave or face consequences for going vigilante. But honestly? It was the best thing that could have happened. Gave me purpose. A way to protect others like Michelle."

"I'm sorry about your friend," Gideon said quietly.

Dacey's expression softened. "Yeah, me too. But at least something good came from it. The Conclave rounded up the remaining hunters, and I found my calling." She stretched, some of her usual energy returning. "Even if it means endless paperwork and dealing with your terrible jokes."

"My jokes are fantastic," Gideon protested.

"Keep telling yourself that." Dacey pulled the files back toward her. "Now, help me figure out what we're missing here."

They bent their heads over the files again, the weight of unsolved murders heavy between them, but now Gideon understood a little better why Dacey pushed so hard, burned so bright. She'd seen first-hand what happened when justice failed. He wouldn't let her down.

CHAPTER 21

Gideon leaned against a pillar outside the hotel's entrance, watching the sky transform. Deep indigo faded to red, then softened into shades of pink that reminded him of the inside of a conch shell.

His mother's voice echoed in his head: "Red sky at night, sailor's delight; red sky in morning, sailor's warning." Every time there was a red sunrise, she'd swear it meant thunderstorms were coming. Given that this was Florida in summer, he figured she wasn't wrong – it basically rained every day here. Though they'd been lucky so far, managing to avoid any downpours since arriving in Millhaven.

Beside him, Dacey checked her watch. "They should be here any minute."

As if summoned by her words, a black SUV pulled up to the curb. The passenger window rolled down to reveal a familiar grinning face framed by wild curls.

"There's my favorite duo!" Wiz called out.

The team piled out of the vehicle – Wiz first, a floral dress making her look like she'd just stepped away from a PTA meeting, though Gideon knew the powerful wizard could level a city block if she wanted. Her magic bubbled and sparkled to Gideon's senses, matching her effervescent personality. Behind her came Santos, his muscular frame filling the doorway before he stepped out with a grace that belied his size. The FBI liaison's Fae telekinetic magic was subtle – just a slight buzzing vibration in the air around him when he moved. MacGuire emerged next, thin and precise in his movements, with his perpetual sneer firmly in place. Gideon's research said gargoyles could transform into eight-foot-tall beings of stone weighing a literal ton, with incredible strength to match. The fact that gargoyles could fly still blew Gideon's mind – how was it possible? It was hard to reconcile that potential with the almost petite man adjusting his glasses in the morning light.

Quinn was last, her dark pageboy bob swaying as she stepped onto the sidewalk. The truth seeker's presence always made Gideon slightly nervous, even though he had nothing to hide. Something about knowing she could detect any lie, no matter how small, was unsettling.

"Can't wait to work with you on your first official Conclave investigation, Gideon!" Santos wrapped Gideon and Dacey in a bear hug, his easy grin infectious.

Wiz wasn't far behind, squeezing them both. "The team's back together! This is going to be fun!"

"Hey! That's *my* line!" Dacey complained with a grin.

"Did Leonhard come?" Gideon asked Wiz, trying not to sound too eager. "I've been hoping to meet the man behind the monitor since our last investigation."

Wiz's smile turned apologetic. "If you want to meet the numerai, you'll need to come to the Savannah Conclave compound. Leonhard doesn't leave his computer-filled ivory tower."

Gideon silently hoped that someday he'd visit the Conclave. His imagination painted a dramatic picture of robed figures holding torches aloft in stone corridors, their voices raised in ancient chants. But he knew the reality was probably more likely to be fluorescent lights and cubicles than a medieval monastery. Still, a man could dream.

Quinn stepped away from the SUV, her heels clicking against the sidewalk as she approached them. Her reserved demeanor was such a contrast to Wiz's exuberance that Gideon sometimes wondered how the team dynamic worked, but somehow it did.

"Good morning." Quinn offered them a reserved smile. "Good to see you again, Gideon."

MacGuire's lip curled into something almost resembling a smile. "I must say, I'm surprised," he said, adjusting his glasses. "With your track record, Dacey, I would have thought this case would be closed by now. Perhaps fresh eyes will help."

Gideon noticed how MacGuire's voice lingered on Dacey's name, his concern transparent in its insincerity. Sensing the tension radiating from Dacey beside him, Gideon shifted his position, partially shielding her from MacGuire's gaze. He now better understood Dacey's aversion to MacGuire – the man was an asshole.

MacGuire was deliberately pushing Dacey's buttons like an annoying sibling might. This clearly wasn't their first clash, and Gideon doubted it would be their last. The hostility seemed personal, though. Professional rivalry? Simple jealousy over Dacey's success? Or maybe something more – a rejected advance, perhaps? Their interactions had a strange undertone, like an old wound that had never quite healed. Gideon filed away a mental note to ask Dacey about it when they had a moment alone. He suspected there was a story there, one that might explain why MacGuire seemed to go out of his way to get under her skin.

"Have you all had breakfast?" Gideon asked, redirecting everyone's attention away from MacGuire. "We could review the case over eggs and coffee."

"Perfect," Wiz said, "but let's drop off our bags first." She headed for the entrance.

"Check-in isn't for—" Gideon started.

Wiz waved her hand dismissively. "Won't be a problem."

Gideon rolled his eyes. "It's good to be the Wiz."

"It really is!" Her giggle echoed across the lobby as she led the team toward the check-in desk.

While they got settled, Gideon secured a table in a quiet corner of the breakfast room, away from the handful of early risers picking through the buffet. The room smelled of coffee and warm pastries, and early morning sunlight streamed through the windows, casting long shadows across the tiled floor.

Quinn settled into her chair with just a cup of coffee while Santos and MacGuire loaded their plates with enough food to rival Dacey's usual portions. Once everyone was seated with their breakfast, Dacey pulled out her laptop and got straight to business.

"Everyone's reviewed the files?"

Quinn nodded, stirring a packet of sugar into her coffee. "Thoroughly. The void magic is unlike anything in our records."

"Good. Anyone notice anything we might have missed?"

Santos shook his head, swallowing a mouthful of eggs. "The pattern is interesting – each victim comes into contact with something or someone, then sometime later goes to sleep and never wakes up. The problem is we don't know how long that window is between initial contact and death. If we knew that timeframe, we could narrow down where they went and who they saw. But right now, the reasons why this is happening and each person's connection is still fuzzy. It's like trying to see through muddy water. We just need a clear view, and I think it'll start to make sense."

"Agreed," Quinn said. "Though the nursing home angle gives us somewhere concrete to start."

Wiz produced a folded paper with a flourish. "Speaking of which – got your warrant for Serenity Living. That's our best lead – I want to take Quinn and start interviewing every person in that building. Staff, residents, everyone. Someone in there has to know something."

"I want to take Gideon and Dacey to revisit the death sites," Santos offered. "Fresh eyes might help. Also, I want to dive deeper into the Heritage Foundation and the Royal Palmetto angle. See if we can unearth something there."

MacGuire shook his head at Santos. "I think the nursing home is a better use of our time, but with the three of us conducting the interviews, we should be able to handle anything that crops up there."

Gideon concealed his relief at escaping having to spend more time with MacGuire, aware Dacey shared his sentiment. The prospect of enduring that perpetual sneer and barely disguised condescension would have been intolerable. A few hours of that attitude would drain anyone's patience.

"Perfect." Wiz pulled out her phone. "I'll start a group chat to keep everyone updated on the interviews. Message if you find anything interesting."

The familiar excitement of a hunt beginning hummed through the air. Gideon caught Dacey's eye across the table and saw his determination mirrored there. Maybe they'd finally start getting real answers with the whole team in play.

* * *

As Dacey pulled away from Eleanor Preston's perfectly manicured lawn, Gideon slouched in the passenger seat. The late morning sun beat down through the windshield, making him wish he hadn't forgotten his sunglasses in his hotel room. They'd spent the last hour essentially harassing Preston's maid, Dolores, who'd already told them everything she knew the first time. Before that, they'd endured Brandon Cho's increasingly irritated roommate, who'd made it clear that he'd be calling in a complaint if they showed up at his door again. Marcus Chauvin's house had been another dead end – nothing new there either. They still needed to check out the tattoo parlor where Chauvin worked, track down Joe's camp in the forest, and visit Willa Wagner's and Grant Vandermeer's houses.

"Well, that was spectacularly unproductive," Dacey said, turning onto Oak Street. Her fingers drummed against the steering wheel in a staccato rhythm that told Gideon she was frustrated.

Santos leaned forward from the back seat. "Sometimes confirming what we already know is valuable, too. We can definitively rule out any new angles from these locations."

"That's a very diplomatic way of saying we wasted our morning," Gideon replied, though he appreciated Santos trying to lift their spirits.

His phone chimed, announcing a message from Vena, and despite it being just text, her excitement practically radiated from the screen:

This void magic is fascinating – unlike anything in any of my references. I'm going to dig deeper into some of the older grimoires. There might be historical precedent we're not seeing yet. Will update you as soon as I find anything concrete!

Gideon couldn't help but smile. Trust Vena to find joy in discovering something that was making their lives miserable. He'd barely finished reading when a second message came through, this one from Wiz:

Halfway through staff interviews at Serenity Living. No one seems to know anything about the deaths so far, but manager Bob Stibbons confirmed Brandon Cho had complained about the death rate. Said Cho thought residents were dying from neglect & had voiced concerns about facility security - apparently it's pretty easy for people to just wander in and out. Also found some financial irregularities in Stibbons' accounting. Looks like he's been keeping the deceased residents on the books for weeks after their deaths to collect their benefit payments. Starting night shift interviews soon. Will keep you posted.

Gideon relayed the information to Dacey and Santos.

"So Stibbons just shot to the top of our suspect list," Dacey said, her hands tightening on the steering wheel. "Financial motive for the deaths, access to the facility, knowledge of the residents' schedules...."

"Also, Vena's excited about having a new magical mystery to solve," Gideon added.

"At least someone's having fun," Dacey muttered, taking the turn that would lead them toward the area where Joe's camp had been. "Though if anyone can dig up evidence that this void magic existed before, it'll be Vena. No one knows magical history like she does."

The car fell silent as they drove, each lost in their thoughts. Gideon closed his eyes and rubbed his temples, trying to ward off the headache that had been threatening since morning.

CHAPTER 22

"Son of a bitch!" Dacey's curse jolted Gideon awake. He blinked, disoriented, realizing he must have dozed off for just a few minutes. Looking around, his mouth fell open in surprise.

A Fourth of July parade filled the street before them, a sea of red, white, and blue blocking their path. A high school marching band's brass section blasted out "Stars and Stripes Forever" while majorettes twirled batons that flashed in the morning sun. Behind the band, a procession of floats crawled down the street, including one covered in flowers that carried several Heritage Foundation members, all holding flower boutiques and waving at the crowds.

"Damn, I forgot about the Independence Celebration today." Dacey muttered under her breath, then added, "We're not getting through that mess. Let me turn around and find a place to park. We'll walk to Joe's camp."

She executed a tight U-turn and, several frustrating minutes later, wedged the car into a spot on a side street several blocks away. They started walking back toward First Street, where the Metro Diner was located, planning to use the space behind the restaurant to access Joe's campsite.

As they approached the parade route, the cacophony of celebration washed over them – children shrieking with delight, the marching band's blaring music, and the Shriners' miniature cars revving as they zipped around. The crowd pressed against the street's barricades, watching the parade and catching candy thrown from the floats.

They came abreast of the parade and paused at the corner, waiting for a break in the procession so they could cross.

"It's time!" A familiar voice screeched.

Astrid stood at the corner, looking even more disheveled than the last time he'd seen her. Her blonde hair hung in tangled knots around her face as if she'd rolled in mud in the middle of a hurricane. Despite the summer heat, she wore two ragged jackets over her dirty clothes. Dark lines covered nearly every visible inch of skin – jagged runes and chaotic markings formed an indecipherable tapestry across her sun-weathered skin.

With frantic movements, she ripped off her jackets and tossed them aside, leaving her in dirty jeans and a tank top. She jabbed a finger at Gideon. "You need to see! You need to understand!" Her voice rose above the parade noise. "This has to happen so you can see – it's the only way!"

Before anyone could react, she spun on her heel and fled down a side street.

"Astrid, wait!" Dacey called out. "We just want to talk to you!"

"Who the hell is that?" Santos asked as they took off after her.

Gideon's feet pounded against the sidewalk as they ran. Ahead of them, a group of parade-goers rounded the corner, miniature American flags waving in their hands. He veered left, jumping onto someone's lawn to get around them. His dress shoes slipped on the damp grass, and he windmilled his arms to keep his balance.

"Sorry! Excuse us!" he called out as they weaved through the group. An elderly woman clutched her flag protectively as they darted past. The sound of the parade grew fainter with each block, replaced by their heavy breathing and the slap of shoes against concrete.

Gideon's lungs burned as they ran. "She's a Völva," he explained to Santos between panted breaths. "Gets visions of the future. They've driven her crazy. She was friends with Joe."

Gideon's toe caught the edge of a curb, and he stumbled, barely catching himself. Behind him, Santos swore as he nearly ran into Gideon's back. They rounded another corner, dodging a couple walking their dog. The poor animal yelped in surprise, straining at its leash.

Up ahead, Astrid's form disappeared around another corner, her tank top a flash of grimy white against the brick buildings.

"Is she half gazelle or something?" Santos panted.

They rounded the corner and pulled up short. Astrid stood on the opposite corner of the street from them, waiting, her wild eyes fixed on them. The quiet felt strange after the chaos of the parade route. Here, they could hear birds singing in the trees that lined the sidewalk, and somewhere in the distance, a car alarm chirped.

Dacey held up her hands. "We just want to talk."

"It's time." Astrid's voice had gone eerily calm.

"Time for what?" Dacey asked.

"Time for you to witness." Astrid's gaze locked onto Gideon. "My spirit is marked, and my reckoning has come. The mountain is calling me away, and you need to witness. I know you don't understand – but it's the only way." Her expression softened for a moment. "This has to happen so you can truly see."

Before Gideon could process her words, Astrid locked eyes with him. Her stare was feral, almost possessed – dark irises filled with a crazed intensity. She sprinted into the street, heading straight toward them, her movements jerky and desperate, boots pounding against the sunbaked asphalt. Her face twisted into something between a grimace and a smile, tears streaming down her cheeks, her skin almost luminous in the bright afternoon light.

Time seemed to slow. Each heartbeat stretched into an eternity. The screech of tires filled the air, cutting through the distant trumpet of brass and the beat of the drums. A blue SUV appeared as if from nowhere. Gideon saw everything in brutal clarity: Astrid's hair whipping across her face, and her arms spread wide, an almost beatific smile gracing her face, the driver's mouth open in a scream.

The impact lifted Astrid off her feet, her body crumpling over the hood before being thrown forward like a rag doll. The thud of her body against metal cut through the parade music. Astrid hit the pavement hard, then rolled to a stop in a crumpled heap, arms and legs splayed like a broken marionette. A single boot, torn free by the force, landed several feet away. Behind them, the band played on, oblivious.

Their shouts and exclamations of shock overlapped as they ran to where Astrid lay crumpled on her back, eyes open but breathing shallow. Dacey dropped to her knees beside her. "Astrid! Can you hear me? Stay with us, okay? We're getting help right now!"

Her gaze found Gideon's face, and her lips moved. "Finally," she whispered, then her eyes drifted shut.

"Astrid! Astrid, open your eyes!" Dacey's voice cracked as she gripped Astrid's hand. "Help is coming, I promise. Just hold on!"

Behind him, Santos was on the phone with emergency services while the driver sobbed, "She came out of nowhere! I didn't mean to – she just ran right out!"

Dacey pressed her fingers to Astrid's neck, her other hand still clutching Astrid's. "She has a pulse. She's just unconscious." Her voice softened as she leaned closer to Astrid's ear. "You're going to be okay. We've got you. Just stay with us."

Magic detonated from Astrid's prone form like a thunderclap. The force drove Gideon to his knees, his chest tight with sudden pressure. The waves hit him mercilessly, each one stronger than the last, battering him like an invisible tide. His ears popped, and the world seemed to tilt sideways. He could barely hear Dacey's concerned voice over the whooshing in his ears.

"Gideon? What's wrong?"

The sensation was unlike anything he'd ever experienced. Where regular magic had texture – Wiz's bubbling sparkles, Santos's subtle vibrations – this was raw chaos. Astrid's magic twisted upward, the spiral tattoo on her chest literally rising from her skin into the air, spinning above her body like a cyclone, gaining speed. The suction of the vortex pulled at him, magical energy howling around them like a hurricane. Each breath felt like inhaling broken glass, and his skin crawled like thousands of insects were marching across it. His magical senses screamed in protest as power built and built, far beyond what any one person should be able to contain.

The maelstrom of energy grew stronger, suctioned from Astrid's body in visible streams that spiraled higher and higher. The air seemed to vibrate, and Gideon's teeth ached from the pressure. His vision blurred at the edges, darkness creeping in, but he couldn't look away from the spectacle before him. The magical whirlwind pulsed with an otherworldly light, threads of power weaving together into a pattern he almost recognized before it all collapsed.

Then, with a sound like a gasped breath, the magical cyclone collapsed in on itself and vanished. The sudden absence of pressure made Gideon's head spin. All of Astrid's magic and life force were ripped from her motionless form, leaving behind a void – a ravenous emptiness where her essence had been drained and devoured. The wrongness hit him like a physical blow. His stomach lurched violently as the hungry nothing reached for him. He doubled over, retching, the darkness pulling at something deep inside him, making him heave again and again. The very air seemed darker around her body, though he knew that was only his imagination.

"What the f—" Gideon fell back, catching himself on his palms. His arms shook so badly he could barely hold himself up. "What the fuck was that?" he choked out, his voice raw with stunned horror.

He crawled toward Astrid's body, every movement an effort against the waves of nausea washing over him. "She's gone. The void is here."

"What?" Dacey's hand was still on Astrid's neck. "What do you mean? She's not—" Her words cut off as she realized Astrid was no longer breathing.

Gideon started to reach for Astrid, then froze, staring at her chest in shock. "The tattoo is gone."

"What tattoo?"

"The spiral tattoo that was on her chest." Gideon's voice shook. "It's gone."

He sat back on his heels, trying to process what he'd just witnessed. In the distance, he could still hear the parade – the cheers and music a surreal counterpoint to the silence that had fallen over their small group. The driver had stopped crying and was talking quietly to Santos, who still had his phone pressed to his ear. But all Gideon could focus on was the void that now resided where Astrid's magic had been and the growing certainty that she had known this would happen.

CHAPTER 23

The ambulance's red and white lights strobed against the buildings, each flash driving a spike of pain through Gideon's skull. He sat on the curb, hands dangling between his knees, watching as the EMTs carefully transferred Astrid into the black bag laid out on the pavement. The sound of the zipper closing around her body was jarringly loud in the quiet street, making him flinch. They lifted her into the ambulance with practiced efficiency. His stomach lurched again at the memory of that horrifying magical void where her life force had been.

The ambulance doors closed with a decisive thud, making Gideon wince.

Dacey and Santos stood a few feet away, conferring with police and EMTs. Gideon caught fragments of their grim exchange – "ran into traffic," "couldn't stop in time," "already called it." Through the open doors of a second ambulance, the driver sat hunched over, wrapped in a silver space blanket with her head in her hands. A paramedic hovered nearby, offering quiet words of comfort. Gideon wondered if the poor woman would ever drive down this street again without seeing Astrid's final moments replaying in her mind.

He was about to try to get to his feet when he heard footsteps approaching. He looked up to see Detective Victor Voss walking toward them. Usually, the basilisk shifter's presence would have his hackles rising, but right now, he was too drained to care.

"Dacey." Voss's measured voice cut through the background noise of police radios and murmuring officers. "I came as soon as I heard."

Dacey turned to greet the detective, her expression softening slightly. "Victor. Thanks for coming." She gestured to Santos. "This is Agent Santos. He's working with us on the case. Santos, this is Detective Victor Voss with Millhaven PD."

Santos extended his hand, which Voss shook firmly. "Detective. Wish we were meeting under better circumstances."

"Likewise." Voss's gaze swept over the scene, lingering on the skid marks on the pavement before settling on Gideon. "What happened here?"

Gideon kept his voice carefully neutral as he described how Astrid had led them on a chase away from the parade, then suddenly ran into traffic. He left out any mention of what he'd sensed or seen magically, sticking to the facts that anyone could have witnessed.

"She was conscious briefly after the impact," Dacey added quietly. "But then she lost consciousness, and we couldn't revive her."

Voss listened intently, his face growing grimmer with each detail. "Do you think this accident is somehow related to your case?" When Dacey nodded, he ran a hand through his dark hair, a surprisingly human gesture for a basilisk shifter. "I'm glad the Conclave is diving deeper into this. Whatever's happening here... it's beyond anything I've ever dealt with before."

"We'll figure it out," Dacey assured him, though her voice lacked its usual confidence.

Voss nodded. "I need to inform Mayor Thorne about this immediately. She'll want to know why there was an incident at her parade." He checked his watch. "I should go handle that now."

"We'll see you at the coroner's later?" Dacey asked.

"Yes. I'll be there." Voss's expression hardened. "Whatever's behind these deaths – we need to stop it before anyone else dies."

They watched him walk away, his tall figure cutting through the gathering crowd of onlookers with practiced ease. Dacey waved goodbye to the officers and headed toward Gideon, phone in hand. "I've got the team on a group call," she said, holding the phone. "Can you tell them what happened?"

Gideon swallowed hard, his mouth dry. "Yeah." He cleared his throat. "Astrid… she led us on a chase away from the parade. When we caught up to her, she just… she ran into traffic. She said that it was time and that we needed to witness. After the car hit her, she was awake for a moment, but then she fell unconscious." His voice cracked. "The magic that came out of her – I've never felt anything like it. It was like a tornado in reverse, made of pure energy, spinning up from her body, sucking away her magic. The spiral tattoo on her chest… it actually rose off her skin into the air above her. It was like a dark whirlpool vacuuming away her essence. And then it all just… collapsed. Everything she was, all her magic, her life force – it got sucked away into nothing. All that was left was the void."

"If there was a spiral tattoo on her chest, it's gone now," Dacey interjected. "We checked."

"What did the tattoo look like exactly?" Wiz's voice crackled through the speaker.

Gideon rubbed his temples. "Like a spiral, kind of like a seashell? But I never got a great look at it."

"Could you draw it?" Leonhard asked. "Send it to all of us?"

"I can try, but like I said, I didn't get the best view. Has anyone ever encountered magic like this before?" Gideon asked. "That kind of… draining darkness?"

Santos shook his head. "Plenty of tattoos are imbued with magic, sure. But I've never heard of one that could drain someone's life force and magic like that. This is something else entirely." He glanced around at the officers securing the perimeter. "Hold on a sec."

He jogged over to a uniformed officer, spoke briefly, and returned with a small notepad and pencil. "Here, draw what you saw. Maybe having a visual will help us."

Gideon took the notepad, his hand trembling slightly as he sketched the spiral pattern. He frowned in concentration, erasing a few lines and redrawing them. He was no artist, but the shape gradually emerged on the paper.

"I'm not very good at drawing," he admitted, "but this is pretty close to what I remember." The rough sketch captured the essence of the spiral. He pulled out his phone and snapped a photo.

"I'm sending this to everyone," Gideon said, quickly texting it to the group.

"Was there anything else on her that might have triggered the event?" MacGuire's voice was tight with concern.

"I did a quick check over her," Dacey replied. "I didn't see anything obvious, but we'll know more after the autopsy…." She trailed off, glancing at the retreating ambulance.

"What killed her?" Wiz asked quietly. "The car or the magic?"

"That's what we're going to find out." Dacey's jaw set with determination. "We'll examine this scene first, then visit the other crime locations before heading to the coroner's office. Dr. Blackwood needs time to complete the autopsy, so there's no point in showing up right away." She turned to Gideon, her expression softening slightly. "But right now, you're going to sit here and rest while Santos and I look around."

"I'm fine—" Gideon started to protest, pushing himself to his feet.

"You just experienced what amounts to a magical bomb," Dacey cut him off. "Sit your ass down and take a breather."

Santos squeezed his shoulder. "She's right, man. Take a minute to recover. We've got this."

Gideon sank back down, watching as they began methodically searching the area. He stared at the ground between his knees, replaying the scene over and over. The way Astrid had smiled right before… The memory made him feel sick all over again.

A pair of familiar shoes appeared between his feet after what felt like hours but was probably only minutes. He looked up to find Dacey standing over him, her face lined with exhaustion despite the smile she'd plastered on.

"We didn't find anything," she said softly. "Blackwood's gonna rush the autopsy, but it'll still take time. We should keep moving forward with our investigation." She held out a hand. "Ready to check Joe's camp, or do you need another minute?"

"Nah, I'm good." He took her hand and pulled himself up, his legs steadier than he'd expected.

The parade had dispersed by the time they made their way back to the Metro Diner, the only sign of its passage a wake of discarded flags and candy wrappers. They hiked behind the restaurant to Joe's camp in silence. The void there had faded since their last visit, barely a whisper compared to the raw wound of Astrid's death. After witnessing a void being created firsthand, this older one felt almost… peaceful. The thought left a bitter taste in Gideon's mouth.

"Come on," Dacey said, tugging at his sleeve. "My blood sugar's crashing, and I need caffeine like you wouldn't believe. Let's grab something to eat."

Gideon nodded, following her lead. His stomach growled, reminding him it had been hours since breakfast. Though food was the last thing on his mind, he knew Dacey was right – they needed fuel for whatever came next. And something told him they'd need all their strength to unravel the mystery Astrid had left behind.

As they walked toward the diner's entrance, Gideon couldn't shake the feeling that Astrid's final words – "This has to happen so you can truly see" – were more than just the ravings of a damaged mind. She'd wanted him to witness her death. But why? He hadn't noticed anything that helped – except for the tattoo and the magical tsunami.

The bells above the diner's door chimed as they entered the restaurant, the smell of french fries and grilled onions wrapping around them like a comforting blanket. But even as Dacey led them to a booth, Gideon's mind kept circling back to that spiral tattoo and how it had risen from Astrid's skin and turned into a vacuum.

Santos slid into the booth across from them as Dacey settled in next to Gideon. He was acutely aware of her fiery warmth pressing against his side, a stark contrast to the cold emptiness he'd felt earlier. The vinyl cushion squeaked as she shifted, pulling a menu from behind the napkin dispenser.

"I think I know why she did it," Gideon said suddenly, his voice low. "Why she killed herself, I mean." He glanced between his partners' faces, seeing the same haunted look he felt reflected in their eyes. "She wanted me to see the tattoo and what it does when the person either falls unconscious or dies. That's why she made sure I was there to witness it. If she already had the tattoo and was doomed – she was on borrowed time already – maybe this was her way of showing us something important."

"Because you're the only one who can see and feel the void magic," Santos said slowly, realization dawning on his face.

Gideon nodded. "I think we should go to Wild Court Tattoos next. That spiral design seems like the key to what happened to Astrid – and maybe the others." He pulled out the piece of paper, studying the drawing again. The simple spiral seemed to mock him. "I want to show this to Chauvin's co-workers and see if they recognize the image. Marcus was a Fae tattoo artist, and now we have evidence of a strange death-tattoo. There might be something we missed there."

"Do you think the tattoo artist was involved?" Santos asked.

"It's possible," Gideon said thoughtfully. "Marcus was the first victim after the nursing home murders. Maybe he or someone at Wild Court created this design. Or perhaps they've encountered something similar before – they might know other artists specializing in spiral patterns. At this point, any lead is worth pursuing."

Gideon's mind wandered back to Astrid's final moments. Her words echoed in his memory: "This has to happen so you can truly see." She'd said that her spirit was marked. At the time, he'd thought she was speaking metaphorically – some cryptic warning about the darkness of her soul. Now, he wasn't so sure. She'd wanted him to witness the tattoo's power, to understand what they were dealing with. But understanding what the tattoo did wasn't the same as knowing how to stop it from claiming more victims.

A server approached their table, notepad in hand. Despite the churning in his stomach, Gideon ordered a grilled cheese and fries. He wasn't sure he could keep anything down, but he knew he needed to try.

Santos picked up the drawing and examined the image.

"It does look like a spiral shell," he mused. "Like a nautilus or a ram's horn snail."

"I'm not completely sure how accurate it is. It's not like I knew to take a good look at it," Gideon admitted. "But that's the best I could do from what I saw."

Dacey drummed her fingers on the table in thought. "Let's eat quick and head to Wild Court Tattoos. I want to get there before the coroner is finished."

CHAPTER 24

Wild Court Tattoos, like half the shops downtown, had been closed for the Fourth of July celebrations when they arrived. Gideon's frustration mounted as they faced yet another dead end. The other crime scenes had proven equally fruitless, confirming his fears.

Gideon gazed out the passenger window of Dacey's car, watching Millhaven streak by in a blur of color and motion. He held his phone in the center of the vehicle, the call on speaker so everyone could hear it. He described the spiral tattoo and the violent magical vortex it had unleashed during Astrid's death to Vena.

"I'm not familiar with anything like what you're describing," Vena said, her voice thoughtful. "Spiral imagery appears in various magical traditions, but none that align with what you witnessed."

"What kind of traditions use spirals?" Santos asked from the backseat, leaning forward between Dacey and Gideon.

"Hmm... Let me see... Celtic magic employs spirals to represent spiritual journeys and rebirth. I've read some documents that some practitioners use them to create portals between worlds. The Māori have koru spirals that represent new life and growth. Egyptian magical practices use spirals to represent the journey of the soul...."

Vena paused. "But none of these traditions involve death magic or the draining of life force you described."

Gideon pinched the bridge of his nose. "So, another dead end?"

"Not necessarily. The seashell aspect is interesting…." Vena's voice grew distant as if she'd turned away from the phone. "I need to look into magical practices involving shells. There might be something there…."

"Let us know if you find anything," Gideon said.

"Will do. Stay safe." The line went dead as Dacey pulled into a parking spot next to the coroner's office.

After years of working at a crematorium, Gideon barely noticed the harsh antiseptic smell of the medical examiner's office – it was just another variation of the clinical scents that had become as common to him as the salt of a sea breeze. The receptionist, a different person from their previous visits, looked up from her computer and dipped her head in greeting. "Dr. Blackwood is expecting you. Go on back."

They found Tabitha Blackwood in the autopsy room, writing notes on a clipboard next to the examination table where Astrid lay. The harsh fluorescent lights cast stark shadows across Astrid's pale form and highlighted the silver of Blackwood's buzzcut. As they entered, the medical examiner looked up, her weathered face creasing into a tired smile.

"And here I was hoping I wouldn't see you folks again so soon," she said, setting down her clipboard.

"Same," Dacey replied with a grimace. She gestured to Santos. "This is Agent Santos, FBI liaison to the Savannah Conclave. We're hoping you found something useful."

"That depends on what you consider useful." Blackwood gestured to Astrid's body. "The injuries from the vehicle impact are extensive – broken ribs, punctured lung, multiple fractures. But none of these injuries should have been immediately fatal."

Gideon's stomach clenched as he forced himself to look at what remained of Astrid. A wave of sorrow washed over him, seeing her like this – almost emaciated, like life had chewed away at her very essence. Her once animated form now thin and broken, her skin covered in crazed, disjointed crude tattoos. Each mark seemed to tell a story of a descent into madness he couldn't bear to imagine.

"We witnessed her death," he said quietly, his voice catching. "There was *definitely* something else at work."

Blackwood's keen eyes fixed on him. "Tell me what you saw."

Gideon described the spiral marking and the magical vortex that had emerged from it, trying to capture the otherworldly nature of his experience. He then pulled out the drawing he had made and handed it to Blackwood.

She studied it carefully. "Interesting. I can say with certainty that none of our other victims had anything like this on their bodies." She looked up at Gideon. "Where exactly was it located?"

Keeping his eyes trained on Astrid's face – peaceful now, so different from the fierce, troubled woman he'd briefly encountered – Gideon pointed to a spot high on her chest. "The tattoo was right here. But it's completely gone now."

Blackwood leaned in to examine the area, then frowned. "You keep referring to it as a tattoo. Are you certain that's what it was?"

The question made Gideon pause. He shrugged. "I didn't get that good of a look at it before it... rose off her chest. From what I saw, it looked like a tattoo. However, you make a good point – until we know exactly what we're dealing with, I shouldn't make assumptions."

The doctor straightened up as Detective Voss's voice drifted in from the reception area.

"Heads up," Dacey muttered. "We're keeping the fact that Gideon's an auramancer under wraps."

Blackwood gave a slight nod just as the detective entered the room. The basilisk shifter's presence seemed to fill the space, though his usual intimidating demeanor was subdued.

"Detective," Blackwood greeted him. "I was just going over my findings with the agents."

Voss approached the examination table, his expression somber as he looked down at Astrid. "She was a regular troublemaker. Public disturbances, disorderly conduct... but this...." He shook his head. "It's a shame to see her like this."

"Did the autopsy reveal anything conclusive?" he asked Blackwood.

The medical examiner shook her head. "Same as the others. Plenty of trauma from the vehicle's impact, but nothing that fully explains the rapid onset of death. No obvious toxins or other immediate causes I can identify."

"Could drugs have played a role?" Voss asked, his voice tight. "She was a known user – meth, heroin, whatever she could get her hands on."

"I don't think so, but I've ordered a full toxicology screening to be sure," Blackwood replied. "Everything points to this following the same pattern as our other victims."

Voss's face darkened as he ran a hand through his hair. "Seven deaths. Seven unexplained deaths in my territory. This is Millhaven, for God's sake – we're supposed to be a safe place where people look out for each other. Things like this don't happen here."

He looked at Gideon and Dacey with worried eyes. "Please tell me you're close to understanding what's happening."

Dacey met his gaze steadily. "We don't have all the answers yet, Victor, but we're not leaving Millhaven until we solve this. Whatever it takes."

"Good. Whatever resources you need, they're yours."

"Thank you. We'll let you know if we need anything." Dacey turned to Gideon. "I think we're done here for now."

Gideon nodded his agreement.

They thanked Blackwood and headed toward the exit. As they reached the morgue lobby, Gideon turned to Dacey. "Since we're next to the hospital, I want to check if Emma Kim is working. She never called after I left my card."

"Emma Kim?" Voss asked.

"The nurse on duty when Marcus Chauvin was brought into the hospital," Gideon explained. "I doubt we'll learn anything useful, but I want to make sure we're not missing anything."

The afternoon sun hit them as they stepped outside, a jarring transition from the morgue's artificial lighting. Heat radiated from the parking lot's black asphalt, the air thick with that distinctive summer smell of softening tar.

Gideon couldn't shake the image of Astrid's body on that cold metal table. The void where her magic had been seemed to echo in his mind, a dark counterpoint to the brightness around them.

He hoped Emma Kim would have something – anything – to add to their understanding of these deaths. But deep down, he didn't think the nurse would remember a patient from almost a month ago.

Santos checked his phone as Dacey led them around the side of the building toward the hospital's main entrance. "I'll update the team about the autopsy findings," he said. "Or lack thereof."

Voss fell into step beside them. "Mind if I join you? I need to speak with a patient about a case I'm working on while I'm here anyway."

"Of course," Dacey said warmly. "We can use all the help we can get."

As they walked, Gideon couldn't help but wonder how long they should continue to keep his abilities and the new information about the spiral magic hidden from Voss. Perhaps he should be brought in. Gideon may not like the man much, but Voss knew Millhaven and might have some insight they desperately needed.

After witnessing Astrid's death, Gideon felt the weight of looming failure pressing down on him. As the only person who could see or feel the void magic at work, he knew it was up to him to solve the case – a burden made unbearable by the knowledge that if he couldn't unravel this mystery, more people might die.

Gideon's mind wandered back to their first arrival in Millhaven when they had naively believed they were merely investigating a series of unusual deaths. He couldn't believe it had only been a few days. But after witnessing Astrid being drained, he now believed that someone or something was actively hunting in Millhaven, using these spiral tattoos to drain people's life force and magic, leaving behind only empty shells and questions.

The emergency department's automatic doors whooshed open,

releasing a blast of cool air. The waiting room was half-full, the usual mix of worried faces and assorted maladies.

Gideon approached the front desk, badge already in hand. "Hi, I'm Agent Nash. Is Emma Kim working today?"

The receptionist tapped at her keyboard and then nodded. "Yes, Emma Kim is here. She's on the third floor, east wing."

Heading toward the elevator, Gideon noticed Voss was still accompanying them. As the doors slid shut, he wondered if the detective's lingering presence had less to do with the person he'd mentioned wanting to interview and more to do with Dacey. The thought brought a frown to his face.

When they reached the third floor, Gideon approached the nursing station with Dacey on his left and Santos on his right. For a moment, the simple formation gave him an unfamiliar feeling of belonging – of being part of a real team. He almost didn't even mind Voss's continued presence behind him.

Three nurses in scrubs looked up as he showed his badge. "I'm looking for Emma Kim?"

A young Asian woman with dark hair pulled back in a neat ponytail stepped forward. "That's me."

"Do you have a moment? I have some questions about a former patient."

"Of course." Emma waved them over to an empty room. "What can I help you with?"

"Do you remember a patient named Marcus Chauvin from a few weeks ago? He was brought in after a bar fight and died during your shift."

Emma's brow furrowed uncertainly. Dacey opened her case and pulled out a photo, which she handed to the nurse.

"Oh yeah," Emma said, recognition dawning. "I remember him. I was working when he coded. It happened so suddenly – no warning at all. He'd been stabilized, and we were prepping him for some scans, about to move him out of ICU. Then boom, he was coding."

"Did you notice anything strange when it happened?" Gideon asked. "Equipment acting up? Did you feel anything unusual?"

Emma gave him an odd look. "No, everything seemed normal."

"Was there anything else you remember from that night? Anything at all? I know it was quite a few weeks ago..."

Emma bit her lip and looked up at the ceiling as if the memories were there. "Not really. I'm surprised I even remember his face. I guess it just stuck with me because it was so sudden and unexpected. It was especially sad because his father had just finished visiting, and I'd told him his son was doing well."

"Father?" Dacey leaned forward. "Marcus's father visited that night. Are you sure?"

"Yes, he introduced himself. I remember him because he had poliosis– I always notice that condition."

"What's that?" Gideon asked.

"It's a patch of white or unpigmented hair."

"Wait... what?"

CHAPTER 25

"Marcus's father had a white patch of hair? Are you sure?" Dacey repeated, looking like a hound that'd found a scent trail.

"Yes… I think so," Emma said, her expression a mix of hesitation and curiosity. She glanced between Dacey and Gideon, clearly unsettled by their sudden intensity about such a seemingly minor detail. "I mean, I'm pretty sure I remember seeing it."

Gideon stepped closer to Emma. "Can you tell me where the streak was located on the man?"

Emma pointed to her temple.

Dacey and Gideon exchanged significant looks. Dacey turned back to Emma. "Did Marcus's father look Hispanic?"

Emma shrugged. "Maybe?"

"If I showed you a picture, do you think you could recognize the man?" Dacey asked.

"I'm not sure, but probably."

"That would be perfect. Thank you, Emma. You've been a great help," Gideon said, giving the nurse a warm smile. "We're going to see if we can get that photo and be back. How late are you working today?"

"I'm here until nine."

After Emma left, Gideon turned to Dacey. "Emma's description sounds like the mayor's assistant. I can't remember his name."

Voss interrupted. "Michael Torres. I know him in passing since I work with the mayor occasionally. He's the only person I know with a white streak in his hair."

"Holy shit! This is crazy. We need to call the group," Dacey said, pulling out her phone. The team answered after barely one ring, and Dacey quickly filled the team in. "Marcus Chauvin's father died years ago, so it *couldn't* have been him visiting. We think it might have been the mayor's assistant, Michael—"

"Torres," Voss supplied. "Michael Torres."

"Wiz, can you get a photo of Torres? We need Emma to confirm it was him."

"Yes, I'm sending Leonhard a text right now."

"Michael Torres?" Quinn's voice sharpened with interest. "That's *very* intriguing. I've interviewed everyone at the facility and hit nothing but dead ends – not a soul knows anything about these deaths. But when I started reviewing the visitor logs, his name jumped out. He's been here consistently, at least twice a week for the past few years, always signing in to visit a resident named Maria Torres. Given the shared surname, I'm assuming they're related."

"Sounds like we need to find this Michael Torres and have a chat," Wiz said.

Voss pulled out his phone. "I'll call the mayor and see if he's at City Hall." He put it on speaker.

"Detective Voss? Why are you calling me?" the mayor's voice came through.

Voss began explaining that they needed to locate Michael, but Dacey swiftly cut in. "Ma'am, I need you to keep this quiet," she said, her voice low and urgent. "We have reason to believe Michael may be behind these deaths. If our suspicions are correct, he's extremely dangerous." She leaned forward. "If he's currently at City Hall, I strongly advise you to leave the building – discreetly. Don't alert him to your departure. Just collect your belongings and exit as if it's the end of a normal workday. If that's not possible, lock your door immediately."

"No, that can't be right. Not Michael," Winnie gasped. "He's been loyal for years. Are you sure?"

"We're not certain, but he's a suspect and should be treated with extreme caution."

"Michael just left a few minutes ago. He went to the Millhaven Food Bank to drop off some paperwork."

After thanking the mayor and instructing her to keep quiet, Dacey asked if everyone on the group call had heard.

"We're heading to the food bank now," Wiz confirmed.

"We'll meet you there," Dacey said, her expression grave. "Remember – if Torres is our perpetrator, he's wielding death magic unlike anything we've ever encountered. Nothing in our records documents this kind of power, and we have no way of knowing how it works or how it might strike. Stay alert and proceed with caution."

* * *

THEY RACED through Millhaven's streets, Dacey taking corners so fast that the car's suspension groaned while Voss called out directions from the backseat. Through the phone's speaker, they could hear the engine of the second SUV roaring as the rest of the team raced to converge on their location.

The food bank was located on the industrial outskirts of town. It was a metal-sided warehouse that was well-maintained despite its utilitarian design. Fresh landscaping dotted the perimeter, with newly planted shrubs and flowers adding life to the grounds. A large vinyl banner hung along one wall, proclaiming "Nourishing Our Community Together" in bold, cheerful letters.

"Everyone clear on Torres's face?" Dacey asked, her voice tight. The photo Leonhard had acquired showed a man in his fifties with soft features and that distinctive white streak at his temple. The same man Emma Kim had positively identified as Marcus Chauvin's mysterious "father".

"Clear," Santos confirmed from the back seat. "Also, Leonhard says he couldn't find any familial connection between Torres and Marcus Chauvin. Or any kind of connection at all."

"Wiz, do you have everything you need for the containment and knockout spells?" Dacey asked through the speaker.

"Ready to go, but there's a catch," Wiz's voice crackled back. "Either we need to catch Torres completely unawares, or you'll have to buy me enough time to work my spells. No shortcuts with this one."

"Listen up, everyone," Dacey's voice cut through the car. "We go in quiet – as Wiz said, the element of surprise is critical here. I want him alive, if possible, but at the first sign he's going to hurt anyone, you have permission to take him out. Clear?"

A chorus of acknowledgments came through the phone. Gideon checked the gun Santos had loaned him, grateful for every hour he had practiced with Silas at the range. He couldn't quite kick the feeling of mortification for needing to borrow a weapon in the first place. Never again, he vowed silently. It had felt like amateur hour. He was going to get approved to carry a gun and never go into an investigation unarmed again.

With practiced movements, he ejected the magazine to verify it was fully loaded and then slapped it back into place. He racked the slide to chamber a round, the metallic sound oddly loud in the tense car. The gun's weight in his hand should have been comforting, but instead, it reminded him of his inexperience.

They parked three buildings down from the food bank. The team's black SUV pulled up behind them, and MacGuire emerged with a handful of earpieces, distributing them efficiently. After a quick mic check, Dacey directed the team to split up.

"Gideon, Voss, and Santos, you're with me around the back. MacGuire, Wiz, and Quinn take the front," she ordered.

They crept along the building's perimeter until the loading dock came into view. The rear of the warehouse was utilitarian and bare – weathered concrete and corrugated metal stretching two stories high. A large roll-up bay door dominated the back wall. Beside it, almost hidden in the shadows, a plain metal door sat recessed into the wall, its dark surface showing years of use from workers coming and going.

"Stay close to me," Dacey murmured to Gideon as they moved toward the metal door, Voss taking up the rear position behind Gideon and Santos. "Since this is your first time running this with the full team – just follow my lead."

The back door yielded to Dacey's touch, thankfully unlocked. She held up a hand, speaking softly into her mic. "Back entrance unsecured. Ready to breach on your mark."

"Front team in position," MacGuire's voice came through. For once, there was no trace of his usual condescension – just the steady, professional tone of someone who'd done this countless times before. "Three... two... one... go."

They stepped through the side door next to the loading dock and entered the warehouse proper, a dimly lit space lined with metal shelving units that stretched from floor to ceiling. Boxes of canned goods, pasta, and dry beans crowded every surface, carefully organized and labeled. Strips of yellow tape marked the floor, creating paths between rows of donated groceries waiting to be sorted. A sign on the wall read, "First In, First Out – Check Expiration Dates!"

They moved in smoothly, Dacey leading with her weapon up. Gideon's heart hammered against his ribs, adrenaline making his breath wheeze in his chest and his vision swim at the edges. He kept his eyes locked on Dacey's back, desperately mimicking her fluid movements, her steady hands, the controlled confidence in every step. He'd never felt more like an imposter – a liability masquerading as a professional.

They moved methodically through the building, clearing each space with silent efficiency – storage closets, a break room lined with lockers, cramped offices with desks pushed against dingy walls. Through their earpieces came the quiet check-ins from the rest of the team, voices barely above whispers as they swept through their assigned sectors. Gideon felt a wave of relief that their section was empty so far, though he could hear the others through the comms, their voices firm but calm as they directed employees to either shelter in place or evacuate.

"Stay in your office, hands where we can see them."

"Exit the building immediately, hands up." Each command was delivered with the kind of authority he hoped he'd someday master.

They rounded a corner into what looked like a sorting area. Folding tables formed a U-shape, their surfaces scattered with half-filled boxes of groceries. Utility carts waited nearby, already loaded with groceries meant for families in need.

Gideon barely choked back a gasp. In the far corner, Michael Torres stood over an unmoving woman sprawled on the floor. Gideon's brain struggled to reconcile the figure before him with the polished city official from the mayor's office. Torres's tie hung loose and askew, his dress shirt dark with sweat and half-untucked. His white-streaked dark hair, which had been neatly groomed at their first meeting, now whipped and danced in a wind that didn't exist. His eyes were wild, almost feral, glancing up and locking with Gideon's. He swayed on his feet, his movements jerky and erratic. The man seemed completely disconnected from reality – Gideon wondered if he was on drugs or was just crazy. Whatever civilized mask Torres had worn in their previous encounter had cracked wide open. His hands were raised over the woman on the floor; his fingers contorted into claws, wreathed in ribbons of sickly green light and swirling mist.

The magic emanating from Torres hit Gideon like a physical force – corrupt and wrong as if someone had distilled disease into pure energy. Gideon's teeth ached, and his skin crawled as waves of sickly-sweet corruption washed over him, carrying impressions of rot and death. Every instinct screamed at him to back away from that poisoned power.

"Freeze!" Dacey's voice cracked like a whip. "Stop the ritual, now!"

Torres straightened slowly, turning to face them fully. His eyes caught the fluorescent light as four weapons trained on him.

"You can't stop this," Michael said, voice trembling with fervor. "I'm too powerful now. Winnie needs to suffer. Ask *her* why it has to be this way. She uses everyone – discards us when we're not useful anymore. Well, she won't make it to the governor's mansion. Not if I have anything to say about it."

The rest of the team filtered from a door on the other side of the room, and Torres jerked like a marionette, his whole body shaking. The green light pulsed brighter. Gideon risked a glance at Wiz, who had pressed herself against the wall, her lips moving in a rapid, silent incantation. He could sense her magic building – a membrane of power expanding outward like a bubble of air rising through water, forming an invisible sphere that pushed against the corrupt flow of energy pulsing from Torres. A containment spell, he assumed, one that would hopefully trap Torres and his deadly power – if she could complete it in time.

"It's over, Michael," Dacey said firmly. "No one else has to die. But we will shoot if you don't stand down."

"You'll have to kill me!" Torres screeched, raising his glowing hands. Gideon felt the competing magics intensify – Wiz's protective bubble straining to grow while Torres's death magic swelled like a tsunami, threatening to overwhelm them all. His finger rested on the trigger, aiming for Torres's shoulder. They were running out of time; the containment spell wasn't solidifying fast enough to counter the murderous power gathering around Torres's hands.

The gunshot next to Gideon's ear was deafening. Detective Voss had stepped up beside him, his service weapon raised. More shots followed – a cascade of thunder that filled the room. Torres's body jerked and twisted, the sickly green light sputtering out as he collapsed. The last thing Gideon saw before the magic died was a look of surprise on Torres's face as if he couldn't believe they'd actually done it.

A high-pitched whine filled Gideon's head, drowning out everything else. He stared down at Torres's still form, at the dark stains spreading across his shirt. His own gun was still raised, trigger unfired. In that moment, when it had mattered most, Gideon had hesitated.

He'd fucking hesitated.

CHAPTER 26

The hotel bar hummed with the usual evening crowd – tired businesspeople unwinding after a long day, tourists planning tomorrow's adventures, and locals seeking refuge from their daily routines. In a corner booth, surrounded by the detritus of shared nachos and various appetizers, Gideon sat with Dacey and MacGuire, though his mind was far from their celebration.

He absently picked at the label on his beer bottle, the paper coming away in damp strips as condensation beaded on the brown glass. Despite staring at the bottle, he saw nothing before him – his mind was still in the food bank.

Through the windows behind their booth, a full moon hung low and heavy in the darkening sky, casting pale light across the palm tree-lined parking lot. Gideon repeatedly found his gaze drawn from the conversation to its ethereal glow. Rather than offering comfort, the moon's presence only emphasized his sense of disconnection, highlighting how surreal the evening felt against the backdrop of normalcy and camaraderie surrounding him.

The scene from the food bank played on an endless loop in his head – Torres's manic gaze, his contorted face, the sickly green light of death magic, the thunderous cascade of gunfire. And his own damning hesitation.

The moon's cold light seemed to mock him, as constant and unwavering as his guilt.

"Earth to Giddy." Dacey's voice cut through his brooding. "What's wrong? You look like someone pissed in your popcorn."

Gideon shook his head, trying to dispel both the memories and the relentless shame that had settled over him since the incident. The tactical part of his brain scrambled for excuses: there had been plenty of other agents to take down Torres; he wasn't the only one who hadn't taken the shot; he wasn't even a fully-fledged Conclave agent yet. Was it truly ethical for him to use lethal force without proper agent status? Yet these carefully constructed justifications rang hollow, doing nothing to ease the gnawing sensation in his gut. Dacey had been counting on him to step up – what if she'd been hurt because he'd choked?

"Come on," Dacey pressed, "you're being a sad sap when you should be over the moon. We saved the day, caught our killer, and nobody else got hurt. That's what I call a win."

Gideon's fingers stilled on the bottle. He glanced between Dacey and MacGuire, hating the idea of admitting his failure, especially in front of the usually smug gargoyle. But its weight sat heavy in his chest, demanding release.

"I hesitated," he finally said, the words bitter on his tongue. "Torres could have killed us all, and I was standing there with my thumb up my ass, unable to pull the trigger. What kind of Conclave agent does that make me?"

"The kind who's been on exactly one raid," Dacey said firmly. "Give yourself a break."

To Gideon's surprise, MacGuire nodded in agreement. "Want to hear something embarrassing? The first raid I ever went on, I puked right outside the target building. My team had to step around it to get inside." MacGuire took a pull from his beer, a slight smile playing on his lips. "They called me Agent Upchuck for *years* after that. Besides, seeing your first death is tough."

"I work in a crematorium," Gideon protested. "I see dead bodies all the time. It's not a big deal."

Dacey snorted at that. "That is completely different than watching a man get shot and die right in front of your eyes. Trust me on this one."

"She's right," MacGuire added. "Looking at a peaceful corpse isn't the same as watching the light go out of someone's eyes. Give yourself a break, rookie."

Gideon studied MacGuire, thrown by this unexpected show of understanding. Maybe he'd misjudged the man. Before he could respond, Dacey's phone buzzed against the table.

"Oh, it's Wiz," she said, swiping to answer. "I hope she has some good news."

She put the phone on speaker. "Hey, Wiz. You're on with me, Gideon, and MacGuire. Tell us something good."

"Well, we've done an initial sweep of Torres's house," Wiz's voice crackled through the speaker.

Gideon leaned forward, forgetting his earlier self-recrimination.

"It's like stepping onto the set of A Beautiful Mind in there. It was clear his mental state was deteriorating."

Gideon struggled to connect the Torres he'd seen at the food bank with the man he'd encountered mere days ago. Physically, the resemblance was intact – same business suit, same clean-shaven face. But behind Torres's eyes, something fundamental had shifted. The corporate professional's measured speech had dissolved into manic ravings, his once-composed features contorting into expressions that seemed barely human. It was as if Torres had become merely a vessel, his body hijacked by something else that used his mouth to channel its madness.

"Notes everywhere – walls, notebooks, loose papers. Most of it's barely coherent, but confessions are mixed in with his rantings against Mayor Thorne. From what we can piece together so far, Torres felt betrayed when he was cut out of some deal involving a hotel."

"That's almost certainly the Royal Palmetto Hotel. Well, that might explain the murders of Willa Wagner, Eleanor Preston, and maybe even Grant Vandermeer," Dacey mused, "but what about the others?"

Wiz sighed heavily. "Some of his writings talk about 'cleaning up the town' and getting rid of the 'riffraff.' That might explain the two homeless victims."

"Some people might consider a tattoo artist riffraff too," Gideon added, thinking of his mother's church and their stance on tattoos. "Have you found any images of the spiral pattern?"

"Not yet, but we're still in the early stages. That reminds me… the green swirling glow we all witnessed around Torres's hands – was it similar to the spiral pattern you observed on Astrid?"

"Not really, but…." Gideon frowned, frustrated at the haziness of his memories. "I never got that good of a look at it – or Torres's hands, for that matter. Even when the pattern rose from Astrid's body and started swirling, the feeling was so overwhelming that I couldn't focus on the details." Silently, he promised himself to do better next time. No matter how powerful or disturbing the magic might be, he needed to observe and remember everything.

"Well, since we interrupted Torres before he could finish his spell, we might never know exactly how he placed it on the victims' bodies," Wiz said. "But hopefully, we'll find some notes or documentation in his house to help us figure it all out. We're going to go through every aspect of Torres's life with a fine-tooth comb." There was a rustling of papers on Wiz's end. "We still need to figure out why he targeted the nursing home residents."

"Maybe he was sacrificing them for power?" Dacey suggested. "Or they had some connection to his mother? Hell, maybe they ate her share of oatmeal or something equally asinine."

"Could be, could be something else entirely. We'll figure it out." Wiz paused. "Gideon, I want you to come by Torres's house in the morning to check for void magic signatures. Don't worry about tonight. You've earned the night off. Good job today, Agent. Welcome to the Conclave."

Hearing Wiz call him "Agent" made Gideon's throat tight. He caught Dacey grinning at him, her smile wide and triumphant.

After they ended the call, Dacey raised her hand to flag down their server. "This calls for more beer. MacGuire, you're staying for another round, right?"

MacGuire pushed his chair back, gathering his jacket. "Normally, I'd love to, but I should head out. Some of us have been up since the crack of dawn." He stood, then paused, looking at Gideon. "You did good today, rookie. Don't let that hesitation eat at you – learn from it and move forward. That's what makes a good agent."

As MacGuire's footsteps faded into the general din of the bar, Gideon turned to Dacey. "Did MacGuire just give me a pep talk?"

"He did," Dacey confirmed, looking amused. "And he meant every word of it. You know, under all that smugness, he can sometimes be a decent guy. But mostly, he's still a pain in the ass."

Dacey slumped back in her seat, running a hand through her hair. "God, I'm exhausted. But at least this investigation is finally over." She lifted her bottle with a tired smile. "To closing the case and catching our killer. And to surviving your first raid, Agent Giddy."

Gideon clinked his bottle against hers, finally allowing himself a small smile. The weight of the day's events still pressed against his chest, but it felt a little lighter now. His gaze drifted to the TV above the bar, where a local news anchor cheerfully reported on city council meetings and weekend weather. There was no mention of a shooting in Millhaven. Logically, he knew the Conclave would keep any hint of magic out of the news – no one outside their organization would ever know today's events. It was strange to think that something so momentous could just... disappear like ripples smoothing out on a pond.

Tomorrow, he'd go to Torres's house and face whatever darkness waited there. Tonight, though – tonight, he'd try to celebrate the win, even if it didn't feel quite perfect.

The low buzz of the bar swirled around them – laughter, glasses clinking, the flicker of sports highlights across the TVs mounted over the bar. Music threaded through it all, some country song Gideon knew his mom liked. It felt surreal how normal everything was after the day's events. Gideon watched as Dacey signaled for another round, her movements relaxed and confident. He envied that ease, the way she could shift from combat to celebration without seeming to carry the weight of what had happened.

But then he caught the slight tremor in her hand as she lifted her beer, the way her eyes occasionally darted to the door – habits of someone who had learned the hard way to stay alert even in moments of peace. Maybe she carried the weight, too, just differently than he did.

The realization was oddly comforting. They were all human –well, mostly human – all dealing with the darkness in their own ways. Maybe that's what made them good at their jobs – not fearlessness or perfect execution, but the willingness to face the darkness again and again, learn from each encounter, and grow stronger with each challenge.

Gideon raised his fresh beer, offering his own toast. "To one hell of a team," he said, and meant it.

CHAPTER 27

The hotel corridor swayed slightly as Dacey pulled Gideon along, her warm hand wrapped around his. Their laughter echoed off the walls, just a touch too loud for the late hour. The pleasant buzz from the beer made everything feel softer around the edges, more dreamlike.

Dacey glanced back at him as they moved, her glossy black hair sweeping across her back like silk. The hallway's dim lighting caught the amber flecks of fire floating in her eyes, making them glow like a banked hearth. A radiant grin lit up her whole face, creating tiny crinkles at the corners of her eyes. Something wild and wonderful lived in that smile, hitting Gideon like a punch to the solar plexus. The crush he'd been nursing for months surged like a wave, threatening to pull words from his mouth that he wasn't nearly drunk enough to say – words about how her smile made him feel like he was falling and flying all at once, how the warmth of her hand felt like coming home, how he'd never met anyone who made him feel so completely alive.

Dacey's foot caught on the corner of the hallway runner, tripping her. Gideon caught her elbow as she stumbled, pulling her close until she regained her balance. Their bodies pressed together briefly, and he felt the heat radiating from her skin even through their clothes.

"My hero," she teased, her hands lingering on his arms, fingers tracing small patterns that sent electricity coursing through his veins. "Always so quick to the rescue."

Fluorescent lights cast an eerie glow over everything, making the hotel's patterned carpet seem to undulate before his eyes. Or perhaps it was just Dacey's intoxicating presence. Or maybe it was the beer. One drink had multiplied into several as they spent hours trading stories, the day's tension gradually dissolving. He wasn't drunk – just pleasantly warm and relaxed, the horror of the food bank incident finally receding beneath the enchantment Dacey seemed to weave around him.

They reached Gideon's door first, and he turned to bid Dacey goodnight, expecting her to continue on to her own room next door. Instead, he found her standing impossibly close, her head tilted back to look up at him. She caught her bottom lip between her teeth, and the gesture sent a bolt of heat straight through him. Something unguarded in her expression made his heart stutter in his chest.

"Dacey?" he managed, but whatever else he meant to say evaporated as she pressed close, her body warm against his. A flash of amber fire rolled through her eyes, wild and alive.

She rose on her tiptoes, one hand sliding up to his shoulder as she drew him down toward her. The phantom scent of scorched spices filled his head, making it hard to think about anything but how her body fit against his and the way her fingers seemed to leave trails of fire wherever they touched.

"Wait," he said, catching her shoulders gently. "You've been drinking. We shouldn't—"

"Shifter metabolism, remember?" Dacey's voice was low and amused. "It takes a lot more than a few beers to cloud my judgment. I know exactly what I want." She traced a finger along his jaw, and he could have sworn sparks followed in its wake. "I've known for a while, Gideon."

The way she said his name, not the usual playful 'Giddy,' sent a shiver down his spine. The realization that she wanted him short-circuited any possible objections he might've voiced.

Before his overthinking brain could kick in, Gideon cupped her cheek and kissed her. Her lips were impossibly warm against his, and when she parted them with a soft sound, he could taste something like cinnamon and woodsmoke. "You taste like fire," he whispered against her mouth.

Dacey smiled against his lips, then pulled back just enough to pluck his keycard from his slack fingers. The door clicked open, and then they stumbled inside, drawn together like magnets. Her skin radiated a scorching heat everywhere they touched, but instead of being uncomfortable, the warmth seemed to sink into Gideon's bones, chasing away the last of the day's gloom.

Her hands slid under his shirt, tracing patterns across his skin, making him shiver despite the heat. His shirt hit the floor, and Dacey's hands mapped the contours of his chest with obvious appreciation, her touch both reverent and hungry. She pulled him down for another searing kiss.

When she finally broke away, her eyes were glowing ember-bright in the dim room. She backed up a few steps, holding his gaze as her fingers worked the buttons of her shirt with tantalizing slowness. As the fabric slipped from her shoulders, phantom wings of fire shimmered into being behind her, a manifestation of her wild emotions. Without thinking, he stepped forward, hand outstretched, drawn to their beauty. His fingers traced the length of one translucent wing, and he was surprised to find it felt like running his hand through sun-warmed water, like touching liquid light itself.

Dacey shivered at his touch, her eyes wide. "You can feel them?" she whispered. "They're not even fully released – most people can't even see them when they're like this, let alone...." She gave him a worried look. "It's not burning you, is it?"

Gideon grinned, still mesmerized by the play of ethereal fire beneath his fingers. "No," he assured her, watching the fire playfully dance around his fingers. "It feels warm. Soothing, actually." He traced another line along the wing's edge, watching it ripple at his touch. "Must be my auramancer ability – probably mutes some of your fire magic, makes it less intense for me than it would be for others."

Something flickered in Dacey's eyes – relief and excitement mingled with something deeper, more profound. Gideon remembered her telling him about life as a bennu shifter, how she had to constantly control her power around humans, always mindful of the raw destructive force that lived beneath her skin. He'd seen the weight of that responsibility in her eyes when she'd had to hold her temper at the rude socialite at the Heritage Foundation meeting. But with him, she didn't have to hold back.

Finally giving in to his urge from the food hall, Gideon caught her hand in his, bringing it slowly to his lips. He pressed soft kisses against her knuckles, his eyes never leaving hers. When she didn't pull away, he turned her hand over, placing another kiss against her palm before trailing his lips along her wrist. Slowly, reverently, he followed a path up her arm, each kiss lingering longer than the last.

Gideon's hands slid down her bare back, drawing her against his chest. Her skin was fever-hot beneath his palms as he bent to press his lips to her shoulder. He traced a path of slow, deliberate kisses across her skin, following the slope of her shoulder up to where it met her neck. Dacey's breath hitched as he continued upward, his mouth mapping the column of her throat. By the time he reached her lips, they were both breathing hard, hearts racing in counterpoint, the air around them charged with electricity and want. Her wings flared wider, wrapping around them as she pulled him back to her lips in a desperate, consuming kiss that felt like diving into liquid fire.

She pulled back suddenly, breaking the kiss with a playful smile that made his heart flip. Her eyes sparkled with mischief as she took another step away from him, giving him a coy look from beneath her lashes. The wings shimmered and rippled with her movement as she turned, reaching behind her back to unhook her bra with deliberate slowness. As she started to turn back toward him, the light caught something on her skin that made Gideon's blood turn to ice.

His hand shot out, catching her shoulder with enough force to make her gasp. Time seemed to stop, the passionate haze evaporating in an instant as his eyes fixed on the mark on her left shoulder blade.

"Wha—?" Dacey started, but the word died as Gideon's ragged "No" filled the space between them. The sound of his horror extinguished her fiery wings like a candle in a windstorm.

The spiral seashell tattoo he knew all too well was on her back, right below her left shoulder.

CHAPTER 28

The spiral pattern stopped Gideon's heart mid-beat. The intricate seashell design seemed to pulse faintly in the low light now that he could see it up close. It was exactly like the one he'd seen on Astrid – the same pattern that had risen from her body and nearly overwhelmed him with its otherworldly power. The pattern that had drained the life and magic from the Völva, leaving nothing but an empty void behind.

"Gideon? What's wrong?" Dacey twisted to look at him, concern replacing the playful heat in her eyes.

His mouth opened and closed, but no words came out.

The spiral pattern rippled slightly, like a heat mirage, and Gideon swore he could feel an echo of that overwhelming void magic radiating from it. They needed help.

"We need to call Wiz," he managed, his voice rough. "Right now."

"What? Why?"

Gideon took a shaky breath, his hands clenching into fists at his sides. "Because someone's marked you. The mark… the void mark. It's —it's on your back. The same way they marked Astrid and probably the others." His voice cracked. "And I don't know how much time we have to save you."

"No." The word seemed to echo in the suddenly silent room. Dacey reached back, fingers searching blindly. "That's impossible. There's nothing there."

"It's right here." Gideon traced the spiral with a shaking finger, feeling the magic bite at his skin – that familiar riptide-like void paired with something else, an undercurrent of something almost Fae. "I can feel it. I can *see* it."

"No." Dacey shook her head violently. "No, I would know if someone—" She broke off, twisting to try to see her own back in the mirror across the room. "I would know. I don't see anything. Are you sure?"

Gideon was already reaching for his phone. "Yes, I'm sure, Dace. I'm calling Wiz." His fingers fumbled with the device, nearly dropping it before he managed to hit the right contact. The rings seemed to last forever before Wiz's voice came through, groggy but alert.

"Gideon? It's the middle of the—"

"Dacey has the mark," he cut in, the words tumbling out. "The void mark. The spiral. It's on her back. I can feel that it is attached to her spirit – to her life force."

A sharp intake of breath. Then, "That's impossible. Torres is dead. His magic would've died with him."

"Unless he had help," Gideon said, the horrible possibility crystallizing as he spoke it. "Unless someone else is involved."

Wiz muttered something that sounded distinctly like a curse in a foreign language. "Don't move. I'm calling everyone. We'll be there in twenty minutes. Don't let Dacey out of your sight."

"I won't," Gideon promised.

The call ended, and Gideon turned back to find Dacey sitting heavily on the edge of the bed, her face pale. He moved to her side, his heart breaking at the lost look in her eyes. Before he could speak, she turned and threw herself into his arms, burying her face against his chest. Her body trembled against his as he held her, one hand moving soothingly up and down her back. Each time his fingers passed over the mark that strange combination of void and Fae magic nipped at them like angry wasps. He sensed a dark whirlpool, immense and looming, pulling at and slowly siphoning Dacey's essence. It made him want to puke.

The knock, when it came, was sharp and urgent. Gideon reluctantly disentangled himself from Dacey, waiting until she'd pulled on a shirt before opening the door. The team quickly filed in – Wiz first, then Santos, Quinn, and MacGuire, all looking rumpled but alert.

"I found it when—" Gideon hesitated, editing quickly. "I noticed it on her back. Dacey can't see it, but it's definitely there."

Wiz handed Dacey a towel. "Show us where," she commanded gently.

Dacey turned, lifted her shirt, and used the towel to cover her front. Gideon pointed to the exact spot. Wiz ran her hand over the area, murmuring something under her breath that made the air crackle. "There's a glamour here," she said finally. "But it's... slippery. Complex. I can't break through it. Frankly, I wouldn't have even noticed if you hadn't told me it was there."

MacGuire frowned, brows furrowing. "How did you not notice this before, Gideon? You've been around her for days now."

"It's very subtle," Gideon said defensively. "I thought it was just lingering magic from her interactions with other Mythicals. Nothing out of the ordinary."

"The glamour is designed to evade detection," Wiz interjected, shooting MacGuire a warning look. "It's crafted to be practically invisible. Even I would have missed it if Gideon hadn't pointed out its exact location."

MacGuire pressed his lips together but nodded, accepting Wiz's explanation.

Wiz waved him closer. "Gideon, tell me exactly what you feel from the mark."

Gideon placed his hand on Dacey's shoulder, trying to ignore how she leaned into his touch. "It's like a whirlpool or a riptide," he said. "The void magic underneath, pulling everything down and in. But there's something else layered over it. Fae magic, but not something immediately familiar. And the mark... it feels like it's attached to her life force, like a leech or a lamprey, feeding off her essence."

"Gideon." Santos's voice was carefully neutral. "Did you notice anything strange recently? Around Dacey, or just in general? Any odd feelings, unexplained sensations?"

"No, nothing."

"Check yourself," Santos said. "Thoroughly. In case—"

The implication hit Gideon like a punch to the gut. He nodded quickly and ducked into the bathroom, stripping to examine every inch of skin in the mirror. Nothing. No spiral, no mark, and no trace of that insidious magic. He dressed and returned to find Dacey finishing what sounded like a recounting of recent events.

"Nothing," he reported and saw several shoulders sag in relief.

"My bennu nature," Dacey said suddenly. "If it… if the mark kills me, I'll just be reborn, right?"

The hope in her voice made Gideon's chest ache. Wiz's expression didn't help. "Don't count on it," she said grimly. "If the mark drains your magic like we think it does, you might not have enough left to regenerate. It could be… a permanent death. We can't risk it."

Gideon's hand tightened involuntarily on Dacey's shoulder. The thought of losing her, of her bright fire being extinguished forever….

"Did you two ever get separated?" Santos asked, his eyes narrowing with focus. "Any time when Dacey was alone?"

"Not really. We've barely left each other's sides since arriving in town. Dacey did wait in the parking lot when I snuck into Serenity Living. But that was only for 15 or 20 minutes." A sudden realization hit Gideon. "Wait. Detective Voss. Dacey was alone with him for over an hour while I was at Vandermeer's office. He could have—"

"We'll track Voss down and question him," Wiz said immediately, pulling out her phone. "I'm calling in a full detainment unit."

"I don't think it's Voss," Dacey said. When Gideon looked at her, she shrugged. "I just don't think Voss put the tattoo mark on me."

"Even so, it won't hurt to question him," Wiz assured her.

"Marcus," Dacey said suddenly. "Marcus Chauvin. He was Fae *and* a sigil tattoo artist."

"Yeah, but it's not a regular tattoo," Gideon said. "Those take hours to create, and except for at night, we've been together almost this whole time. Besides, we've only been in town a few days, and your skin is completely smooth – no redness, no scabbing. A real tattoo takes time to heal. We've been together almost this whole time – I don't know how anyone could've done this to you without me noticing."

"Could someone have gotten into her room while she was sleeping?" Santos asked.

"No way," Dacey said firmly. "I would've reacted, made a ruckus. Gideon would've heard something – his room is next to mine."

"Not if they used a spell to knock you out first," Wiz pointed out.

Dacey shook her head. "Gideon would've sensed someone casting magic that close to his room. Wouldn't you?"

Gideon felt touched by Dacey's faith in him. Shaking his head, he ran a hand through his hair. "We shouldn't rule anything out yet. We're dealing with magic we don't fully understand."

"We'll have Leonhard check the hotel's CCTV footage," Wiz said.

"Even if it's not a regular tattoo. It looks like one, right? And it feels like Fae magic. Could it be Chauvin's magic you're feeling?" Dacey asked.

"I'd like to go check Chauvin's house," Gideon said. "The magic does feel Fae in nature. Now that I've been able to touch the mark, I'd like to take another look around the place." He could feel the urgency building in his chest, the need to act, to do something.

"I'm coming with you," Dacey started to rise, but Wiz pushed her gently back down.

"No. You need to rest. I'm calling in the Conclave's medical team. You need to stay here so we can figure out how to detach this mark from your magic without causing harm." She fixed Dacey with a stern look. "We don't know how long the magic takes to work. We may have to put you into a stasis spell to halt the progress of the spell. We're going to need to monitor you closely."

"I'll go with Gideon," Santos volunteered.

"Count me in, too," MacGuire added, stepping forward.

Gideon knelt before Dacey, lifting her chin with gentle fingers until her eyes met his. The fear he saw there, so foreign on her usually confident face, made his heart clench. He thought of Astrid, of her sacrifice, of her cryptic warnings. "A marked spirit," he muttered, the words hitting him like a physical blow as their meaning finally became clear. Astrid had said that Gideon needed to see. She'd known somehow – had perhaps even given her life to give him this chance to save Dacey.

"Hey," he said softly. "I'm going to figure this out. Just stay awake for me, okay? I'll fix this. I promise."

Her fingers gripped his briefly, fire-warm and trembling.

Gideon turned to Wiz and commanded, "Don't let her go to sleep. No matter what. As far as I can tell, the magic doesn't activate until the person falls unconscious. As long as Dacey is awake, we can fix this."

Wiz dipped her chin in agreement. Then Santos was at his shoulder, urging him toward the door, and Gideon had to let go of Dacey. He cast one last look at her as they left. She was putting on a brave face – spine straight, chin lifted, eyes sparking with defiance – but he could see right through it. The tension in her shoulders and the way her smile didn't reach her eyes – all of it betrayed how terrified she was.

He would not let her fire go out. Not while he still drew breath.

CHAPTER 29

Gideon surveyed the chaos scattered across Chauvin's living room, his shoulders throbbing from the relentless search. Sliced-open cushions and pillows had disgorged their stuffing across the hardwood like fresh snowfall. Every framed photo stood dismantled, the prints and frames meticulously examined. Empty video game cases lay discarded after a thorough inspection. He'd even upended the couch, shredding its protective underside to probe every spring and crevice. Emptied drawers had surrendered their contents to the growing disarray. The walls stood naked, with even the baseboards pried away in their desperate hunt. Yet for all this destruction, their only reward was a single drawing pad filled with rough sketches of that damned spiral mark.

He'd immediately sent photos of the images to the team, but it only confirmed what they already suspected – Chauvin was somehow involved. Fat lot of good that did them with the Fae tattoo artist dead and beyond questioning. His fingers tightened on his phone, knuckles white with tension. The team had been texting updates throughout the night, but none were good. The Savannah Conclave had managed to gather a few specialists – a shaman from Jacksonville, a sigil tattoo expert from Tampa, even a Mythical medical practitioner from Orlando – but no one had made any real progress with Dacey.

Adding to their frustration, no one had been able to locate Detective Victor Voss yet. They needed to question him about the time he was alone with Dacey. MacGuire had called the precinct multiple times, checked Voss's apartment, and even tried his usual haunts, but the detective wasn't answering his phone and hadn't been home. His absence now, when they desperately needed information, raised more than a few eyebrows. The timing seemed suspicious at best.

Gideon's phone buzzed, Dacey's name lighting up the screen. His heart lurched as he stepped outside, suddenly aware of the pale morning light washing over Chauvin's front yard. Had they been at this almost all night?

"Hey," he answered, trying to keep his voice steady.

"Hey, yourself." Dacey's voice was warm but ragged around the edges. "Find anything useful?"

"Not really. Just the sketches. You doing alright?"

"Good, all things considered." She attempted a light tone that didn't quite land. "The coffee here is terrible, though. I think the hotel's been buying the cheap stuff."

"How's the tiredness?" He couldn't quite keep the worry from his voice.

"It's there, but not too bad." There was a rustle on the other end as if she was shifting position. "Wiz and the others don't think I'm in immediate danger as long as I stay awake. But...." She hesitated. "They want to put me in stasis by noon if we haven't figured something out by then. Wiz has called in an entire containment team to oversee the whole process. It's a lot to deal with. Giddy... I'm scared."

Gideon kicked a terracotta planter by the door, pain shooting through his toe as the pot tumbled down the front steps and shattered against the concrete path. Its withered fern sprawled lifelessly among the fragments.

Turning away from the broken pot, he kept his voice deliberately upbeat. "Hey, listen to me, Dacey. You're the toughest person I know. You've faced worse than this before. And you pulled through. You always do." He took a deep breath, steadying himself. "I'm not going to let anything happen to you. None of us will. We're all working on this, and we'll figure it out. Trust me on that. Just hang in there for a little longer." Then he added, "Besides, we need to figure it out before the weekend. We have to – my mom invited you to her Fourth of July cookout on Saturday."

"Really?" The surprise in her voice was evident. "I thought Stella hated me."

"Nah." Gideon leaned against the porch's railing. "She was just being protective after… everything. But she wants a fresh start. She knows how important you are to me."

"Yeah?" The warmth was back in her voice, genuine this time. "You're important to me too."

Gideon's heart stuttered. He opened his mouth, the words he'd been holding back rising to his lips – that she was more than important, that somewhere between the monster hunting and the near-death experiences, he'd—

"Dacey!" Quinn's voice cut through the background. "The shaman wants to try something."

"Sorry," Dacey said quickly. "I've got to go."

"Of course. Keep me posted on how you're feeling, okay?"

"Will do."

The line went dead, and Gideon tilted his head back, staring at the morning sky. The soft blue seemed to mock him with its serenity. His chest felt like it was being crushed in a vice, each breath harder than the last. He'd faced down murderers, battled creatures from a demon realm, and even survived thinking he was going insane from what he thought were hallucinations – but he'd never felt this helpless. So utterly and completely useless.

The mark was killing Dacey. With every passing second, it was draining away her essence, her magic, and her life. All he could do was stand here, surrounded by worthless bits of paper and dead-end leads, as the clock ticked inevitably toward noon.

The door creaked behind him, and Santos stepped out, his clothes rumpled and dusty. He sighed heavily, running a hand over his face. "I don't think there's anything else to find here, Gideon. We've torn the place apart."

Gideon turned to him, jaw set with grim determination. "Then let's go tear his workplace apart instead." His voice was steel, determination dripping from every word. "Every fucking inch if we have to."

Santos nodded, no hesitation in his expression. "I'll tell MacGuire to bring the car around."

As Santos pulled out his phone, Gideon cast one last look at the brightening sky. Somewhere in this city was the answer they needed. The key to saving Dacey. And he would find it, even if he had to dismantle every building brick by brick.

He refused to consider the alternative. He refused to imagine a world without Dacey's fire, her laughter, and her unwavering strength. He would not lose her – not to this, not to anything.

Time, though, was running out. And with each passing minute, the void mark pulsed its hungry rhythm against Dacey's skin, counting down to a darkness from which there might be no rebirth. The thought made his jaw clench tight enough to ache.

CHAPTER 30

Gideon marched up the path to Wild Court Tattoos, gripping the worn edges of Chauvin's sketchbook so tightly his knuckles were bone white. Santos and MacGuire flanked him like twin shadows, their footsteps echoing his determined stride. The small building had an industrial artsy vibe – vibrant murals adorned one side of the building and potted plants lined the entrance. The shop radiated the kind of creative energy that usually drew Gideon in and made him want to study every piece of artwork. But it all felt hollow against the cold panic coiling in his chest today.

The cheerful jingle of the door chime felt like an insult. Morning light streamed through the front windows, catching on framed artwork and making the polished hardwood floors glow.

The receptionist's eyes went wide as she took in his expression, whatever greeting she'd been about to offer dying on her lips. Her multiple piercings caught the light as she leaned back slightly in her chair. Gideon couldn't blame her – he could only imagine what he looked like after hours of searching, running on nothing but coffee and desperate determination.

He pulled out his badge, forcing his voice to remain steady. "I need to speak with everyone who worked with Marcus Chauvin." The words came out clipped, more demanding than he'd intended. "And access to his workspace."

The woman nodded slowly, her dark-lined eyes darting between the three agents. Her fingers fidgeted with one of her facial piercings – a small silver hoop through her bottom lip. "I… I can call—"

Gideon was already pulling out the sketchbook, flipping it open to one of the spiral drawings. "Have you seen this before? Did you ever see Marcus working on anything like this?"

She peered at the sketches, tension visible in the set of her shoulders. After a moment, she shook her head. "No, it doesn't look fam—"

"What about any strange visitors or clients?" Gideon pressed, turning to another page. "Anyone who seemed particularly interested in his work, or—"

"Is there a problem here?" The familiar voice cut through Gideon's questioning like a blade.

He turned to find Violet DuBonne standing in the doorway leading to the shop's back. Where she'd worn ripped jeans and a faded band t-shirt at their meeting days ago, she channeled pure rockabilly glamour today – a high-waisted pencil skirt and cherry-print blouse. Her red-tipped hair was styled into a sleek pompadour with the sides smoothed close to her head. The brilliant koi fish still seemed to swim up and down her arms, the intricate scales catching the light with each subtle movement.

"Agent Nash." Her voice was cool but carried an edge of wariness. "What brings you back?"

"We've had some developments in our investigation, and we now believe that Chauvin was not just an innocent victim."

"I see. We're here to help, though I'd appreciate it if you'd be a bit gentler with my receptionist. Katie doesn't deserve to be interrogated first thing in the morning." She raised an eyebrow, the friendly rapport of their previous meeting notably absent. "You know I'm always willing to help, but if this isn't a friendly and polite visit, you might want to come back with a warrant."

Gideon's chest tightened, the urgency of Dacey's situation warring with the knowledge that antagonizing potential witnesses wouldn't help anyone. He took a deep breath, consciously unclenching his jaw. "I apologize," he said, looking first at Katie and then at Violet. "One of our colleagues was injured. We have reason to believe Marcus was connected to the people responsible."

Something flickered in Violet's expression, like someone preparing themselves for bad news. She gestured for Gideon to continue.

He held out the sketchbook. "Have you seen these before? Did you see Marcus working on these designs?"

Violet stepped closer, studying the spiral patterns with careful attention. After a moment, she nodded. "Yes, actually. I saw him working on similar designs a few times. Think he might have left some more sketchbooks in the break room."

"Did he ever give anyone a tattoo with this spiral?" Gideon asked, trying to keep the desperate edge from his voice.

Violet tapped her chin thoughtfully but shook her head. "Not that I can recall. Marcus had been with us for years, so I didn't feel the need to review every piece he did. He was one of our most experienced artists, and clients specifically requested him for his custom sigil work."

Santos stepped forward. "I can go with you to check the break-room if that's alright?"

"I'll talk to the other artists," MacGuire added, giving Gideon a look. Gideon assumed that MacGuire was taking point with talking to the other artists because he was worried that Gideon wouldn't be able to keep his cool. "Gideon, why don't you take a look at Marcus's station?"

Gideon glanced down at the sketchbook, suddenly aware of how tightly he was gripping it. He forced his fingers to relax, handing it over to MacGuire with a short nod. The familiar weight of failure pressed against his chest – this felt like another dead end, with more precious minutes slipping away. But losing control wouldn't help Dacey.

He took several deep breaths as he made his way to Marcus's empty station, trying to push back a vision his mind conjured of

Dacey in that hotel room, fighting to stay awake as the void mark slowly drained her life away.

Gideon examined Marcus's tattoo station methodically, carefully checking every cabinet and surface once again. The upper storage compartments contained the expected supplies – needles, inks, and cleaning materials – all neatly organized, though he noticed several empty spaces in the ink storage tray. One drawer was empty, its barren interior raising questions in his mind about what might have been stored there. He made a mental note to ask Marcus's colleagues about the drawer's previous contents, though he suspected they probably would not know. The bottom cabinet stuck slightly as he pulled it open, revealing a stack of paperwork and a couple of flash books filled with samples of Chauvin's work.

Setting aside the paperwork, he pulled out the first flash book. The leather cover was well-worn, and its pages were dog-eared from frequent use. Page after page revealed classic designs – anchors wrapped in banners, roses coiling around daggers, and eagles clutching skulls in their talons. Celtic knots, complex tribal designs, and pinup girls smiled coyly from every page. Each design spoke of technical skill, but none bore any resemblance to the spiral spirit mark he sought.

The second book's leather was still stiffer, lacking its predecessor's softened edges and stains, indicating that it was newer. Here, Chauvin's style had transformed – gone were the bold outlines and classic imagery, replaced by intricate geometric patterns.

Gideon slowed his search, studying each design more carefully now. Some of the spiraling patterns made his heart rate spike. Still, each time he looked closer, they resolved into something entirely mundane –nested circles forming lotus patterns, mandalas, or hexagonal grids. Though these designs came closer to the style of the spiral spirit mark, none quite matched what he was looking for.

With a growl of frustration, he tossed the final portfolio back into the drawer, his usual careful handling forgotten in a moment of anger. The heavy book hit the back of the cabinet with more force than he'd intended. A hollow knock caught his attention as the drawer's back panel shifted slightly.

Heart hammering, Gideon rapped his knuckles against the back of the drawer, confirming his suspicion. Carefully, he pried off the false back, revealing a small notebook wedged in the narrow space. Opening it revealed pages of seemingly random letters and numbers that meant nothing to him. It looked like something a mad scientist would create.

"Santos! MacGuire! Get in here!" Gideon called out.

They rushed over, and he showed them his discovery. MacGuire leaned in, studying the cryptic contents. "This looks like code."

Santos grinned. "Good thing we know a numerai. There's not a code on earth that Leonhard can't crack."

As Santos and MacGuire discussed the logistics of scanning and transmitting the notebook to Leonhard, Gideon noticed an argument across the shop. Two employees he'd met last time he'd been at the shop appeared to be bickering. The heavily tattooed man with short, dark hair was confronting the woman with curly, blonde hair.

"Jordan, you can't just take things from my station without asking," the man said firmly.

"I didn't take anything, Danny," Jordan protested.

"My gloves, Jordan. I know you took them. I can literally see them at your station. You know you need to keep up with your own supplies instead of always borrowing everyone else's."

Gideon watched as Jordan sheepishly returned Danny's box of gloves. Danny grumbled under his breath but seemed more annoyed than angry. Something tickled at the back of Gideon's mind.

Jordan started complaining about ADHD, but Gideon couldn't hear the words through the sudden ringing in his ears.

"Wait," Gideon called out to Jordan. "Have you taken anything from Marcus's station?"

Jordan hesitated, starting to deny it, but Gideon cut her off, stepping into her space. "Don't fucking lie to me. This is a matter of literal life and death. Did. You. Take. Anything. From Marcus's station? Anything at all?"

Looking contrite, Jordan admitted, "Just a couple of vials of ink and some transfer paper." She paused. "The paper was crap anyway; it didn't take ink evenly. It's not a big deal; it's not like Marcus needs that stuff now."

Lightning seemed to course through Gideon's veins, his head buzzing. "Do you still have the paper?"

Jordan faltered under his intensity. "I threw it away, but... it might still be in my trashcan."

"Show me."

Jordan led him to her station and pointed to a trash can in the corner. Gideon dug through the contents until he found a stack of papers at the bottom. As he pulled them out, he stared in shock. Each sheet bore the spiral image in perfect, crystal-clear detail.

"Do these look blank to you?" he asked Jordan.

She looked at him like he was losing his mind. "Yes, they're blank."

Without a word, Gideon grabbed a tray and a vial of black ink from Jordan's station, ignoring her protests as he poured the ink into the tray. He carefully laid one of the sheets into the ink. The black liquid seeped into the paper, except where the spiral image was drawn, creating a stark negative image.

"Can you see it now?" Gideon asked Jordan.

She nodded, shocked and speechless. Beyond her, Santos and MacGuire stared in disbelief. Gideon held up the paper. "*This* is the mark that's on Dacey."

CHAPTER 31

Gideon's hands shook violently as he set the transfer paper down on Jordan's station and nearly dropped the sheet. Steadying himself with a deep breath, he pulled out his phone, snapping several photos of the stark negative image where the black ink had revealed the hidden spiral. He sent the pictures to the team group chat, along with a brief explanation of what they'd found.

"I need some air," he rasped, his voice sandpaper rough. The tattoo shop's walls seemed to constrict around him, closing in with suffocating pressure. The weight of how close yet still so far they were from saving Dacey threatened to crack his composure.

Santos clasped Gideon's shoulder with a steady hand. "Take your time, brother. MacGuire and I will keep combing through the shop. We've got this."

Gideon nodded sharply, not trusting himself to speak as he pushed through the front door. The Florida heat hit him like a punch, drawing beads of sweat under his arms and temples. At least there's a breeze, he thought inanely, watching cars cruise past on the street. The traffic was much lighter now that the Fourth of July celebrations had passed, leaving the roads relatively clear in the late morning sun.

The sharp trill of his phone made him jolt. Leonhard's name

flashed across the screen, and Gideon's heart rate kicked up another notch. He turned back toward the shop's front window, catching Santos's eye through the glass. He mouthed 'Leonhard' and pointed to his phone. Santos dipped his head in acknowledgment, already turning to signal MacGuire.

"Leonhard," Gideon answered, trying to keep the desperate edge from his voice.

"Gideon." Leonhard's usually precise tone sounded frazzled. "How certain are you that this image matches the mark on Dacey's back?"

Santos and MacGuire pushed through the door to join him just as Gideon replied, "One hundred percent certain – it's an exact match."

A harsh breath crackled through the phone. "It's as bad as I feared, then. The mark – it's a Fibonacci spiral. I should have realized it when you said it looked like a nautilus shell. That's one of the most famous examples of a Fibonacci spiral in nature."

"I don't know what that means," Gideon cut in, running a hand through his sweat-dampened hair. "What's a Fibonacci spiral?"

"It's a logarithmic spiral where the growth factor is related to the golden ratio," Leonhard explained, slipping into a professorial tone. Gideon huffed in annoyance, still not understanding a word the numerai had just said. "It's based on the Fibonacci sequence, where each number is the sum of the two preceding numbers. Look, it's simple math – you start with two ones. Add those together, you get 2. Then take that 2 and add it to the 1 before it, giving you 3. Then add 3 and 2 to get 5, then 5 and 3 make 8, 8 and 5 make 13. The numbers grow exponentially – by the twentieth number, you're already in the thousands. When you transform those numbers into an image, it creates a spiral. The spiral grows outward following this principle, creating a perfect ever-expanding curve. They appear everywhere in nature – pinecones, sunflower seeds, fiddlehead ferns, galaxies, hurricanes...."

"How does this information help me save Dacey?" Gideon interrupted, his patience fraying.

There was a heavy pause before Leonhard continued, his voice grim. "The spiral isn't just mathematical – it's being used as a magical vortex. The precise mathematical properties of the Fibonacci sequence create a perfect energy drain, pulling life force and magic from the victim in an ever-expanding spiral. It's... elegant, in a horrifically cruel way."

"A drain to where?"

"Someone out there has a corresponding mark," Leonhard explained. "A matching Fibonacci spiral that acts as an anchor absorbing all that stolen power. After this many victims...." He trailed off. "Well, they must be incredibly powerful by now. And with Dacey's rebirth magic and connection to fire, she's probably their most potent target yet."

"How do I track them?" Gideon demanded. "How do I detect this kind of magic?"

"That's the problem," Leonhard said. "The magic signature would have traces of both Fae and void energy, but it's designed to be virtually undetectable until it activates. When Dacey's mark begins to drain, you might be able to track the energy flow if you know what to look for. However, as you witnessed, the final drain happens quickly, so you would need to be close to the anchor to track them. However, it's probably too late at that point, and once the transfer is complete...." He sighed. "It's like a computer virus that erases itself after execution. The magical signature disappears. All it leaves behind is a void."

"So you're telling me I have to find someone with a matching spiral tattoo somewhere in this whole damn town?" Gideon's voice cracked with barely contained rage. "A mark that's probably hidden, that I can't even detect until it's too late? It's like trying to find—"

"No, Gideon," Leonhard cut in, a strange urgency in his voice. "You're not looking for the mark – you're looking for someone who understands this math. This isn't basic geometry. The Fibonacci sequence, the golden ratio – these aren't just numbers. Whoever created this mark has an advanced understanding of theoretical mathematics *and* advanced magical theory. These aren't arbitrary curves."

Gideon could hear papers rustling on Leonhard's end of the call. "The spiral follows a logarithmic progression with a precise growth factor of phi, the golden ratio. One miscalculation in the coefficients, even by a fraction of a decimal point, and the whole thing would collapse. The siphoning process exploits properties of holomorphic functions to ensure conservation of energy during transfer. If the spiral isn't mathematically perfect, you'd get catastrophic results – either an implosion killing the caster instantly or an explosion as the energy goes haywire. You're not looking for just anyone with a tattoo. You're looking for someone who could create this. The mathematical precision required to create this is staggering. The golden ratio image must be exact to create the energy vortex, and the calculations involved in maintaining the power transfer without destabilizing the—"

Gideon stopped listening, his mind suddenly racing as pieces clicked into place. The phone slipped from his nerveless fingers, but Santos's telekinetic power caught the device before it hit the pavement.

Gideon turned to face his partners, his eyes wide. "I know who it is."

CHAPTER 32

Gideon raced down First Street, the engine straining as he pushed it well past the speed limit. His knuckles were white on the steering wheel as he wrenched it hard to the right, tires squealing as he turned onto the road that led to city hall. The imposing façade of Millhaven's city hall loomed ahead, its white trim and tall windows gleaming in the late morning sun.

"Jesus Christ," Santos muttered from the passenger seat, one hand braced against the dashboard. In the back, MacGuire had gone completely silent, his typically haughty expression tight with tension.

Gideon didn't slow as he approached the building. The vehicle jumped the curb, coming to a jarring stop with one tire planted firmly on the bottom step of city hall. He was out of the car before the engine had fully settled into idle, leaving the driver's door hanging open as he took the front steps two at a time.

"Sir! You can't park there!" A uniformed security guard emerged from behind his desk in the lobby, moving to intercept them. "This is—"

"I've got this," Santos called to Gideon, already reaching for his badge. "Go!"

Gideon didn't hesitate, pushing past the guard with MacGuire close behind. As he started up the main staircase, he heard Santos's steady voice explaining their presence to the flustered guard.

"What if you're wrong?" MacGuire's voice carried up from a few steps behind as he caught up, slightly winded from the sprint.

"I'm not." Gideon's jaw was set as he rounded the landing between floors.

He barely registered the framed photographs lining the stairwell walls – decades of Millhaven history reduced to a blur of black and white as he raced past. His shoulder clipped someone coming down the stairs, sending papers flying. He heard MacGuire calling back an apology but didn't slow his pace.

The second floor opened into a familiar corridor. Polished hardwood stretched out before them, partially covered by deep red runners. The same gold-leafed antique chairs lined the walls, their ornate wooden frames gleaming in the light from the tall windows. Michael Torres's familiar face was absent from the mayor's reception desk. Instead, a young woman in her late twenties looked up at their arrival; her brown hair pulled into an elegant twist.

"Good morning, how can I—" she began, rising from her chair.

Gideon blew past her desk, MacGuire on his heels. They headed straight for the frosted glass door with its gold lettering.

"Wait! You can't just—" The receptionist's protests cut off as Gideon grabbed the door handle and pushed it open.

The wave of wild mountain witch magic hit him like a physical force – more potent than it had been just days ago. Mayor Thorne sat behind her massive desk, Detective Voss and her husband standing on either side as they leaned over what looked like paperwork. All three heads snapped up at the interruption.

"Agent Nash." The mayor's perfectly shaped eyebrows drew together in a frown. "Please let my receptionist do her job. If you need to speak with me—"

"I know it's you." Gideon's voice was flat, cutting through her practiced political tone.

"What are you talking about?"

"I know you're behind all of this."

The mayor settled back in her leather chair, studying him with sharp eyes as she steepled her fingers on the polished desktop. After a long moment, she turned her attention to the doorway. "Everything is fine, Samantha. Please close the door and return to your desk. I still need you to finish going through those emails."

"Yes, ma'am." The receptionist nodded, pulling the door shut with a soft click.

Mayor Thorne rose slowly from her chair, smoothing her dark suit skirt. "Tell me what you think you know."

The magic rolled off her in waves now – dark, seductive, coercive tendrils reaching for his mind. Gideon felt the weight of it pressing against his thoughts, urging him to confide everything. He let his shoulders relax slightly, allowing her to believe her magic was taking hold.

Although he could feel the charismatic pull of the mayor's magic, he wasn't as affected as the others in the room. The mayor's magic couldn't penetrate his defenses completely. She didn't know he was an auramancer, and the natural resistance that came with his abilities was shielding him from the worst of her influence. Mayor Thorne was too cocky and too confident in her power to consider someone might resist her. He kept his expression carefully neutral, grateful for the advantage and determined not to give it away.

"Your sister Willa created the math of the spiral tattoo," he said, keeping his voice steady. "The one that drains people. Marcus Chauvin put the designs on transfer paper for you." He watched her face as he continued. "You used Michael Torres and had him access the nursing home to begin draining your first victims – the residents. Then you moved on to bigger targets – Marcus himself, Eleanor, Brandon Cho, who worked at the nursing home and started asking too many questions about the deaths. A couple of homeless people. Even your own sister."

The mayor's brown bob swayed as she nodded, looking almost impressed. Gideon risked a glance at MacGuire, and his heart sank. The gargoyle shifter's eyes were slightly glazed behind his glasses, the mayor's persuasive magic wrapped tight around him like invisible chains. He could feel it also trying to bind him, pressing against his defenses.

"This is what you're going to do." Mayor Thorne's voice was silk over steel. "You're going to cover up my involvement in the deaths. Once your agent dies, you'll convince everyone it was residual magic left by Michael Torres. You'll make sure no one suspects me. You will do what*ever* it takes to make that happen. You must protect me at all costs – that is your only objective."

"Yes," MacGuire responded immediately. Gideon quickly echoed him, careful to keep his expression compliant.

A smile curved the mayor's lips. "Once this last person is drained, I should have enough power to secure the governor's office. Your agent friend will be the last victim for a while – at least until I'm ready to try for the presidency." She waved a manicured hand toward the door. "You can go. Call me if anything relevant comes up." Her smile widened to a grin. "And don't forget to vote for me."

The weight of her magic was crushing now, like an anchor dropped on his soul. But underneath the surface of compliance, Gideon's mind raced. Everyone in the room was thoroughly spell-bound to protect Winnie. Even if he could break free, he'd have to fight through all of them to get to her.

"Keep me posted on whether your colleagues back off," the mayor added as MacGuire turned toward the door.

Gideon started to follow, his peripheral vision catching the gun holstered at MacGuire's hip – right within reach.

Time seemed to slow.

Without letting himself think too hard about what he was about to do, he moved.

His hand shot out, fingers fumbling for a split second with the stiff leather retention strap on MacGuire's holster. The angle was awkward – his wrist bent uncomfortably as he worked to release it – but adrenaline hurried his movements. The strap popped free with a barely audible snap. His fingers closed around the grip of MacGuire's weapon before the gargoyle could register the movement. MacGuire was just beginning to turn toward him, his expression shifting to surprise. In one smooth motion, Gideon drew the gun free, clicked off the safety, and brought it up level with the mayor's forehead. Her eyes widened in genuine shock – the first real emotion he'd seen from her – as he squeezed the trigger.

The gunshot was deafening in the enclosed space. For a split second, Gideon saw a small, neat hole appear in the center of Mayor Thorne's forehead. Then, her accumulated magic exploded outward in a concussive blast that lifted him off his feet and slammed him into the wall. The impact drove the air from his lungs as darkness crowded the edges of his vision.

The last thing he saw before losing consciousness was the mayor's body crumpling across her desk, papers scattering in the magical windstorm that howled through the office. As his eyes slipped closed, he sent a silent prayer that he'd been fast enough to save Dacey.

Then everything went black.

CHAPTER 33

Gideon came to with a groan, his head throbbing where it had connected with the wall. Papers drifted around the room like oversized snowflakes, carried on the lingering currents of wild magic. The mayor's body lay sprawled across her desk, dark blood pooling beneath her head and dripping onto the carpet in a steady rhythm.

The office door burst open. Santos charged in with his weapon drawn, the receptionist Samantha close behind him. Her piercing scream shattered the eerie quiet, bouncing off the wood-paneled walls.

Santos kept his gun trained on the other occupants of the room, his gaze never wavering as he moved sideways toward Gideon. With his free hand, he reached down and helped Gideon to his feet, steadying him as he swayed. Through the window's reflection, Gideon caught a glimpse of himself – blood matting his hair and clothes covered in dust from the magical explosion.

MacGuire stirred at the noise, pushing himself up from where he'd been thrown against a filing cabinet, pressing his fingers to his temples. The mayor's husband was curled against the wall, rocking back and forth as silent tears streaked down his face.

Detective Voss dragged himself off the floor and dropped heavily into a righted visitor's chair, the leather creaking under his weight. Sweat beaded on his forehead as he ran trembling fingers through his hair. "I can't believe that bitch…." he muttered, his voice rough. "All this time…."

"Everyone stay exactly where you are," Santos commanded. He turned to the receptionist, who stood frozen in the doorway, hands pressed to her mouth, and flashed his badge. "Miss, I need you to return to your desk. Don't let anyone else in here until I tell you otherwise."

She nodded jerkily and backed out, closing the door with trembling hands.

Santos surveyed the chaos of drifting papers and the mingled smells of burnt paper, blood, and spent magic.

"What the hell happened here?" he asked, carefully stepping around a toppled filing cabinet.

Gideon leaned against the wall, massaging his knee. "She was controlling them all," Gideon explained. "The mayor's magic was strong enough to make everyone protect her and cover up what she'd done. She was going to have us all help her get away with the murders."

"It's true." Voss stared at his hands, voice barely above a whisper. "I've been under her control for a month. Everything I did… everything she made me do…. I was the one who put the spell on Joe and Astrid. And I put one on Chauvin after I'd beaten him. *I killed them*. Oh God! I put one on Dacey, too – she's in danger!"

"Relax," MacGuire said, his tone unexpectedly gentle. "With the mayor dead, the spell should be completely inert. Dacey's safe now."

Voss slumped in his chair, the tension visibly draining from his body as relief washed over him.

Santos surveyed the scene with practiced calm. "I need someone to explain this from the beginning."

Gregory Thorne wiped tears from his face, taking a moment to collect himself. "She started with the nursing home residents," he said, his voice hollow and distant. "Did it during a community outreach visit. All Winnie had to do was press a piece of paper with the invisible spell against someone's skin and say the activation phrase – *Potentiam rapio* – 'I seize power.' That's all it took."

Santos's expression hardened as Gregory continued.

"She used the power from those first victims to boost her natural abilities – enough to enchant me and Michael. Once she had Michael under control, she used him to mark at least a half dozen more of the seniors at the home. As their life force drained away, she gained enough power to ensnare Detective Voss."

"And then she had Voss start eliminating loose ends," Gideon said, the puzzle pieces falling into place. "Starting with Marcus Chauvin, who drew the spiral image for her."

Voss nodded silently, shame evident in the slump of his shoulders.

Gregory rubbed his temples as he continued. "When Brandon Cho grew suspicious about the nursing home deaths and filed a formal complaint, she and Michael intercepted him after work. She made him compliant while they applied the mark." His voice cracked. "Then she used her position as mayor to squash any investigation into Serenity Living."

"What about Eleanor Preston?" Gideon asked.

"Winnie targeted her after a Foundation meeting," Gregory explained. "Preston was vocal about opposing Meridian Hospitality's involvement in the Royal Palmetto restoration. Winnie couldn't let her block that project – Meridian had promised to back her gubernatorial campaign if she delivered the deal."

"And Grant Vandermeer?" Gideon pressed, recalling the businessman's death.

Voss spoke up, his voice leaden with guilt. "Torres handled that one. He pressed the transfer paper against the back of Vandermeer's hand after a zoning meeting."

"And the mayor's sister, Willa?" Santos asked quietly.

Gregory Thorne let out a choked sob, sliding down the wall to sit on the floor. "Winnie... my wife... she had her own sister marked." He looked up, his eyes red-rimmed. "Willa and Winnie developed the mathematical framework for the spiral mark together. But Willa only intended it to extract magical energy from enchanted artifacts, never from living beings. When she figured out that... when she realized Winnie had perverted her work to drain life from people instead of objects... she was furious. Winnie decided to eliminate her own sister rather than face possible exposure."

His face contorted in anguish. "She used me. She preyed on my friendship with Willa. Made me place the mark while we were together at the university."

"But what about Torres?" Gideon asked. "How did he end up taking the fall?"

Voss shifted uncomfortably in his chair. "After the Heritage Foundation meeting, when Dacey informed the mayor that you guys were bringing in reinforcements, Winnie panicked. She decided to use Torres as a scapegoat. She commanded him to write those incriminating notes we found scattered throughout his home, then ordered him to go to the food bank where he'd be caught 'in the act.'"

He paused, swallowing hard. "She also gave me specific instructions to stay close to you two and... and to make sure Torres didn't survive the encounter."

"Jesus," Santos muttered, running a hand over his face. "This is going to be a nightmare to cover up."

"I don't care," Gideon said flatly. "As long as Dacey is okay."

Santos studied him for a long moment, then pulled out his phone and put it on speaker. "Wiz? We've got a situation."

"Santos!" Wiz's voice burst through, words tumbling out in her typical rapid-fire fashion. "You'll never believe what just happened! There was this weird flash of magic around Dacey, and suddenly, she said she felt better – not tired at all anymore. We were about to put her in stasis when—"

"The mayor's dead," Santos cut in. "She was behind all of this. Gideon shot her."

After a beat of silence, Wiz let out a whoop that had Santos yanking the phone away from his ear. "That explains it! The magical backlash of her death must have broken all her spells. I'm sending

Quinn and the rest of the containment team to help clean up, but I'm staying with Dacey. We still need to monitor for lingering effects."

Relief washed through Gideon. Worth it. It was all worth it.

"Gideon?" Dacey's voice came through, slightly distant but clear. "Are you there?"

He took Santos's phone and turned off the speaker. "I'm here. Are you okay?"

"I should be asking you that." Her smile was audible, though tinged with worry. "I can't believe you shot Winnie. For me. What if you'd been wrong?"

"I wasn't." The certainty in his voice surprised even him. "I knew it was her. But even if I hadn't been completely sure...." He swallowed hard. "You're worth the risk."

"I want to come see you," Dacey said softly. "But Wiz has threatened to sit on me if I try to leave. Says she needs to monitor me for at least a few hours."

"Then I'll come to you." Gideon glanced at Santos, who nodded.

"Go," Santos said, taking back his phone. "I've got this. The cleanup team will be here soon. Don't worry about the mayor – this is not my first rodeo. I'll come up with a cover story. We just need to secure the building, and we'll get it figured out."

MacGuire had recovered enough to steady himself, though his hands still shook. "I'll round up the witnesses and secure them. Then I'll lock down this floor."

Gideon hesitated at the door. "Santos...."

"I know." Santos waved him off. "Just go. Check on your partner. We'll sort out the details later."

Outside the mayor's door, Gideon spotted Samantha arguing with the security guard, doing her job of keeping people away. Gideon's steps quickened as he headed for the stairs.

His head ached, and he would be covered in bruises, but knowing Dacey was safe made Gideon feel weightless. He searched himself for guilt or remorse over taking the mayor's life but found none. Perhaps those feelings would surface later, but he doubted it.

The political fallout would keep the Conclave agents busy for quite a while. He imagined there would be investigations, cover stories, and mountains of paperwork. But right now, none of that mattered.

The morning sun hit him as he exited City Hall. His car still sat awkwardly with one tire on the bottom step and the driver's door hanging open. In the distance, the first sirens approached.

Pulling away from the curb, he spotted Quinn emerging from the lead black SUV in a convoy, striding purposefully toward the building with a few agents following closely behind. She barked an order to secure the perimeter while two police cruisers with flashing lights took position on either street corner in front of the building. Let them handle it, he thought. He had somewhere more important to be.

The hotel wasn't far – ten minutes if he obeyed traffic laws, less if he didn't. Gideon's hands tightened on the steering wheel as he accelerated through a yellow light. He'd already broken enough rules today. A few traffic violations hardly seemed worth worrying about.

Dacey was waiting.

EPILOGUE

Gideon wiped his sweaty palms against his jeans yet again, his eyes fixed on the side gate of the backyard. The summer air was filled with the aroma of sizzling meat and the steady hum of conversation. His mother's laughter, bright and happy, rang out as she mingled with the neighbors who had joined her Fourth of July barbecue.

Any minute now, Dacey would arrive. The thought sent a fresh wave of nervous energy through Gideon. Thankfully, she'd had no residual effects from the spiral mark – Wiz's team had monitored her closely in those first 24 hours after the mayor's death, but the magic had dissipated cleanly, leaving her healthy and whole. Still, the memory of how close he'd come to losing her made his heart clench.

Pulling his memories away from those dark thoughts, Gideon looked around the gathering. He couldn't help but smile, watching his mother gesturing animatedly as Pastor Simon and several members of her church helped serve food to the guests. Her easy laughter mixed with theirs as she chatted with Mrs. Henderson from next door. After years of cramped apartments and shared walls, seeing his mother with a real house – complete with a white picket fence and the beginnings of a garden she'd always dreamed of having – made his chest tight with happiness. His mom deserved this – all of it.

His phone buzzed in his pocket, and he nearly dropped it in his haste to check the screen. But it was just Santos.

Found Willa Wagner's notebooks in the mayor's study. Mathematical proofs for the spirit mark. Leonhard's having a field day with the calculations. He's also already cracked the code in Chauvin's notebook – it had the formula to create an 'invisible' sigil ink that has the whole Conclave excited for future possibilities. You owe me a drink for dealing with Leonhard's endless theorizing.

Gideon typed back a quick acknowledgment, his mind drifting to the revelations of the past couple of days. The sisters had made a breakthrough by combining Willa's mathematical formulas with the little-known magical principles of Franz Mesmer's work on "animal magnetism" and hypnosis. Gideon had been shocked to discover that Mesmer, known to most of the world as merely an eccentric 18th-century German physician, had been a powerful warlock whose theories about invisible life forces and hypnotic enchantment had a foundation in genuine magical practice.

Gideon typed back a quick acknowledgment, his mind drifting to the revelations of the past couple of days. The web of lies and manipulation surrounding Winnie Thorne had been breathtaking in its scope. Now that her victims had been freed from her magical control, the disturbing picture had fully emerged.

According to Gregory and Voss, the spirit mark took half a day to two days to fully drain its victims, depending on their health, magical strength, and natural resistance. When they'd questioned why Dacey had been targeted, Voss believed it was because of her magical strength – with Dacey as a final victim, the mayor would have gained enough power that she wouldn't need any more sacrifices – at least until she decided to make a run at the oval office. Dacey had been convenient, powerful, and in the wrong place at the wrong time.

Gideon's phone buzzed again, and his heart skipped when he saw Dacey's name. A text from her read simply: *Just arrived.*

"Ma!" he called out, already moving toward the gate. "She's here!"

He rounded the corner of the house, boots crunching on the gravel path, and there she was. Dacey stood on the other side of the gate in a yellow sundress that made her skin glow, a casserole dish in her hands. The sight of her made his breath catch – especially when she looked up, and he caught the familiar warmth in those brown eyes, the way the sunlight caught the unusual amber flecks in her irises.

"Hey," she said softly, shifting the dish to one hand.

"Hey, yourself." He reached for the gate latch, suddenly hyper-aware of his movements. They hadn't had a chance to talk about what had happened in his hotel room. The memory of her skin under his hands, of desperate kisses and half-shed clothes before he'd spotted the spiral tattoo, still made his pulse race.

"I'm so glad you could make it," he said, taking the dish from her – some kind of cobbler, judging by the smell.

Dacey tucked a strand of hair behind her ear. "Are you sure your mom is alright with me being here? I mean, after the last time I saw her...."

"Are you kidding? She's thrilled." He gestured toward the backyard with his free hand. "I've talked to her, and she understands how important you are to me."

The slight smile Dacey gave Gideon made his heart triple its beats.

"Are you ready?" Gideon asked, offering his elbow for Dacey to take.

Dacey threw him a look that managed to be both amused and slightly panicked. Something warm unfurled in his chest, chasing away the final lingering shadows of the past week.

She turned to face him fully, and suddenly, he was very aware of how close they were standing – close enough to see how her eyes caught the fading sunlight, turning those amber flecks to fire.

"Gideon...." She hesitated, then squared her shoulders like she was heading into a firefight. "About what happened in the hotel room, before... everything. I just wanted to—"

His mother's voice rang out. "The burgers are ready! Everyone, grab a plate!"

Dacey jumped slightly, then laughed, shaking her head.

Gideon started to tug her toward the backyard. "We should probably…."

"Are you sure I'm welcome here?"

"Absolutely. Come on, Dacey. It's gonna be fun."

Dacey laughed, then groaned. "I think we need to pick a new phrase. I swear that one's cursed."

"Nah. It's turned out true every time. I always have fun with you."

To Gideon's amazement, Dacey blushed.

The sun was setting, painting the sky in shades of pink and gold. Soon, fireworks would be launched from the park downtown. His mother had already set up chairs facing that direction.

Tomorrow, there would be more paperwork. More investigations into the depth of Winnie Thorne's schemes. More questions about magic and power and corruption. But right now, at this moment, there was just this: his mother's laughter, his neighbors' children playing, Dacey's hand warm in his, and the promise of something new beginning.

It wasn't just fun.

It was pretty damn close to perfection.

AFTERWORD

Writing a novel is never a solitary journey; this one is no exception. I am grateful to the many people who helped bring this story to life.

First, my heartfelt thanks to my beta readers, who provided their time, insight, and honest feedback. Your suggestions and encouragement made this a book better than I could have created alone.

To my family, thank you for your patience, love, and unwavering support. This book exists because you believed in me.

And to you, my readers, thank you for choosing to spend your precious time in the Mythical world. Your enthusiasm for stories makes this writing journey worthwhile.

* * *

A note about Millhaven: Those familiar with central Florida might recognize that Millhaven is heavily inspired by the charming town of Sanford. I chose not to use Sanford's actual name because I've taken *considerable* creative liberties with the setting, including turning the mayor into quite the villain! I feel compelled to assure everyone that the real mayor of Sanford is probably a lovely person who doesn't orchestrate murders or engage in shadowy real estate schemes. At least, not that I'm aware of!

Real Sanford landmarks inspired several locations in the novel:

The Millhaven Food Depot drew its inspiration from Henry's Depot, a fantastic food hall housed in a historic building that once served as a train station.

The Royal Palmetto Hotel is based on the Mayfair Hotel. Built in 1925 during Florida's land boom, the real Mayfair was once a luxurious Mediterranean Revival-style hotel that hosted celebrities and wealthy snowbirds escaping northern winter. After serving as a naval training center during World War II, it has gone through various incarnations over the decades.

Edelweiss Hall is based on Hollerbach's, my favorite German restaurant in central Florida.

First Street Social is inspired by Tuffy's Music Box & Lounge, which has a great music venue and even features a hidden tiki bar inside.

The Metro Diner in my novel is a nod to Sanford's Colonial Room, where the comfort food and small-town atmosphere have fueled both my body and my imagination.

The marina in the book is based on Sanford's actual marina, where my sailboat is docked. The sailing school, its determined owner, and her rescue macaw are also inspired by the real sailing school where I took lessons.

While the town, people, and events in this novel are fictional, the spirit of Sanford – its charm, history, and sense of community – is very real, and I'm grateful to this special place for inspiring Millhaven's creation.

ABOUT THE AUTHOR

Gwen DeMarco is an avid reader, coffee snob, sailing enthusiast and a lover of all things nerdy. Gwen loves to write paranormal romance novels with a focus on the weird and wonderful.

Gwen is happily married to her high school sweetheart and has two teenage children. She can often be found with her nose in a book and a glass of wine or mug of coffee in her hand.

Sign up to her mailing list and receive a **free** copy of a novellas: one from the Kingdom of Erishum Trilogy and another from the Sophie and The Odd Ones series.

To learn more, please visit my website and sign up for my mailing list to receive updates at www.GwenDeMarco.com

ALSO BY GWEN DEMARCO

Sophie Feegle Series

Sophie and The Odd Ones

Portents and Oddities

Odd Times for Sophie Feegle

Against All Odds

Odds and Ends

Auras & Embers Series

Gideon Bean

Spirit Marked

Kingdom of Erishum Trilogy

The Mudlark

The Gutter Shrike

The Dying Wilds

www.ingramcontent.com/pod-product-compliance
Lightning Source LLC
Chambersburg PA
CBHW020322030826
48979CB00022B/782

* 9 7 8 1 9 6 3 9 0 6 0 5 9 *